# THE
# A TIME TO
# SLAUGHTER

# THE BROTHERS O'BRIEN
# A TIME TO SLAUGHTER

## WILLIAM W. JOHNSTONE

### with J. A. Johnstone

**PINNACLE BOOKS**
Kensington Publishing Corp.
www.kensingtonbooks.com

PINNACLE BOOKS are published by

Kensington Publishing Corp.
119 West 40th Street
New York, NY 10018

PUBLISHER'S NOTE
Following the death of William W. Johnstone, the Johnstone family is working with a carefully selected writer to organize and complete Mr. Johnstone's outlines and many unfinished manuscripts to create additional novels in all of his series like The Last Gunfighter, Mountain Man, and Eagles, among others. This novel was inspired by Mr. Johnstone's superb storytelling.

All Kensington titles, imprints, and distributed lines are available at special quantity discounts for bulk purchases for sales promotions, premiums, fundraising, educational, or institutional use. Special book excerpts or customized printings can also be created to fit specific needs. For details, write or phone the office of the Kensington special sales manager: Kensington Publishing Corp., 119 West 40th Street, New York, NY 10018, attn: Special Sales Department; phone 1-800-221-2647.

ISBN-13: 978-0-7860-3108-5
ISBN-10: 0-7860-3108-5

First printing: January 2013

10  9  8  7  6  5  4  3  2

Printed in the United States of America

First electronic edition: May 2014

ISBN-13: 978-0-7860-3109-2
ISBN-10: 0-7860-3109-3

# Chapter One

Black was the sky and bitter the wind, but Silas Creeds felt no chill, for the wind was not colder than he and the sky no blacker than his killer's heart. Truth to tell, he was highly amused. In the dead and dreary winter of 1888, he was not in the New Mexico Territory to kill a man, but to return a runaway woman to her rightful owner.

This was a first for him, and the cause of his mirth.

From a rise studded with pines, he looked down on the Dromore ranch. Pyramids of wind-blown snow lay at the bases of each trunk as though the trees had dropped their drawers in preparation for a scamper down the hill. His thoughts turned to the job at hand. How does a man born to the gun treat another man's trophy woman?

Well, he could truss her up and throw her behind his saddle, Creeds decided. Or he could loop a noose around her neck and drag her after his horse.

Neither method struck him as satisfactory. He shook his head, a smile playing around the corners of his thin scar of a mouth. It required some serious thought. Why did Zebulon Moss want the treacherous little whore back anyhow? It would've been a lot simpler to put a bullet into her and have done. Serve her right.

Creeds sighed. Ah well, Zeb knew his own mind and he set store by the little baggage, so there was an end to it.

A lone rider hazing a Hereford bull toward a cattle pen near the big plantation house took his attention. The puncher showed a shaggy wing of gray hair under his hat, but the turned-up collar of his sheepskin hid his face.

Creeds grinned and slid the Winchester from the boot under his left knee. He drew a bead on the rider and had him dead to rights. A head shot, easy at that distance. "Pow!" Creeds said quietly.

The puncher rode on and Creeds shoved the rifle back into the leather. There was to be no killing on this trip. "Just bring my woman back," Zeb had said. He was paying the money, so he got to choose the tune.

Creeds scanned the ranch again.

A big plantation house with four pillars out

front, white-painted fences and corrals, a bunk-house for seasonal punchers and the single hands, a commissary, and a row of eight neatly built cabins for the married men.

Creeds nodded. No doubt about it, those were civilized folks down there and that meant they'd be fat and sassy and easy to kill.

Set apart a ways from the other buildings was a timber structure with a V-shaped shingle roof and a low bell tower. Smoke from its iron chimney tied bows in the wind and even from where he sat his horse Creeds heard the noisy laughter of children. The building was painted red and that amused him greatly. "Well, well, well, ol' Zeb's information was correct . . . Trixie Lee is out in the boonies, teaching snot-nosed brats in a little red schoolhouse."

That was a far cry from working the tinpans and cowboys up Santa Fe way. And an even farther cry from being Zebulon Moss's kept woman, bought and paid for.

Creeds shook his head. He had to smile. Damn, this was getting better and better. A real challenge.

He was a tall, scrawny man, dressed in the ankle-length black coat he wore summer and winter. On his head, he sported a battered silk top hat he thought became him, and a long woolen muffler in the red Royal Stuart tartan was wound twice around his turkey neck. He'd taken the scarf off a tinpan he'd shot a spell back, but he couldn't remember the exact circumstances of that killing. After a while they had a way of all running together.

Apart from the rifle under his knee, Creeds showed no other weapons. But the pockets of his coat were lined with buckskin and in each nestled a Colt double-action Lightning revolver in .38 caliber. A careful man, he'd bobbed the hammers of both guns so his draw would not be impeded.

Creeds had killed seventeen men. One he did remember was good ol' Charlie Peppers, who was reckoned by them who knew to be the fastest man with a gun south of the Picketwire.

After the fight, Creeds had taken Charlie's title and his left ear as a trophy. He'd also bedded his woman, but that ended badly when he'd had to shoot her after she came at him with a knife in her hand, crying rape.

All in all, Creeds considered himself the West's premier gunfighter, and no one cared to argue the point with him.

Silas Creeds was trespassing on Dromore range and knew men had been shot for less, but it didn't trouble him in the least. He was confident of his gun skills, and such fears were for lesser men. He rode past the big house, skirted the corral where the Hereford bull was penned up, then crossed fifty yards of open ground to the red schoolhouse.

He drew rein and studied the front of the building, a flurry of snow spinning around him. Because of the iron-gray sky the windows on either side of the door were opaque and stared back at him like lifeless eyes. Inside the kids were quiet, probably studying their ciphers, he guessed. Or was Trixie telling them about the good old days in Santa Fe?

After a while he stood in the stirrups and yelled, "Trixie Lee! Come out!"

The children's voices raised in an excited babble and Trixie hushed them into silence.

"Trixie Lee!" Creeds yelled. "Get out here! I won't tell you a second time."

The door opened a crack and the woman's voice called out, "What do you want, Creeds?"

"Me, I want nothing, Trixie. But good ol' Zeb wants his woman back in his bed. He says he's hurting for you real bad, if you get my meaning."

"I'm not going back," Trixie called out. "I'm not going anywhere with you, Creeds."

Creeds relaxed in the saddle and smiled. "Trixie, Zeb paid two hundred dollars for you, fair and square as ever was. You're his property. Now get the hell out here or I'll come in after you."

"You heard the lady. She's not going anywhere with you."

The gunman's head turned like a striking snake toward the handsome young man who lounged against the corner of the building. The man's sheepskin was open and he wore a belted Colt.

Creeds' yellow, reptilian eyes glowed. "Who the hell are you?"

"Me? I'm the man who's throwing you off this property."

"Give me a name." Under Creeds' sparse mustache, his thin lips were peeled back from his teeth. "Damn it, boy. I never did cotton to gunning a nameless man.

"Name's Shawn O'Brien. I'm co-owner of this ranch, and you're on it, Creeds, which is causing me no little distress."

"So you've heard of me, O'Brien?"

"Some talk"

"What did you hear?"

"That you're a tinhorn killer who'll cut any man, woman, or child in half with a shotgun for fifty dollars."

"Hard words, O'Brien. And payment for such words don't come cheap." A wrong-handed man, Creeds slipped his left hand into the pocket of his coat.

But suddenly he was looking into the muzzle of Shawn's Colt.

"Mister," Shawn said, "when you bring that mitt

out, either have a prayer book in it or nothing at all."

As slow as molasses, Creeds' long-fingered hand spidered out of his pocket. "All right. You got the drop on me, O'Brien."

"Seems like."

"I want to talk with Trixie."

"You've already done that, and she's not interested in anything you have to say."

Creeds, irritated that he'd been shaded on the drop by a hick with cow crap on his boots, turned away from Shawn and yelled with a vicious edge to his voice, "Trixie! Get the hell out here!"

The triple click of Shawn's cocked Colt was an exclamation point of sound in the snow-spun morning. "Mister, I warned you—"

But he bit off his remaining words when the schoolhouse door opened and Trixie Lee stepped outside.

Creeds grinned. "Good to see you again, Trixie. Now get up on the back of this here hoss. We got some travelin' to do."

The girl shook her head. "I told you I'm not going anywhere with you, Silas."

"And I told you that Zeb wants you back."

"Zeb doesn't want me." Her fingers touched the deep scar that ran from the corner of her left eye to her mouth. "He just can't handle the thought that a woman would even think about running out on him."

"That doesn't signify with me, Trixie. But Zeb paid two hundred dollars for you, more than your puncher friend here makes in a year. The way I see it, he ain't getting his money's worth what with you lighting a shuck for a schoolhouse on a hick ranch an' all."

"I'll pay him back. Tell him that. It may take me a couple years, but I'll repay every last cent of his money."

Creeds shook his head. "He wants his woman, not the money."

"Then he can go to hell," Trixie spat out. "And tell him to take you with him."

"You heard the lady," Shawn said, stepping away from the corner of the building. "Now fork that bronc on out of here and don't even think about coming back."

Creeds smiled and glanced at the sky. Lifting his top hat, he revealed a bald head covered with a red bandana. "Oh, I'll be back, cowboy, count on it. No man gets the drop on Silas Creeds and lives to boast of it."

Holding the hat with his right hand inside it, he brushed off a few flakes of snow from the crown.

A moment later, a bullet slammed into the hat.

# Chapter Two

The bullet hit the holstered derringer under the crown, and rammed the sneaky gun with venomous force into Creeds' hand. The man yelped, let the top hat drop, and shook his stinging fingers.

"I seen that tinhorn trick for the first time twenty years ago. It didn't fool me then and didn't fool me now." Grim old Luther Ironside, the Dromore *segundo*, walked from the corner of the schoolhouse behind a smoking Colt. "You heard Mr. O'Brien, Creeds. Now git off his damned property."

Creeds was livid, raging beyond anger. The gunman's face twisted into a demonic mask of hate as he stepped along the ragged edge of insanity. He was enraged enough to draw.

"Try it, Creeds." Ironside's voice was low and dangerous. "See what happens." Snow flurried around him and his gray hair tossed in the wind. He looked like an Old Testament prophet come to justice.

Creeds was game, but he backed off like a snail into its shell when he saw Ironside adopt the classic gunfighter pose, right arm extended, the revolver steady in his fist, left foot forming a T behind the heel of the right, deciding he didn't want any part of the tall old man. Not that day. "Mister, I'll be back and I'll kill you."

Ironside nodded. "Yeah, you do that, sonny. But wait until them fingers o' your'n have straightened out some. A blowed-up sneaky gun stings like the dickens."

Creeds swung back to Trixie. "Last chance."

The girl shook her head, turned on her heel, and rushed back into the schoolhouse.

"I'm going, O'Brien," Creeds said. "But I'll be back and I'll bring down the fires of hell on this place."

Shawn picked up the man's hat and handed it to him. "You'll need that. Keep your head warm."

The gunman cursed, then swung his horse away and was soon swallowed by cartwheeling snow, winter darkness, and distance. His threat hung in the air and made the morning foul.

\* \* \*

"We should've killed that feller, Shawn," Ironside said. "I figger I taught you better than that."

"I thought about it. But it didn't seem to call for a shooting."

"Damn it, he had a sneaky gun,"

"Yes, he did at that. Why didn't you kill him, Luther?"

Ironside was silent for a moment, but couldn't find an answer. Finally, he said, "Well, your brother Jacob would've gunned him right off."

"Probably."

"No probably. Jake would've gunned him fer sure."

"Yes . . . he . . . would . . ."

Ironside snorted like an angry bull. "Hell, Shawn, you're not listening to me."

"I'm thinking, Luther."

"Thinking, huh? Well study on this—if you've got the drop on a man never let him take his hat off. I teached you that a long time ago."

Shawn smiled. "I guess I must've slept through that lesson."

"I guess you did, an' it near got your fool head blowed off."

"But you were around to save me, Luther, as always."

"Damn right I was, as always."

Shawn quickly stepped close to the old man, taking him by surprise, then laid a smacking kiss on Ironside's unshaven cheek. "You're my hero, Luther." He grinned.

Ironside rubbed his cheek as though he'd just been stung by a hornet. "Damn it, boy, don't ever do that again."

Shawn laughed and walked toward the schoolhouse.

Ironside watched him until he opened the door and stepped inside. Only then did Ironside smile. God knows, he'd tanned their hides often enough doing it, but he'd taught his O'Brien boys right. No doubt about that.

When Shawn stepped into the school, the black eyes of a dozen kids turned to him. All were the children of the Dromore vaqueros, and their education was one of his father's pet projects.

His spurs chiming in the sudden hush, Shawn walked to the front of the class. He smiled at the teacher he knew only as Julia. "We have to talk."

The woman nodded, realizing that the morning's events had changed everything. She turned to her class. "Children, the snow is getting heavier. I'm letting school out early today."

The kids had learned enough English to understand the gist of that. They cheered before stampeding out the door in a wild tangle, perhaps fearful that Miss Julia might change her mind.

After the children left, Julia said, "I guess I've got some explaining to do."

Shawn nodded. "Trixie Lee to Miss Julia Davenport is quite a leap. It confuses a man."

"Julia Davenport is my real name. I was Trixie Lee when I worked in Zebulon Moss's saloon in Santa Fe. He gave me that name and I've always hated it."

"All right. Tell me about it," Shawn said, his chin set.

But Julia saw no accusation or judgment in his eyes. Rather she saw a reined patience, a man waiting for what was to come. She wiped off the chalked blackboard with a yellow duster, giving herself time to collect her thoughts and leaving circular white smears that matched the color of her face.

Shawn came from a direction she didn't expect. "Did Moss give you the scar on your face?"

Julia turned then shook her head. "No, no, he didn't."

Shawn waited. The only sound in the room was the whisper of the north wind around the eaves and, far off, the voices of the children.

"My mother did that with a carving knife," Julia explained. "It was part of a carving set that had been a wedding present to her and Pa."

"What happened?"

"She went crazy. Mad, I guess you'd say. Pa failed at everything he'd tried in life, including the poems he wrote that nobody ever published. Farming on the Kansas plains was his last chance to make good. Have you ever been in Kansas?"

Shawn shook his head.

"It's a flat, lonely place, grass as far as the eye can see and not a tree in sight. Well, Ma stuck it out for five years—five years of drought, prairie fire, torrential rains, blizzards, whirlwinds, locusts, rattlesnakes, and gray wolves, to say nothing of horse thieves and begging, destitute Indians." Julia smiled. "What is it they say? 'In God we trusted, in Kansas we busted.' That's how it was with us, and with our poverty came not only hunger but the death of hope."

"When you talk about Kansas, you shut your eyes," Shawn said.

"I'm seeing it again, just like it was, so lonely and bleak."

"And it finally drove your ma mad?"

"Yes. I guess it was the loneliness that drove her mad, that and the constant prairie wind. The wind blows day and night and it never stops, not for a moment. Then one day, she went outside the cabin and screamed and screamed and we thought her screams would never end. Finally Pa took her inside and she was quiet for a few days. I mean she didn't speak or eat; she just stared and stared at nothing. Then, on the Sabbath, after Pa had read from the Bible, Ma got the carving knife and stabbed my little sister Bethany through the heart. She slashed at me and gave me the scar on my face, then she cut her own throat."

Julia blinked, seeing pictures she didn't want to see. "There was blood everywhere. The cabin was full of blood, red, scarlet blood on the floor, on the walls, all over Pa, all over me. Then Pa roared as though he was in pain and he held Ma and my sister to him for a day and a night and then another day. We buried the bodies away from the house, but shallow because the ground was hard with frost. The coyotes came and took them and we never found anything of Ma or Bethany again."

"I'm sorry," Shawn said, knowing how inadequate that sounded.

Julia took a breath and continued. "After that we moved to Dodge, where Pa thought he might prosper in the dry goods business, but he died of nothing more serious than a summer cold within a year."

Shawn stepped to a side window and looked outside. Sky and earth were the same shade of dark purple and snow cartwheeled through the sullen day, driven by a wind cold as a stepmother's breath. Julia had lit the oil lamp on her desk, but its dull orange glow did little to banish the gloom shadowing the schoolhouse.

"So you were left alone in the world," Shawn said. "You were just a child, I guess."

"I lived as best I could for a while, then I jumped a deadheading freight to Wichita. I couldn't find a job so I worked the line for the next three years for a four-hundred-pound gal I knew only as Big Bertha. That's where Zeb Moss found me. I'd just reached my seventeenth birthday."

"And he gave you a new name," Shawn said.

"And a job. He paid Bertha two hundred dollars for me and made me a hostess in his saloon in Santa Fe. He said with my scarred face I'd have freak value to customers who valued such things."

"So after a while you ran away and came here?"

"Not for a couple years. I became Zeb's kept woman and he never let me out of his sight. Then I read an advertisement in the newspaper about a teaching job and answered it. I made my break from Zeb when Colonel O'Brien wrote, telling me the job was mine."

"You sent references to the colonel," Shawn said. "Pa said you were obviously a genteel young lady of good breeding and that you'd worked as a tutor back East."

Julia smiled slightly. "Say what's on your mind, Shawn. Tell me I'm not a genteel young lady at all. I'm just a cheap whore and now my pimp wants me back."

# Chapter Three

Julia Davenport's words stung Shawn O'Brien like wasps, yet he had to push her and discover why the colonel could make such a mistake. "Your references were impeccable. You sent three letters of recommendation from good Boston families that fooled even Pa, and he's not a man easily hoodwinked."

Julia looked like a woman in pain. "The letters were forged by a Caddo Indian by the name of Billy One Wing. He's got only one arm, but he's the best counterfeiter in the business. He gets a lot of work from Zeb, and I gave him mine. I trusted Billy because he doesn't like white men and knows when to keep his mouth shut."

Shawn nodded. "He must be good to have fooled the colonel."

"Billy One Wing could fool anybody." Julia

took her cloak from the peg on the wall and threw it around her shoulders. She doused the oil lamp, then said, "Well, shall we go see the colonel?"

"You're a good teacher, Julia. Everybody agrees on that."

"My ma taught me to read and cipher. The rest I know comes from books."

"I'll talk to the colonel first," Shawn said. "Prepare the way."

"What difference does it make? You know he'll fire me and throw me out of Dromore."

"If he does, what will you do?"

"I don't know. Run somewhere else, I guess. Just keep on running until Zeb Moss tires of chasing me."

Shawn thought for a moment, and then said, "Everything blew up this morning, Julia. Under different circumstances I would've said nothing to the colonel about your past, but suddenly you're a danger to Dromore. You heard Silas Creeds. He means to do us harm if he can."

"I understand, Shawn. You must do what you have to do. I'll survive."

"I'll talk to him," Shawn offered again. "When we go back to the house, just go to your room and wait."

"For what?"

"For whatever the colonel decides."

"Is he down on whores?"

"He's down on anything or anyone that's a threat to Dromore."

"And that includes me?"

"Yes. I'm afraid it does,"

Julia nodded. "Then I'll do as you say."

She and Shawn walked to the door, but Julia stopped and looked up at the tall O'Brien brother. "Knowing what you've learned about me, could you love a woman like me, Shawn?"

Shawn smiled. "What kind of question is that to ask a man?"

"It's simple enough. Could you love a woman like me?"

"I don't know."

"Is it the scar? In your eyes am I the troll that lives under the bridge?"

"No, you're a beautiful woman, Julia. I think that scar adds to your attractiveness, not detracts from it."

Julia absorbed that. "The reason I asked is I want a man to love me one day."

"One day a man will, depend on it."

"But not you?"

"I've still got growing to do, Julia. Maybe a few years from now I could, but not right now."

"An honest answer."

"It's how I feel."

"Will you give me your arm when we walk to the house?"

"I'd be honored," Shawn said.


"So she's a whore," Luther Ironside said to the others gathered in the parlor of Dromore. "Damn me, but I knew it all along. I can just tell, you understand?"

Colonel Shamus O'Brien winced. "Luther, you think every woman is a whore until she proves otherwise, usually to your disappointment."

"Shawn, how seriously do you take Silas Creeds' threats?" Samuel, Shawn's oldest brother, looked at him in earnest.

"He's a killer, Sam," Shawn said. "I take anything he says seriously and so should you."

"Damn, I should've plugged him when I had the chance," Ironside whined.

"If it's not him, it will be somebody else," Shawn said. "Zebulon Moss wants his woman back and he'll kill to get her."

"Why?" Samuel asked. "I mean, she's a pretty woman, even with the scar an' all, but if what I've heard about Moss is correct, he's rich enough to get any woman he wants."

"How do you know, Sam?" Patrick, Shawn's brother, asked.

"You mean about Moss?"

"Yeah. How do you know he's rich?"

"He owns half of Santa Fe. I heard that the last time I was up that way, and there are some who reckon ol' Zeb got his start in the bank robbing profession. Of course they don't say it out loud. Silas Creeds is just one of the thugs he hired to keep his business interests running smoothly."

"You mean his saloons?" Shamus asked.

"Saloons, opium, prostitution, the protection racket, you name it. Zeb's got a dirty finger in a lot of pies."

"Enough about Moss," Shawn said. "We're supposed to be talking about Julia Davenport."

"Hell, get rid of her, I say," Ironside said. "We don't want a whore teaching our kids. God knows what she'll tell them."

"Luther," Shamus said, "may I remind you that when you served in my regiment in the war you ran a few rackets of your own, including, but not limited to, selling rotgut whiskey to the new recruits and acquiring fancy women for their officers. And if memory serves me correctly, you and the quartermaster regularly traded coffee and flour to the Rebs for cigars, chewing tobacco, and Confederate scrip and made a tidy profit doing it."

Ironside opened his mouth to speak, but the colonel held up a silencing hand. "As for teaching, you taught my sons about whoring, drinking, cussing, gun fighting, and riding fast horses. Readings from Holy Scripture were notably absent from your curriculum, as was righteous instruction on the path to eternal redemption."

Satisfied that he'd stated his case in an exemplary fashion, Shamus sat back in his wheelchair. "Now, Luther, no more about who should teach who, please. You are hardly qualified to have any opinions on the matter."

Patrick grinned. "I bet you're sorry you spoke, Luther."

Ironside growled something under his breath and Shamus said, "What? What was that?"

"Nothing," Ironside said. "I didn't give my opinion on nothing."

"And I should hope not," Shamus said. "The very idea."

"Do you gentlemen mind if I say something?" Samuel's wife Lorena interrupted.

"Please do," Shamus said, scowling at Ironside. "It will be a pleasant change to hear someone talk common sense for a change."

"We hired a teacher, not a past," Lorena pointed out. "As it happens, Julia is an excellent teacher and the children love her. What more can we ask of her?"

"Hear, hear," Patrick said.

"I don't think it's for men, including you, Luther, to sit in judgment on her. It was men who used and abused Julia in the past and if you send her packing, you'll be continuing that abuse, all of you."

"Hear, hear," Patrick said again.

Shamus looked at him. "Patrick, don't say that again." To Lorena he said, "There is a possibility that she could—"

"Probability," Shawn interrupted.

"Bring danger to Dromore. How do you address that, Lorena?"

"Colonel, you've never shied away from danger before."

"True, but Miss Davenport is not kin. She's a stranger to us. But she's an employee of this ranch and deserves a fair hearing. She's our schoolteacher and an important part of Dromore, no doubt about that." Shamus turned to his sons. "Patrick, Samuel, and Shawn, your opinions, please."

"What about me?" Ironside said.

"You've already made your feelings known, Luther," Shamus said.

"But I've changed my mind, Colonel. What Lorena said about us being no better than the men who abused her in the past kinda rang true with me."

"A most singular change of mind indeed, Luther," Lorena said. "But of the greatest moment." She looked around the study. "Well, what do the brothers O'Brien think?"

Shawn cast his vote. "I'm for keeping her right here at Dromore."

"I agree." Patrick nodded.

"That sets fine with me," Samuel agreed.

"Colonel?" Lorena looked to her father-in-law.

"I'll think on this and give you my answer in the morning," Shamus said. "I will pray to Our Lady of Good Counsel and beg her advice on this matter."

"Good. She's a woman." Lorena smiled.

"And the virgin mother of God," Shamus said.

# Chapter Four

Gray old Uriah Tweedy came down from the Manzano Mountains astride a buckskin mustang leading a one-eyed Missouri pack mule. He turned in the saddle for a final look at the trail he'd taken.

"Sleep tight, ol' Ephraim," he yelled. "I'll be back in the spring."

Now that the bears were hibernating in their deep dens there would be no more hunting until they woke in spring sunshine and once again roamed the wild lands.

As the snow swirled around him and the wind sighed cold, Tweedy dreamed of a soft bed with sheets and blankets and a bright patchwork quilt to keep the winter gloom at bay. And eggs. Sunnyside up. Fried in butter with thick slices of sourdough bread on the side and more butter, sweet and yellow as corn silk.

But when he camped that night, Tweedy's supper was as it had been for the past six months, bear meat and bacon so old the fat was sloughing off the lean, and little enough of that.

After he ate, Tweedy crouched over a hatful of fire and contented himself with coffee, his pipe, and fond memories of the slender, graceful Hopi woman he'd lived with for nigh on five years. He'd named her Kajika, which in Hopi meant Walks Without Sound. She was half bobcat, half cougar, and all woman, and she'd made his days comfortable and his nights memorable. The Mescaleros had stolen her and though Tweedy searched high and low, he never found her again.

He sighed and stirred the fire with a stick, sending up a shower of sparks that glowed bright scarlet and then died. It was a hell of a thing to lose a woman like that, a woman who walked without sound.

He heard a sound. A twig cracked in the snow-flecked darkness and Tweedy stood, his .44-40 Henry in his hands. "Is that you, ol' Ephraim?" he called out. "You should be abed."

Only the creak of the wind and the hush of the falling snow could be heard.

"Ephraim, have you come for me?" Tweedy said into the night. "Have you counted how many of your kin I've shot an' skun and come for a reckoning?

"Drop the rifle, old man, or I'll drill you square."

"That ain't Ephraim," Tweedy said. "It's a skunk."

"Drop the rifle, I said." The man's voice was harsh and commanding, in no mood for conversation. "There's two Winchesters on you and we don't miss much."

The men came at Tweedy from his right and left, their rifles at the ready.

Tweedy let go of the Henry and it dropped at his feet. "Surprised you didn't gun me straight off. Ain't that the way of trash like you?"

The man to his right spoke first. "Thought about it, but we need your fire and grub and we don't much feel like dragging your carcass through the brush in the dark. That'll keep until mornin'."

"Considerate feller," Tweedy said under his breath.

Two men stepped into the firelight. They wore ragged mackinaws and jeans and looked as though they were missing their last six meals. Both had the wary, watchful eyes of predators and the Winchesters in their hands were oiled and well cared for.

"Sit, pops," the older of the two said. He wore

a moth-eaten fur cap, the earflaps tied under his chin, and his feet were bound with rags, as were his companion's.

Tweedy reckoned that a man who can't afford boots was poor indeed. "What do you want from me?"

"Whatever's your'n."

"I ain't got much."

"Hoss, mule, rifle, shoes on your feet, clothes on your back, we'll take it all," the man said. "It's a sight more'n we got."

"Coffee in the pot, boys," Tweedy said, playing the kindly old-timer. But the man who hunted black bear and grizzly for a living had learned to pay close attention to everything around him, and his pale blue eyes searched for an opening. With riffraff like those two, just a second of time was all he'd need. When Uriah Tweedy put his mind to it, he was a sudden, dangerous man and he'd planted more than a few who'd figured otherwise. He was seventy years old, tough as a trail drive steak, and as enduring as an Apache.

And he was salty. Too salty to allow a couple of yellow-bellied curs rob him of what was his.

"What you got in your poke, pops?" The older man nodded to the burlap sack resting against Tweedy's saddle.

"Bear meat, sonny," Tweedy said. "I had bacon, but that's all gone. Was half rotten anyway."

"Then pour us coffee and burn us a couple bear steaks."

The younger man was anxious to get on with it. "Joe, I say we gun the old coot. He's got eyes that have seen more'n their share o' killing."

"Hey, pops, you're creeping the hell out of my cousin Link," the man called Joe said. "Now what am I gonna do with you, huh?"

"No man wants to die," Tweedy said.

"Yeah, but I reckon you've already lived your three-score-and-ten, old-timer, so you're long overdue fer dying." Joe looked at the younger man. "All right, Link, after he cooks for us, I'll gun him. I never was much of a trail cook myself." Joe smiled. "That set all right with you, pops?"

"Do I have, like, any choice in the matter?" Tweedy asked.

"Sure you do, pops. You kin get shot in the head or the belly." Joe grinned. "Life's just full of choices, ain't it?"

"Well, I'm not partial to getting gut shot," Tweedy told him.

"Then I'll put a bullet in your head," Joe said. "Unless you ruin them steaks, that is."

"I've got salt in my possibles bag," Tweedy offered. "You like salt?"

"Everybody likes salt, you crazy old bastard," Link snarled. "Get it out and salt that bear meat."

Tweedy knuckled his forehead. "Right away, sonny. Just don't start shootin' at ol' Uriah."

"Old man's tetched," Link said to Joe. "When you kill him, you'll be doing him a favor."

"Ain't that the truth, cousin."

Those were the last words he ever uttered.


Tweedy picked up the buckskin possibles bag and pretended to root around inside, continuing to play the part of a confused old-timer.

Then he moved. In one fluid, graceful motion he grabbed a Green River knife from the bottom of the bag and flung it at Joe. The five-inch blade slammed into the man's throat to the hilt and Joe's eyes popped wide; he knew he was a dead man.

Tweedy didn't hesitate for a second. He threw himself at the Henry rifle Joe had tossed aside and rolled on his back, the gun coming up fast. Link stood paralyzed for an instant, his eyes on his cousin down on hands and knees, gagging blood and phlegm.

Tweedy needed no more time than that. He fired, cranked the rifle, and fired again, both bullets crashing into the center of Link's chest. But the young man was game and managed to trigger a despairing shot at Tweedy. Hit high on his left shoulder, Tweedy rolled again and levered the Henry. But he had no need to shoot. Link was down and wasn't moving.

With a mortally wounded man's desperation, Joe tried to pull the knife from his throat, his bloody mouth wide in a silent scream.

Tweedy rose, stepped to the man's side, and booted him onto his back. Joe's unbelieving eyes stared at the older man. Joe was stunned by the manner and circumstance of his death.

"Mister," Tweedy said, no sympathy in him, "I'm too old a cat to be played with by kittlins."

Joe closed his terrified eyes and death took him.

His Henry up and ready, Tweedy stepped to Link. The boy, who looked to be no more than seventeen, was as dead as he was ever going to be.

Shaking his head, Tweedy surveyed the scene of carnage. It was a sorry thing to die for a mustang hoss and a one-eyed mule.

The pain from his bullet wound set in and he breathed through gritted teeth. The ball was deep, too deep to dig out by himself. He needed help badly.

He tilted back his head and yelled into the night, "Ephraim, you leave me alone now, you hear? Ol' Uriah is hurtin' and he don't need no wintertime bear adding to his misery."

It was not in Tweedy's nature to ask the help of anyone, but getting shot changes a man's attitude fast. With fat flakes of snow feathering around him, Tweedy remembered there was a big ranch somewhere to the northeast. Dromore, that was it. Maybe they were caring folks who would tend a wounded man. Snow or no snow, he'd ride through darkness for Dromore.

Maybe they'd put him in a bed with a patch-work quilt.

# Chapter Five

The morning was dark and cold and the air smelled of raw steel. Snow flurried in the wind and the top of Glorieta Mesa was lost behind cloud. Shamus O'Brien sat in his wheelchair, looking out the window of the parlor. He turned and looked around the room. "I've thought it over and I've decided that Miss Julia Davenport can stay on at Dromore as our schoolteacher. Any objections?"

The brothers O'Brien were silent.

"Luther?" Shamus asked.

"It's fine by me, Colonel," Ironside answered.

"Then it's settled," Shamus hit his fist against the arm of his wheelchair. "Lorena, are you satisfied?"

She nodded. "You came to the right decision, Colonel."

"Quite so. As you said, who are we to judge her?"

"Hear, hear," Patrick said.

"Patrick, I do wish you'd stop saying that." Shamus scowled. "Makes you sound like a damned Englishman."

"Sorry, Pa," Patrick mumbled.

"Hear, hear," Shawn said, grinning.

Shamus ignored that and spoke directly to Samuel. "Have you heard from your brother?"

"As far as I know Jake's still riding shotgun for the Simmons and Smyth stage line up Denver way. I haven't gotten a letter since the last one."

"But that was a month ago," Shamus argued.

Samuel nodded. "Jake's not much of a hand at letter writing."

"I worry about Jacob," Shamus said. "I guess we all do."

"Jake can take care of himself," Ironside said. "I taught that boy all I know and like me he's hell on wheels with a scattergun. Damn right."

Normally that would've given Shamus an opportunity to berate Ironside about his teaching methods, but Patrick saved the older man from yet another tongue-lashing when he said, "Rider coming."

Shawn stepped to the window and looked out into the snowy, iron-gray morning. "Looks like he's riding hurt."

"Jesus, Mary, and Joseph," Shamus said, crossing himself. "It's not Jacob, is it?"

"No. Older man. He's wearing a bearskin coat and leading a pack mule." After a few more moments of observation, Shawn said, "Damn, he looks all used up."

"Shawn, you and Patrick help him inside," Shamus instructed. "Maybe all that ails him is cold and hunger."

"I done fer the two bushwhackers, but I took a bullet in the shoulder, so maybe they done fer me." Uriah Tweedy sat in the kitchen of Dromore with the O'Briens and Ironside.

"Luther, what do you think?" Shamus asked.

"He's a scrawny old rooster, but he's got some meat on his shoulders, and the ball's still there, Colonel."

"We can send to Santa Fe for a doctor," Shamus suggested.

"We should do that, Colonel," Ironside agreed. "This man will need attention after I cut the bullet out of him."

"There's no other way?"

"No. If it stays inside him much longer it could poison his whole body."

"Gangrene?"

"It's a possibility, Colonel."

Tweedy took a gulp of brandy then said to Ironside, "You done this afore, sonny?"

"Yeah, during the war a few times. Dug minié balls out of cavalrymen."

"How many of your patients survived?"

"Oh, in round numbers, about half."

Tweedy nodded. "All right, then cut away, sonny. I like them odds."

"I'm about the same age as you, so don't call me sonny," Ironside said irritably.

"Luther, is it?"

"Yeah."

"Then cut away, sonny."

"Pat, Shawn, help Luther get Mr. Tweedy onto the table," Shamus ordered.

"Beggin' your pardon, Colonel, but I'm right comfy where I am." Tweedy smiled, but beads of perspiration appeared on his forehead and his breathing was quick and shallow.

Shamus saw that Tweedy was hurting and asked, "Can you do it there, Luther?"

Ironside nodded, then said, "Cletus, get more brandy into him. A lot more."

"Now you're talking my language . . . Luther," Tweedy said.

"I'll be drinking right along with you," Ironside said. "Damn right."

Lorena helped Ironside remove Tweedy's buckskin shirt and under vest, revealing a muscular chest and wide shoulders.

"You look real good for an old-timer," Ironside said, smiling under his mustache. "Not as scrawny as I thought."

"Huntin' bear ain't for sissies, sonny." Tweedy winced. "I can't move my shoulder. How's it look to you?"

"About what you'd expect," Ironside said. "It don't look good, kinda like a big red mouth."

"You'll be just fine, Uriah," Lorena said, angling Ironside a killer look. "Now drink some more brandy and we'll soon get the bullet out."

"Real nice to have you here, ma'am," Tweedy said. He glared at Ironside. "Some folks just ain't sympathetic by nature, I reckon."


Luther Ironside, slightly drunk, had an ordinary table knife in his hand. It was a time for digging, not cutting. Lorena held an oil lamp to give him more light.

Shamus and the O'Brien brothers were reduced to interested spectators, though Patrick held the brandy decanter, should Tweedy or Ironside's courage falter.

"You ready?" Ironside said to Tweedy, the knife poised over the ragged wound.

"Have at it, sonny." The man held up his glass. "About now I'm feeling no pain."

"Me neither," Ironside pointed out, plunging the knife deep into the wound.

Tweedy's breath hissed through his clenched teeth.

"Damn, it's in there far." Ironside probed with

the tip of the knife and blood welled around the blade. "Hold on there, old-timer. This ain't going to be easy."

"Easy fer you," Tweedy said, openmouthed.

"Pa," Patrick whispered, "are you sure Luther's done this before?"

"He's done it," Shamus said. "How well he's done it, I don't know."

Lorena leaned over and wiped blood from the wound. Ironside dug around inside again. Lorena's face was pale, her eyes wide, understanding Tweedy's pain.

"I feel it," Ironside said. "I feel the ball."

There was a tap at the door.

Tweedy was tough and he had sand, but the man was in a lot of pain and it showed. "For God's sake, sonny. Dig the damned ball out of there."

"It's stuck, damn it." Sweat beaded Ironside's forehead and his right hand was covered in blood to the wrist. "It's stuck, stuck, stuck."

Another *tap-tap-tap* sounded at the door.

Tweedy's tortured breath hissed in and out of him with a sound like a boiling steam kettle.

*Tap-tap-tap.*

"Somebody answer the damned door," Ironside yelled.

Samuel rose and quickly opened the door. "Oh, it's you, Julia. You've come at a bad time."

"Samuel, who is it?" Shamus leaned to one side.

"Miss Davenport."

"Then let her in. I'm sure Lorena could use some help."

Julia stepped into the room, her face puzzled.

"We have a wounded man here," Shamus said. "Luther is trying to get the ball out."

Julia could see only the back of Tweedy's head. She walked closer and Lorena gave her a grateful smile. "It's deep," she said.

Recognition dawned on Julia's face. "Why that's Uriah Tweedy."

"As ever was, Trixie," Tweedy said, gasping. "It's right . . . nice . . . to see you again." He scowled at Ironside. "You're a damned butcher, sonny."

"Hell, man, I'm doing my best." Ironside turned to Patrick, "Give me a swig of that brandy, Pat."

"And me," Tweedy rasped out.

"That's the last thing you need, both of you." Julia pushed Ironside out of her way. "I'll do it. Lorena, wipe off the wound. And Patrick, pour the brandy over my fingers."

The woman held out her hand and Patrick liberally doused it with the alcohol. To Tweedy she said, "Uriah, this will hurt, but only for a moment."

"Do what you have to do, Trixie. I got a worse hurtin' put on me than ol' Ephraim ever done."

"Brace yourself, Uriah," Julia said softly, and plunged her long, slender finger into the wound.

Tweedy ground his teeth as sudden agony hacked at him. He didn't cry out, though his face was a twisted mask of torment.

"Got it!" Julia cried. Her finger came out of the wound, the rifle bullet caught in the crook of the top joint of her bloody index finger.

Tweedy looked close to fainting, but his ordeal was not yet over.

"Uriah, there's a piece of buckskin in there. I felt it," Julia said. "It's got to come out, too."

"Hell," Ironside said, "bullets kill a man, not buckskin."

"I must remove it," Julia insisted. "It's dirty and could cause an infection."

Ironside looked at the bear hunter. "Tweedy?"

"She's right. It's got to come out."

"Stupid, if you ask me," Ironside grumbled. "Digging buckskin out of a man."

"No one is asking you, Luther," Shamus said. "Miss Davenport, please proceed."

The piece of buckskin was only the size of a dime and it took Julia several endless minutes to find and remove it. By then Tweedy had reached the limit of his endurance and was barely holding on to consciousness.

"You all right, Tweedy?" Ironside asked.

The man nodded.

"Good, because this is gonna hurt like hell, but it will clean the wound."

Before Tweedy could utter the NO! that formed in his mouth, Ironside poured brandy over the raw, tattered wound.

The shock of pain was too much, and Tweedy could no longer hold on. He closed his eyes and plunged into darkness.

"Luther, was that necessary?" Lorena hissed, her eyes flashing anger.

Julia said, "Mr. Ironside is not much of a surgeon, I agree, but he's right. The alcohol will help fight infection."

Ironside nodded. "Damn right." He looked down at his unconscious patient. "Now what do we do with him?"

"You'll help the ladies get him into bed, Luther." Shamus looked at Julia wiping blood off her hand. "I want you to stay on at Dromore as our teacher, Miss Davenport."

The woman was surprised. "I came here to tender my resignation. I don't want to be a burden to you."

"You are not a burden, dear lady, I assure you."

"Did Shawn tell—"

"Yes, he told us. As Lorena said, I hired a teacher, not a past. I hope you will reconsider and stay on at Dromore."

Julia's face lit up. "Oh, I do. I can't wish for anything more in the world."

"Then the matter is settled. Now get that poor man into bed." Shamus glared at Ironside. "God knows, he's suffered enough."

# Chapter Six

After stopping overnight, the snow returned with a vengeance in the morning. Silas Creeds sat his horse on the same ridge he'd sat when he caught his first sight of Dromore. He had two men with him, a couple frontier toughs who'd both killed their man in the past. Mercy Larch was a sure-thing back shooter and petty thief and his partner, Luke Manston, was younger but of the same stripe.

"We do it fast, boys," Creeds said. "Just in, grab the woman, then out and gone. Understand?"

"This woman, is she pretty?" Manston asked.

"Real pretty," Creeds replied.

Larch leered. "Big ones?"

"Big enough."

"Do we get to try her?" Manston wondered.

"Sure, boys, sure," Creeds said. "Then she tells

Mr. Moss and trust me, you'll never screw another woman again."

Manston spat a stream of tobacco juice over the side of his horse. "You could've said it plain, Creeds. You'd no call to cut up nasty."

"Tellin' it like it is, boys," Creeds said bluntly. "Now are you gonna earn your fifty dollars or are we gonna sit here an' chaw the fat all day?"

"We'll see it through, Creeds," Larch said. "But it's a hard thing to be close to a pretty woman on the trail and not get a piece of tail."

"Well, that's the way it is," Creeds said. "Zeb Moss don't like anybody messin' with his women."

That was a fact well known, and Larch kept silent.

"Right." Creeds kneed his horse into motion. "Let's get 'er done."


The thermometer on the Dromore stable door hovered a couple degrees above freezing, but ice laced both banks of the creek that ran close to the house. The day was a somber watercolor in shades of gray and black and only the snow-blurred, red tint of the schoolhouse was visible in the gloom.

Creeds, a muffler tied over his top hat and knotted under his chin, led his men directly to the school door, trusting in the murk to keep them hidden from anyone inside the house. It was unlikely people would venture outdoors too often, but he was prepared to shoot anyone who tried to stop him.

He swung out of the saddle and barged into the schoolroom, Larch and Manston close behind him. Because of the weather, only a handful of students were present, but the men ignored them and went directly for Julia.

The woman backed away from them, opening her mouth to scream. A vicious backhand from Creeds silenced her. Realizing trouble, the students ran quickly out the door.

Creeds watched the kids running away and snarled to one of his men, "Get her damned cloak. I don't want the lady to freeze to death."

Revealing surprising strength, he draped Julia's unconscious body over his shoulder and walked out into the snow. He draped the woman over the front of his saddle, then mounted up. "Let's get the hell out of here. Those damned brats will play hob."

The three men galloped north for Santa Fe. Ahead of them lay ten miles of rugged, broken country, the kind of terrain that discourages a posse and aids the hunted.


Julia Davenport groaned and tried to lift her head. She saw the snowy ground under her streak past at a galloping speed and felt Creeds' hand on her back, holding her down.

"Stay right where you're at, or I'll club you with the butt of my gun."

The motion of the horse and her uncomfortable position made talking difficult, but the woman said, "Where are you taking me?"

"Hell, you know where," Creeds said, a grin in his voice. "Zeb is pining for you something awful."

Julia tried to struggle free of the man, but he kept her pinned down. "I swear, Trixie, I'll bash your brains in if you try that again."

The woman quieted, but Creeds knew he had a problem. Around him lay a land of pine-covered mountains and dark gorges, all of it under a blanket of snow. This was not long-riding country and his mount would soon tire carrying its extra burden. If they were to reach Santa Fe before dark he needed to get Trixie on a horse, and the sooner the better.

Creeds turned and studied his back trail. He saw only the empty land, the falling snow, and the clouds shrouding the mountain peaks.

He eased up on his horse, slowing to an easy canter and let Larch and Manston get ahead of him. They were muffled to the ears in sheepskins, their heads bent against the keening wind, seeing little, hearing nothing.

He fired twice, his gun hand extended in front of

him. The bullets hit the men in the space between their turned-up collars and the bottom of their hats. It was remarkable shooting in less than ideal conditions, but Silas Creeds was no ordinary gunman. Such gun skill came to him as naturally as breathing.

He slipped his boot out of the stirrup, raised his right knee, and pushed Julia off the saddle. The woman fell on her back onto the snow and lay stunned for a moment. Then she scrambled to her feet and tried to run in her high-heeled, lace-up boots and heavy winter dress.

Creeds put a bullet a yard in front of the woman's feet and said, "The next one will be right between your shoulder blades, Trixie."

Julia froze where she was and Creeds ordered, "Go round up the black and lead it over here. And grab one of them sheepskins. You're going to need it if we don't reach Santa Fe by sundown."

Stepping around the dead men, their bodies already dusted with snow, Julia grabbed the reins of the black mustang and led it toward Creeds.

"Get a coat, like I told you," the gunman said.

Julia shook her head. "They're dead. I don't want to touch them,"

Creeds shrugged. "Then freeze." He motioned with his hand. "Get up on the hoss. Make any fancy moves and I'll kill you."

"What would Zeb say about that?" Julia scoffed.

"I dunno. I guess I'd have to kill him, too. Now get on the goddamned hoss."

She picked up her cloak and placed it around her shoulders. As the day grew colder, its thin wool would provide little warmth but she would not take clothes off a dead man.

"Let's ride," Creeds said. "We've got some hard country to cover."

Julia heard, but said nothing. Inside she was dying a little death.

# Chapter Seven

A shawled señora, holding a small boy by the hand, pounded on the door of the big house at Dromore.

The butler answered and before the man could speak, the woman said, her eyes frantic, "She's been taken."

"Who's been taken?"

"Miss Davenport." The woman looked down at the boy. "Tell him, Ignacio."

"Three men came and took her away," the boy said.

The woman crossed herself. "God help her, señor. She's gone."

"You better come inside," the butler said. "It's cold out there."

Left alone in the foyer, the woman looked around her. She'd been in the house before with her vaquero husband, but the marble floors, oak paneled walls, and grand staircase never ceased to amaze her.

She recognized the men who burst out of the study and stepped quickly toward her. Mr. Samuel, tall and handsome, and Mr. Shawn, handsomer still, with his yellow hair and piercing blue eyes.

"What happened, señora?" Mr. Shawn asked.

"Ignacio was in school and—" Uncertain of her English, she broke off and looked at her son. "Tell Mr. Shawn, Ignacio."

"Three men took her away. They came into school and grabbed Miss Julia and took her away."

Shawn kneeled beside him and took Ignacio's cold hand. "What did they look like?"

"Two men wore big coats, sheepskin coats like *mi papá*. One had a long black coat and a hat"—the boy raised his hand above his head—"this high."

"Silas Creeds," Shawn said, rising. "He's taking Julia back to Santa Fe and Zeb Moss."

Samuel glanced out a window near the door. "It's blowing up a blizzard out there and he won't get far. We'll saddle up come first light."

"No, Samuel, I'm doing this alone," Shawn said. "I feel I was responsible for Julia's safety and I should've realized this might happen. I'm going by myself."

"The hell you are," Samuel said. "You could freeze to death out there."

"We could all freeze to death out there." Shawn's eyes met his brother's. "I've got it to do, Sam."

"We'll see what the colonel has to say."

"No, don't tell Pa. Don't tell anybody until I've gone." Shawn stepped quickly to the stairs and as he mounted the steps two at a time threw over his shoulder, "Rustle me up some grub, Sam. And don't forget the coffeepot."

"But Shawn—"

"Do like I say. And do it quietly."


The snow had whitewashed the land and there was no trail for Shawn O'Brien to follow. But he doggedly headed northwest, figuring he was following the same path as Silas Creeds.

An hour later, Shawn was still well south of Sun Mountain and the light was changing. The sun had long since given up the struggle and by late afternoon the darkness began to crowd close. The north wind iced the snow on the front of his sheepskin, and above the muffler around his throat and mouth, his cheeks were red and raw. Juniper and pine stood on the high country slopes like white-haired old men who had wandered into the area and lost their way in the cloud mist.

Shawn looped around a meadow, wary of open country, then swung north again along an eyebrow of game trail through the trees. His eyes scanned ahead of him, watering in the cold, as he tried to envision Creeds' every step. Was the gunman just ahead of him, watching him with his finger on the trigger?

The windswept emptiness before him gave the lie to that question. Creeds was either in Santa Fe already or he'd gone to ground for the night.

Shawn wondered how Julia was holding up. Not well, he imagined. This high country cold could be hell on a woman.

He bitterly berated himself for leaving her alone. He should've known a man like Creeds would not give up so easily. There was no one to blame but himself, Shawn decided. But beating his breast and whining mea culpa would not help anybody, especially Julia.

With his head bent to the wind and snow, he rode on, a tiring horse under him and the pitch-black night looming ahead of him.

The two mounds of snow were not a natural phenomenon of wind and weather. Nor was the paint mare standing off a ways, its saddle slung under its belly.

Shawn O'Brien dismounted and with his gloved

hand scraped snow off one of the mounds. He uncovered the toes of a pair of boots, then moved to the other end of the mound, where he cleared snow off a man's face. The features were blue, and black shadows showed under the eyes and in hollows of the bearded cheeks. The frozen eyes were wide open. After doing the same to the other body, Shawn stood. Both men had been shot neatly in the back of the neck and one of their horses had been taken.

This was Silas Creeds' work. He'd needed a horse for Julia and had casually murdered two men to get it.

Snow swirling around him, Shawn stepped to the paint, uncinched the saddle, and let it fall to the ground. He removed the horse's bit and bridle, then patted the animal on the neck. "You're on your own, girl. Good luck to you."

The paint shook its head, then trotted south.

"As good a direction as any, hoss," Shawn said.

The bodies lay in a narrow clearing and shadows were already gathering among the pines. Shawn glanced at a sky as black as coal, here and there streaked with narrow bands of pale gray. There was no letup in the snow, and the icy wind tugged at him and snatched away his breath.

Reluctantly, Shawn decided he needed to find shelter. A man exposed to the elements overnight could freeze to death without even knowing it.

He swung into the saddle again and continued north along the game trail. After fifteen minutes, frozen to the marrow of his bones, he beheld a joyful sight, a ruined, burned-out log cabin just a hundred yards off the trail. Only two walls still stood, forming a right angle, but a huge cottonwood overhung the corner and promised a roof of sorts.

When Shawn investigated, he found that only a dusting of snow had fallen into the corner. A narrow stream was nearby, sheeted with thin ice but still flowing freely underneath.

He unsaddled his horse and led it to an area under the trees where the snow was thin. The horse was mountain bred and knew how to fend for itself and was already grazing on thin grass as Shawn walked back to the cabin.

Working quickly, he gathered up some dry, charred wood, built a hatful of fire in the corner, and put the coffeepot on to boil. He inspected his grub sack and discovered that Samuel had packed a small loaf of sourdough bread and a couple of thick slices of roast beef. He'd also wrapped three cigars in grease paper and dropped those inside.

Shawn nodded. All in all, Sam had done just fine.

\* \* \*

At first light Shawn took to the trail again, riding north into wind, snow, and cold, roofed by clouds that looked like sheets of curled lead. Santa Fe was just five miles ahead of him and he needed an excellent plan.

The trouble was, he did not have one.

# Chapter Eight

"As much as I would take great pleasure in watching you beat her, she is already flawed goods," Halim Ali said, tracing a line down his left cheek with his forefinger. "The great Sheik Abdul-Basir Hakim would not care to see her pale skin damaged further." Ali shrugged and spread his small, elegant hands. "We must think of the woman's price at the Zanzibar slave market, you understand."

"Then rest assured she will not be harmed," Zebulon Moss said.

"Where is the lady in question?"

"Locked up in the basement of my saloon."

"Ah, there is one thing more," Ali said. "The girl should not be used until Sheik Hakim inspects her and makes his judgment. If he refuses the woman, then you can throw her to your men. Is this clear to you?"

"Perfectly," Moss said. "I won't let a man with unbuttoned pants get within a mile of her."

"Then that is well." Ali smiled a small smile, showing small teeth.

Moss raised the silver coffeepot from the table. "More?"

The Arab shook his head. "No thank you. American coffee is not to my taste. It's a vile, barbaric brew."

"You don't drink liquor?"

"My religion forbids it," Ali said.

Moss leaned back in his huge, red leather chair. "How did you find out about me?"

"In San Francisco. At the Barbary Coast, I believe the place is called."

"It is. Now go on."

"Sheik Abdul-Basir Hakim's schooner the *Nawfal* recently raised anchor in the Embarcadero. He already has a score of Chinese girls on board and a few blacks, but what he most desires, and what our clients pay large sums for, are white women, preferably virgins with yellow hair."

Moss grinned. "Not too many virgins around Santa Fe."

"Sheik Hakim will sell them as virgins nonetheless."

"You still haven't answered my question, Ali. Why did you come to me?"

The Arab studied Moss before he answered. The man was exactly as he'd been described, a giant standing well over six feet, broad, muscular shoulders, black hair, and piercing blue eyes. His nose looked as though it had been broken at least twice and there was a scar above his right eyebrow. Moss's gray frockcoat was open and Ali caught a glimpse of the ivory handle of a revolver in a shoulder holster.

It was said along the Barbary Coast that Zebulon Moss had killed two dozen men with brass knuckles, blackjacks, knives, guns, and his bare hands. He was described as the most dangerous, ruthless man in the West, and Ali believed it. Moss was also said to be very wealthy, and Ali believed that, too, judging by the red velvet and polished brass opulence of his office. It was vulgar, of course, but expensive nonetheless.

Ali realized he'd been quiet for too long as he saw sudden blue fire in Moss's eyes and the man's voice sounded as though it had just been honed on a whetstone. "I asked you a question, mister."

"A thousand pardons, sir. I was gathering my thoughts." The little bug-eyed Arab, dressed in a high-button suit, celluloid collar, and striped tie, smiled. "Your reputation along the Barbary Coast is that of a man who gets things done. We were told that when you were in San Francisco you shanghaied more sailors for the New York hell ships than any man alive, and that you once controlled so many brothels you employed two hundred women."

"Half that number, and most of them were Chinese." Moss shrugged. "The good thing about Chinese whores is that they're expendable. They only last a year or two."

"Yes, indeed. And white women?"

"Yeah, some of those, some of the time. Who told you all this?"

"A tavern owner by the name of Bill Gasper, for one."

"He's still alive? I heard he'd been hung by vigilantes years ago."

"No, he's still among the living,"

"He's a rum one is ol' Bill. Cut your throat for a dollar."

"Was he correct, that you can you supply Sheik Hakim with white women out of Santa Fe on a regular basis?"

"How many does he need?"

"As we already agreed, five or six on this shipment, twice that number on subsequent deliveries." Ali read the question on Moss's face. "Mr. Moss, you have an excellent geographical situation, close to the Sonora coast of Old Mexico, and we've been assured you can lure women to you."

"I can. Or I'll shanghai them. Either way your boss will have his quota."

"Then, on behalf of Sheik Hakim, I look forward to doing business with you."

"A thousand dollars a head, mind," Moss said. "That's my price."

"Yes, but only for those who meet our standards. The rest you can sell in Mexico and still turn a profit."

"They'll all meet your standards. I don't deal in shoddy goods."

"Then the only one in doubt is the scar-faced woman."

"Trixie will meet your standards, Ali. She knows how to please a man." Moss smiled. "Even a flea-bitten Arab."

Ali smiled faintly. "Mr. Moss, I am but dirt under your feet and therefore do not mind, but do not say such words to the great and noble Sheik Abdul-Basir Hakim. He has a quick temper and has killed two score men and countless women with the sword."

Zebulon Moss was unimpressed. "I'll keep that in mind."

The basement of the Lucky Lady saloon had been hewn out of solid rock. No bigger than a jail cell, it was dark, dank, and dreary. An iron cot stood against one wall, a slop pail against another, and nothing else.

Zeb Moss took the flight of stone steps leading down to the room, the oil lamp in his hand splashing a dim yellow light on the damp walls.

The bed creaked as Julia Davenport got to her feet and waited to speak until Moss stood in front of her. "You've come here to beat me, Zeb. I tell you now, you can beat me senseless but it won't do any good. I'm not your woman any longer, nor do I wish to be ever again."

Moss smiled, huge white teeth gleaming in the gloom. "I'm not here to beat you, Trixie. Nor do I want you. Hell, I've already got another woman, and she's a sight prettier than you." As cruelly as he could, he added, "And her face ain't scarred."

"Then what do you want from me?" Julia said. "Let me go."

"I need you, Trixie."

"For what? You don't need anyone."

"It's true that I don't need your body any longer, but I do need the thousand dollars you represent. A few of my business ventures have not gone well of late."

"What the hell are you talking about, Zeb?"

"I'm selling you, my dear."

"I didn't think I was worth that much."

"You're not, but my Arab friends think otherwise."

Julia was an intelligent woman, and she knew immediately what Moss was saying. "You're selling me into slavery?"

"Bravo!" Moss said. "How very perceptive of you, my dear."

"Zeb, you can't do that to me!"

"Oh, but I can. You're destined for the Zanzibar slave market. I'm told it's a very pretty island off the coast of East Africa. You'll like it there. Sunny all day long, I'm told."

"That can't happen . . . the authorities . . ."

"What authorities? The Americans don't care and the British thought they'd shut down the Zanzibar slave markets, but they still prosper." Moss smiled. "As do the officials fresh from London who turn a blind eye to what's going on. I believe some of them get quite rich off the slave trade."

Julia felt a spike of real fear. "You'll never get me there alive."

"That is a matter of complete indifference to me, Trixie. I get paid when I deliver you to the Arabs. As to what happens after that . . . well, I just don't give a damn."

Julia was unable to talk, but Moss spoke into the silence. "Look on the bright side, Trixie. You'll end up in a brothel or some rich Arab sheik's harem. You'll be kept alive until your prettiness fades and your body sags, say in two, three years."

"You filthy rat!" Julia shrieked. She lashed out at Moss, but he caught her wrist and pulled her close to him. "You ran away from me once, Trixie. You won't get a chance to do it a second time."

The woman wrenched free, then sat on the

bed, her face in her hands. When she looked up at Moss her face was streaked with tears. "Zeb, have mercy on me. Let me go. Please, let me go back to being a schoolteacher."

Moss snorted. "A whore schoolteacher. I never heard the like." He turned and walked to the steps, then stopped. "You'll end your days as a plaything for horny men. See, Trixie, some things really never change."

# Chapter Nine

Near the Santa Fe plaza, Shawn O'Brien checked into a small hotel with the luxury of a kiva fireplace and a thick native rug on the floor. The bed was soft and clean and there was a plentiful supply of logs for the fire. Normally, he would've been content, but worry over Julia gnawed at him and gave him no peace.

His only plan was to visit every saloon and cantina in the city, starting with those owned by Zebulon Moss. It was likely he'd put Julia back to work in one of his own establishments, but he could have stashed her away in some other smaller place until the threat of rescue had passed. The city's many brothels didn't enter into Shawn's thinking. Julia was Moss's woman and he wouldn't degrade her in that way.

Shawn wore a sheepskin coat, shotgun chaps, boots, and a battered Stetson and could pass for an ordinary puncher in town on a tear. Around his waist, belted high in the horseman's style, his gun belt carried a long-barreled .44-40 Colt. In the right pocket of his coat he dropped a Smith & Wesson .32 caliber sneaky gun, as Luther Ironside had taught him.

"You go into a shooting scrape with a feller you reckon is faster than you, put your hands in the pockets of your coat and tell him you don't want to fight," Ironside had said. "Then when he starts to strut around and sneer at you and brag on himself, whip out the sneaky gun from your pocket and cut loose. Keep shootin' at his belly until he drops and there ain't no more brag left in him."

Stepping out of his room, Shawn smiled at the memory. Luther had a way with words.

The desk clerk looked up from a ledger when Shawn stopped in front of him. "Can I help you, sir?"

Shawn asked for the names of Zebulon Moss's saloons and the clerk, a rodent-faced man with sly eyes, said, "If you're looking for wine, women, and song, then the Lucky Lady is the place. If you want peace and quiet, then try the Gentleman's Club on Lincoln Street. No ladies are allowed, but they serve only the finest liquors and Cuban cigars."

After nodding his thanks, Shawn stepped into the muddy street. Despite the funneling snow there was a steady pedestrian traffic and a few freight wagons made their slow, creaking way through the crowd, Mexicans in bright serapes at the reins.

Lanky cowboys and bearded and booted miners rubbed shoulders with businessmen wearing velvet-collared coats and ogled the languid señoritas gliding past, their beautiful black eyes seductive and knowing. The white Santa Fe belles were just as bold, dressed in the height of fashion, their bustles huge, tiny hats perched on top of swept-up, ringleted hair.

Above it all was a constant babble of conversation in Spanish, English, and a half dozen other languages. The cold air smelled heavily of peppers and spices for sale in booths lining both sides of the street.

Shawn stood for a while on the steps outside the Lucky Lady, taking in the sights, aware that he was acting like an openmouthed rube. More than a few kohl-lashed eyes turned in his direction and the bolder belles coyly smiled at him, their teeth white in moist pink mouths.

Santa Fe had snap aplenty, Shawn decided, but he wasn't there for pleasure and that weighed on him.

After one last glance at the bustling street, he turned on his heel and stepped into the saloon.

The Lucky Lady was a long, fairly narrow building with a full-length mahogany bar behind which hung two French mirrors. A piano and small stage were at the far end, along with the usual assortment of tables and chairs. Unusual for a New Mexico saloon, a whale's jawbone adorned the wall opposite the bar. A narrow staircase led to the upper floor and the small, curtained rooms where the whores plied their trade.

Three bartenders lined the bar, magnificent creatures with slicked-down hair and curled mustachios. Each wore a brocade vest and sported a diamond stickpin in his cravat.

It seemed, Shawn thought, that Moss treated his male hired help well.

Although the day was dark, by the clock it was still early afternoon and the sporting crowd was still abed, gathering their strength before making their appearance at the witching hour. Two gray-haired businessmen stood at the bar talking in earnest tones and a puncher crouched at a table, nursing a beer, a hangover, and a broken heart.

A pair of young Texas guns caught and held Shawn's attention as they looked him over with insolent, challenging eyes. Dressed like the businessmen at the bar, down to the elastic-sided boots and plug hats, they didn't have weapons in view, but the cut of their coats suggested their tailor had made an adjustment for shoulder holsters.

It was not in Shawn's interest to tangle with a couple gents who sported big Texas mustaches and gold watch chains and had hired guns written all over them.

Pretending an indifference he did not feel, Shawn stepped to the bar and one of the magnificent mixologists smiled at him. "What will it be, mister? The beer is cold, the whiskey is bonded, and we have a large selection of the finest cigars."

Shawn ordered a beer and a Cuban cigar that he took time to light. Then, behind a curling cloud of turquoise smoke, he said, "I'm looking for someone."

"Aren't we all." The bartender had quick, intelligent brown eyes and at one time could've been anything.

"Her name is"—Shawn was about to say Julia, but stopped himself in time—"Trixie Lee."

"Is that a fact?" the bartender said, his face guileless. "I haven't seen Trixie in a six-month." He turned and called down the bar, "Miles, Pete, either of you seen Trixie around?"

Both men shook their heads, and the bartender said, "Plenty of pretty girls will be in come dark, cowboy. You can take your pick."

"Trixie is a friend of mine," Shawn said. "We go way back."

"Mister, Trixie has a lot of friends." The man retreated down the bar, where he and the other bartenders exchanged glances and slight shakes of the head.

Worried that he'd tipped his hand, Shawn

pretended to be unconcerned and stepped to the door as though looking through the stained glass would give him a different perspective on Santa Fe and its denizens. As a precaution, he unbuttoned his coat. He had much more confidence in the Colt .44-40 on his hip as a man killer than he did the .32 in his pocket. After a while he turned and had to step around the outstretched feet of one of the guns, who grinned at him. The other gunman said, "Trixie ain't around anymore, cowboy. Maybe you should try Albuquerque."

Shawn nodded. "I'll remember that the next time I'm there."

"Um . . . maybe you should leave today. It takes time to find a woman in a big city," the man said in a Texas drawl. He smiled without warmth. "Like leave right now."

"Thank you for the advice," Shawn said, "but I enjoy it around here. The town has snap."

"Ah, that's a complication." The Texan looked at his companion. "Is that not so, Mr. Tabard?"

"Indeed it is, Mr. Bohan."

"Well, when you boys sort it out, let me know," Shawn said.

"Impertinent, don't you think, Mr. Tabard?" Bohan inquired.

"I'd say so, Mr. Bohan."

Bohan rose from his chair, uncoiling like a slender, lithe serpent. His black eyes met Shawn's. "The air around Santa Fe has just gotten unhealthy for a man of your inquisitive nature."

"You mean you want me to leave?" Shawn asked. "Pack up and ride on out of Santa Fe, and me only arrived?"

Bohan nodded. "Just that."

"Which of you two boys is faster with the iron?" Shawn said around the cigar clenched in his teeth.

"What the hell are you talking about?" Bohan grumbled.

"It's a simple question. Who's quicker on the draw and shoot? Mr. Bohan, meaning you, or Mr. Tabard?"

"We're both fast, cowboy, faster than you know."

Shawn nodded and pulled his coat back from his gun. "So it doesn't really matter who I kill first, huh?"

Alarmed, the two businessmen stepped away from the bar out of the line of fire.

The brown-eyed bartender reached for something, his face grim. "Cowboy, you're not killing anybody." He pointed the business end of a Greener shotgun at Shawn. "Now you just slide on out of here. The beer and cigar are on the house."

Shawn arched a brow. "What about Mr. Bohan and Mr. Tabard? Will they give me the road and let me slide in peace?"

"I've got your back," the bartender said. "I've got faith in this here scattergun and every gentleman in this establishment knows it."

"Just remember, what I said still goes," Bohan cautioned. "You're a questioning man and that can get you killed in Santa Fe."

Shawn said nothing, but he turned and left a dollar on the bar. "I pay my way."

The bartender nodded. "Ease on out. Real nice and friendly, like you're saying so long to kinfolk."

Without a glance at the two gunmen, Shawn walked to the door, his spurs ringing in sudden, hostile silence, and stepped outside. The snow, heavier now, blustered around him and there were fewer people on the street, the belles and señoritas having fled to where it was warm.

Asking about Julia had touched a nerve with the two gunmen, presumably employed by Zebulon Moss. Shawn was convinced the girl was in Santa Fe, hidden away somewhere. But where was he going to find her?

He had no answer to that question, no answer at all.

# Chapter Ten

Shawn O'Brien woke from sleep, immediately awake and aware.

From somewhere in the hotel he heard a clock strike two, then leave an echoing silence. He listened into the night and heard the wind shivering along the street outside and smelled the ever-present aroma of spices and the metallic tang of snow.

The clock hadn't wakened him, he was sure of—

There it was again! A soft fall of footsteps in the hallway outside, muffled by the rug. That's what had wakened him. A couple drunks returning late maybe? Or something else?

Shawn slid the Colt from the holster by his bed and rose to his feet. Pulling his pillow into the middle of the bed, he covered it with the quilt until it looked like a man deep in peaceful slumber. He padded across the room in his long-handled underwear and dragged the easy chair to the foot of the bed to serve as a barricade. Flickering scarlet light from the fire played across the white ceiling of the room and the burning log cracked and sent up a shower of sparks.

Shawn crouched behind the chair, a flimsy enough barrier, and waited, his eyes on the door. It had a lock, but no key, the proprietor of the hotel having long since decided there was no profit in continually replacing keys taken by careless guests.

There was faint thud as a booted toe accidentally hit the bottom of the door, immediately followed by a muted, "Shh . . ."

Shawn swallowed hard, then wiped the sweat from his gun hand on the leg of his long johns. Fear, sharpened by anxiety, spiked at him and his mouth was dry as mummy dust.

The door handle turned.

His revolver up and ready, Shawn kept a steady gaze on the door. Sweat beaded his forehead and suddenly the room felt hot. Snow drifted past the window.

Slowly . . . one low creak at a time . . . the door opened a couple inches. Then two more . . . then a few more . . .

In the ruby fire glow Shawn saw the barrel of a

gun ease through the opening, then a man's hand, his finger on the trigger.

Shawn jumped to his feet, the Colt in his hand bucking and spitting flame like a blue dragon.

A man shrieked and the gun disappeared. The heavy thud of a body hitting the floor was followed by the pound of running feet.

Shawn crossed the floor in three long steps and threw the door open wide with his left hand, his Colt cocked in the other. Despite the darkness, it was easy to recognize the sprawled form of the man called Tabard, elegant even in death.

Doors opened along the hallway and a woman yelled, "Get the sheriff."

Another screamed, probably thinking it was the ladylike response to a shooting.

Shawn took a knee beside the body. He'd hit Tabard twice in the chest, the bullets so close he could've covered them with the palm of his hand. His third shot had hit the doorjamb and driven a dozen splinters into the gunman's cheek that stood out like porcupine quills.

A plump man wearing a hastily donned dressing gown flapped past on carpet slippers. He looked in horror at the dead man and then at Shawn and hurried his pace.

"And good evening to you, too," Shawn said after him.

But the man made no answer, his fat buttocks bouncing like pigs in a plaid sack.

"My name is Tim Woodruff. I'm Sheriff Shern's deputy," said the man with the star on his chest and the iron on his hip. "Andy Shern is an early-to-bed man and he don't turn out unless I send for him."

Shawn nodded at the body on the floor of the hotel hallway. "There were two of them and this one tried to kill me."

"So you say." Woodruff pointed out.

"Yes, so I say."

Woodruff was a big man, heavy in the belly, and he didn't kneel beside Tabard, content to bend a little as he studied the body. "Good shooting."

"He didn't give me any choice."

Woodruff motioned for them to step into Shawn's room. He thumbed a match into flame and lit the oil lamp on the table by the bed. "Need some light in here." He looked at Shawn, his eyes as dark and flat as chocolate buttons. "His name is Lou Tabard. Him and his sidekick Rance Bohan drifted into town a three-month ago and went to work for Zebulon Moss. Heard of him?"

"I reckon I have. He's a big man in this town."

"He's a big man in any town." Woodruff nodded

in Tabard's direction. "That one killed a miner in the Lucky Lady a couple weeks ago. Everybody said the tinpan drew down on him first, so that was that. But folks said it was a real pity because Andy Brown left a real nice wife and a passel o' young ones."

"Then he should've stayed out of saloons." Shawn was full of advice.

Woodruff nodded. "There's always that." He reached under his mackinaw and produced a tally book and a stub of pencil. He licked the lead, then said, "Name?"

"Shawn O'Brien."

Woodruff seemed surprised. "You wouldn't be kin to Colonel Shamus O'Brien down to Glorieta Mesa way?

"I would. I'm his son."

"Know a tough old reprobate by the name of Luther Ironside?"

"He's the colonel's segundo and close friend. They founded Dromore together, with my ma, of course."

"Ironside's as mean as they come," Woodruff said. "And he sure loves his whiskey and the ladies." The lawman shook his head. "I swear when he sets his mind to it he can raise more hell than an alligator in a drained swamp."

"Not the man I know," Shawn said. "Luther

spends more time with his Bible and doing good works than anyone else in the territory."

Woodruff smiled. "Yeah, and that's the biggest big windy I've heard in a coon's age."

"You plan to arrest me, Woodruff?" Shawn was tired of the conversation.

"Well, that's up to Sheriff Shern, but I reckon not. It's as clear as mother's milk that it was self-defense, or so you say."

"You don't believe me?" Shawn said, his anger flaring.

"You say it was. Who's to say otherwise? You were the only witness."

"Not the only one. There's Rance Bohan for a start."

Woodruff shook his head. "Then he'd have to confess that he was here, outside your room, when the killing went down. No, ol' Rance will claim he was asleep in bed with a whore when this happened."

The deputy stuck his head into the hallway and said to the wide-eyed crowd that had assembled, "One of you men get Masheck Pettwood over here. Tell him I've got business for him." To Shawn he explained, "He's the undertaker, and a damned good one, too."

"I'm sure Lou Tabard will be happy about that," Shawn said. "Wherever he is."

\* \* \*

Pettwood, a scrawny crow of a man wearing a clawhammer frock coat and a somber expression, removed Tabard's body and told Woodruff that he'd charge the city at his normal rates and supply a planed pine coffin "at cost."

"Damned robber," Woodruff said after the man had gone. "I'd lock him up, but I might need him my ownself one day." He stepped to the bottle of whiskey Shawn had left on the dresser and poured a glass. "I don't know if it's too late or too early, but I need a heart-starter." Over the rim of the glass, he said, "Get out of town, O'Brien."

"Are you telling me to leave, Deputy?" Shawn said.

Woodruff refilled his glass. "No, not me, but you've killed one of Zeb Moss's boys and he won't let that go. Son, when you gunned Tabard, you ran out of room on the dance floor."

Shawn let that go. "I'm looking for Trixie Lee."

Woodruff's eyebrows crawled up his forehead like a pair of hairy caterpillars. "What do you want with Trixie?"

"It's a long story."

"She ain't here. I mean, she isn't in Santa Fe."

"Where is she?"

"Hell if I know. Whores are like gamblers, they stay for a while, then drift."

"Zeb Moss kidnapped her from our ranch," Shawn said.

"Is that so? It don't seem hardly possible since he hasn't left town in months."

"It was one of his men, tall skinny feller by the name of Silas Creeds."

A less steady man would've spluttered whiskey all over the front of his vest. As it was Woodruff contented himself with an unbelieving shake of the head. "O'Brien, when you go after folks you believe in starting at the top, don't you?"

"When I find Creeds, I'll have found Julia . . . I mean Trixie."

"When you find Creeds he'll gun you for sure. He's always on the prod."

"Where is he, Deputy?"

"I don't know and if'n I did know I wouldn't tell you. Boy, you're not in Creeds' class when it comes to the draw and shoot."

"I'll take my chances," Shawn declared.

Woodruff shook his head. "Not in my town you won't. Come first light get out of Santa Fe. And I don't mean after your pork chops and eggs. I mean I want to see a heap of git between you and this town come midday."

"I'll take that advice under consideration." Shawn folded his arms across his chest.

"I'm not advisin', boy, I'm tellin'. I'm an easy-going man and I probably won't gun you if you ain't left by sunup, but Zeb Moss sure as hell will."

Woodruff laid his glass on the dresser and stepped to the bullet-holed door. "You heed me, boy, or Mash Pettwood and you will become real good friends."

# Chapter Eleven

The mighty sea wolf Abdul-Basir Hakim stood at the port rail of his anchored schooner and studied the curving Mexican coastline a hundred miles north of the city of Mazatlan and the Tropic of Cancer. Protected by the Baja Peninsula to the west and the Sierra Madre to the east, the Gulf of California was dead calm, the cobalt sea shimmering in hard winter sunlight. His skin was tanned almost black by the sun and his great beak of a nose and hazel eyes gave him the look of a piratical hawk. He took the telescope from his eye and said, "They return."

A dory rowed by two men crossed the sparkling sea at a fast clip toward the *Nawfal* and its waiting commander.

Hakim put the glass to his eye again and studied the village on the shore. Yes, he decided, there was some kind of fiesta going on. The plaza was full of people, their clothes a riot of color against the drab stucco buildings. Faintly, almost lost in distance, he heard a band play with more enthusiasm than skill.

He nodded. Where there was a fiesta there would be women, and at least a few of them would surely be pretty and shapely of body enough to command a good price. The sheik turned to his second-in-command, a scar-faced rogue he'd saved from a French gallows. "A fiesta, Najid."

The man smiled, showing few teeth and all of those black. "Good news, lord." Hassan Najid had no need to say more. He, like his master, knew the implications of such a celebration.

Unlike his men, who were dressed in the striped shirts and black bell-bottom pants of English seamen, Hakim wore the blue robes of a Bedouin. At his left side hung a gold-hilted *saif*, the terrible curved scimitar of the Middle East. The sheik was proud to say that two score men had fallen to his sword in many battles.

The dory bumped alongside the schooner then a seaman scrambled over the rail. The man bowed and Hakim said, "Well?"

"A wedding, lord," the seaman said.

"And the bride?"

"Very lovely, lord. And there are other pretty

young women there." The seaman smiled. "And some hags."

"And the men? What about the men?"

"No more than thirty of fighting age."

"Are they armed?"

"They are sheep, lord."

Hakim gave that some thought. Like many successful warriors, he was a cautious man and carefully weighed the odds before entering battle.

Finally he turned to Najid and said, "Lower the longboat. You and eleven others will go with me. The men will use their swords and pistols this day."

Najid gave a deep salaam, then turned away, shouting orders. Within minutes, the longboat was lowered and a dozen heavily armed seamen scrambled on board. Hakim, his naked blade across his knees, took his usual place at the bow.

That he was outnumbered did not enter the sheik's thinking. His men were the elite of his corsairs, tough desert warriors born and bred for war. They would make short work of a rabble of Mexican peasants.

The longboat followed the surf and ground to a halt on a narrow stretch of shingle beach between half a dozen upturned fishing boats. The village, a rambling collection of adobe buildings built around a central plaza, lay fifty yards from shore.

Hakim stood on the beach and studied the village through his telescope.

The plaza was crowded with people dancing to music the sheik did not understand or appreciate, a far cry from the sweet flute airs of his homeland.

One girl stood out above the rest. Dressed in white, she was obviously the bride, and her hair, as black and glossy as a raven's wing, hung unbound to her waist, swaying like a thick sable curtain as she danced.

Sheik Hakim nodded and smiled. Such a bride would bring a fine price at the Zanzibar slave market. He turned and addressed his men. "I want the girl in white and all the other women present. I will make my selection in the plaza."

"And the men, lord?" Najid asked.

"Kill them all. Spare the hags and the *atfal.* We do not make war on children this day." Hakim raised his sword. "Forward!"


The corsairs hit the village like a ripsaw through soft pine.

Women screamed in terror as their men were cut down one by one.

The groom, a slender, handsome young man,

tried his best to protect his bride and got a sword in the guts for his attempts. He died hard, using the last of his strength trying, and failing, to come to grips with his attacker.

Shrieking, the bride kneeled beside her fallen husband and took him in her arms and soon her dress looked like blood on snow.

Hakim, huge and powerful, cut down three cowering peons one after the other, laughing, enjoying the slaughter. His sword was not a silent weapon. The steel blade announced its coming deathblow with a thin whisper, and for a dozen Mexicans it was the last sound they heard on this earth.

The village blacksmith, taller and more muscular than the others, made a stand at his forge and dashed out the brains of two of Hakim's men with a hammer.

Enraged, the sheik ordered him taken alive and lost a third man when the smith rammed a corsair's head into the anvil, splitting the man's skull so his brains spilled onto the floor. But finally the giant was wrestled to the ground where, bloody but defiant, he was bound hand and foot with ropes.

When the slaughter was over, the sand of the plaza was scarlet with blood from the sprawled, butchered bodies. The fountain in the middle of the square ran red, the legs of a headless corpse sticking out of the basin. Above the village the sky was blue, the sun bright, but the air was tainted with the metallic smell of blood, and the birds shunned the place.

Hakim's corsairs herded the bride and a dozen other girls to the beach. The women were terrified, some crying uncontrollably while others stood, stone-faced, in shocked silence.

The sheik ordered the women to be pushed into a line, then strolled past them, pausing at each one to study her face and figure. In the end he settled on the bride, a beautiful girl named Consuelo Spinoza, and three others.

"Take them to the ship, then return," he ordered Najid, whose sword hand was crimson to the wrist. "See no harm comes to them or you'll pay with your head."

The longboat pulled away with the hysterical women on board, grieving for lost fathers, husbands, or lovers.

Sheik Abdul-Basir Hakim watched them leave and was well satisfied. If that infidel dog Zebulon Moss had agreed to provide more, his trip would be profitable indeed.

He turned away from the shore. He had a score to settle.

He ordered the blacksmith brought before him and his corsairs forced the man to his knees. The Mexican was defiant; no fear in him. That was good. Hakim would not defile his blade with the blood of a coward.

One swift stroke of the sheik's sword and the blacksmith's head jumped from his body and rolled in the sand. Hakim's men cheered and Hakim acknowledged them by smiling and holding his bloody sword aloft.

By the beards of his forefathers, it had been a fine morning's work.

# Chapter Twelve

Shawn O'Brien put on his hat, then washed, dressed, and shaved in the chill dawn light. The fire had burned down and was a pile of cold gray ashes. The windowpanes were etched with ferns of frost and outside, snow flurried in the street, hurried along by an icy wind blowing off the Sangre de Cristo Mountains to the east. The black morning promised a blacker day.

Shawn punched the empty shells from his Colt, reloaded then buckled his gun belt around his hips. He shrugged into his sheepskin, left the room, and headed downstairs in search of coffee and breakfast.

At this early hour there were only a few people in the dining room, but the killing of Lou Tabard had created a stir and all eyes were on the tall, slim young man in shotgun chaps and sheepskin whose Mexican spurs chimed as he found a table and sat down.

Shawn met stares with a stare and his fellow diners quickly dropped their eyes and suddenly found the food on their plates to be of the greatest interest.

"What can I get you, cowboy?" the waitress, a plump, motherly woman with the endlessly suffering expression of people with sore feet, asked.

"Coffee, please, ma'am," Shawn said, smiling.

"You've been raised right, young feller," the woman said. "You hungry?"

To his surprise, Shawn realized he was. Luther Ironside always said that a killing ruined a man's appetite, but he was having the opposite reaction.

Before he could give her his order, the waitress said, "How about steak and eggs? It's the only thing they can halfway cook right in this dump."

"Sounds good to me," Shawn said.

The woman waddled away and returned a few moments later with a coffeepot. The coffee was hot, strong, and bitter, just the way Shawn liked it. The food, when it came, passed muster as edible.

He lingered over coffee and his first cigar of the morning, reluctant to leave the warmth of the dining room, where a large log fire burned. His attention was drawn to a woman who stepped into the room and hesitantly looked around, as though looking for someone. She wore a hooded cloak with a sprinkling of snow on the shoulders and top of the hood that almost completely covered her face.

The woman turned in Shawn's direction and their eyes met. Looking at her face, he realized she was a young, pretty brunette, her cheeks rouged by the outside cold.

The girl made up her mind about something and walked directly in Shawn's direction. Always keen to meet a pretty woman, he rose to his feet and the girl said, "Mr. O'Brien?"

"Yes I am, but you can call me Shawn."

"May I sit?"

"Of course."

Shawn stepped around the table and pulled out a chair for the woman. After she was seated, he regained his own chair and said, "What can I do for you?"

"I shouldn't be here," the woman said, glancing over her shoulder. She still had the hood of her cloak pulled over her head.

"I'd say that makes two of us." Shawn smiled.

"My name is Minnie Dennett and I'm a friend . . . was a friend . . . of Trixie Lee."

"Do you know where she is?"

"I'm not sure, but I think so."

"Coffee?"

"No, thank you."

Shawn waited to let Minnie think about what she had to tell him. Her eyes were brown, worried.

Finally the woman said, "I work for Zeb Moss at the Lucky Lady saloon."

"Hostess?"

"Something like that."

"Go on, Minnie."

"There's a cellar at the rear of the saloon. It's accessed by a trapdoor on the floor. Zeb stores his beer barrels in there to keep the beer cool."

Then, anticipating what Minnie would say next, Shawn said, "And that's where Jul—Trixie is?"

"Yes, I think so."

"But you don't know so."

"I believe I heard a woman's voice down there, talking to Zeb. It might have been Trixie's voice, but I'm not sure."

"How the hell do I find out? The saloon never closes."

"That's why I came to talk to you this morning. The Lucky Lady will close early tonight to let carpenters work on the floor behind the bar. Stuff spills back there and some of the floorboards are rotted."

"Will the carpenters be there all night?"

"No. I heard Zeb say that he wants the job done by midnight. Then he told the bartenders they should open up tomorrow morning at seven."

"That's enough time for me to get in there and find Trixie."

"Yes. I mean, if she's who I heard."

"I'd bet the farm on it, Minnie."

The woman nodded, but said nothing more. After a lengthy silence she said, "The saloon only has one back door. I'll try to leave it open for you. If I can't, you'll need to find another way in."

"I'll find a way," Shawn said.

Minnie rose to her feet. "I must go now. I can't risk being seen with you." Then, after a moment's hesitation, she added, "Zeb Moss plans to kill you, Mr. O'Brien."

"I figured that when two of his guns tried it last night."

The woman nodded. "Rance Bohan is a dangerous man and now he hates you. All of Zeb's hired gunmen are dangerous."

"I'll make sure to step around them," Shawn said, smiling.

"Good luck, Mr. O'Brien." Then Minnie was gone, walking quickly across the dining room to the door.


The clock tower in the plaza struck one as Shawn stepped out of the hotel into the night. A few flakes of snow drifted in the icy air, and his breath smoked as he crossed the empty street to the alley running between the Lucky Lady and the general store next door.

Stepping into the alley, he smelled the rawness of the night and the dank odor of wet mud and ancient vomit. He made his way carefully, but still his boots hit empty bottles that clanked and rolled, alarming the rats that scuttled along the baseboards of the saloon. A mist hung in the air, gray as a ghost.

At the rear door of the saloon, Shawn stood still and listened in the silence. No sound came from inside, though earlier hammers had pounded and saws rasped so loudly he'd heard the racket from his hotel room.

He reached out a gloved hand, turned the door handle, and gave a little push. The door creaked open. A drift of mist entered into the saloon and he followed it inside, stopping immediately, trapped by darkness. After a few moments he slid one tentative foot ahead of him, then another, like a man crossing a frozen pond.

*Clang!*

A spittoon bounced away from Shawn's booted toe and clattered and gonged as it tumbled across the wood floor. He froze and held his breath, waiting for . . . he didn't know for what. Voices, yells, running feet, gunshots . . . maybe any of those.

But all he heard was silence and the slow *tick . . . tick . . . tick* of the railroad clock above the bar.

After Shawn's thudding heart settled and he could breathe normally again, he made his way carefully across the floor. Disoriented, he hoped he was headed in the right direction. What he needed was a lamp. Better to take the chance on being seen than fumbling around in the dark.

And suddenly there was light.

To Shawn's left, Zeb Moss turned up the wick of an oil lamp, illuminating Rance Bohan and two other hardcases lined up in front of the bar. All four men grinned at him, the muzzles of their shotguns aimed right at his belly.

"Don't even think about it, O'Brien," Moss said. "We'll cut you in half before you can clear leather."

Shawn let his right hand drop from his holstered Colt. "Minnie." The name was like bitter gall on his tongue.

"She told you she works for me, O'Brien," Moss said. "What did you expect? You're not the first man to let a pretty face make a fool of him."

"Damn. I should've known," Shawn grumbled, playing along.

"Yes, you should've. Now unbuckle the gun belt, let it drop, and kick it over here."

Shawn did as he was told, then Moss said, "Since you're so all-fired determined to find Trixie, I'm going to oblige you." He nodded toward the rear of the saloon. "Walk that way, real slow and easy."

Shawn knew he couldn't save his life by bluster and threats of the vengeful wrath of Dromore. Men like Moss were savvy, hard as nails, and afraid of nothing.

He walked slow and easy.

When he reached the stage, Moss ordered Shawn to stop and looked at his men at the bar. "If he tries a break or makes a fancy move, gun him."

"Looking forward to it, boss," Rance Bohan said, grinning at Shawn with teeth too perfect to be anything but store bought.

Moss walked behind the stage and after a moment yelled, "Bring him here, boys."

A shotgun butt slammed into his back, urging Shawn in the right direction. When he joined Moss again, the man was holding the trapdoor open. "Hey, Trixie!" he yelled. "Here's a friend of yours come to visit for a spell!"

Moss nodded to the opening in the floor and again Shawn was prodded until he stood on the edge of the opening, a rectangle of blackness just beyond his toes.

"Comin' down, Trixie!" Moss yelled.

He pushed Shawn hard in the small of the back. Unable to keep his balance, Shawn fell into the dark void. The last words he heard before the trapdoor slammed shut were Moss's shouted, *"Vaya con Dios, amigo!"*

Shawn O'Brien hit every hard, timber step on the way down—and there were a dozen of them.

He cartwheeled, all arms and legs, thumping, bouncing, first his back hitting, then his front, then his head . . . then his back again.

Finally he thumped onto the floor, sprawled, and lay still.

"Shawn, are you all right?" The voice came from a long way off, at the far end of a tunnel.

"Shawn, speak to me."

His eyes fluttered open and he looked into Julia's concerned face, lit by the dim light of an oil lamp. "Damn, those steps are hard. If I ever find the man who built them, I'll shoot him."

"Can you move?" the woman said. "Do you have any broken bones?"

Shawn's head throbbed and his brain seemed as though it had ground to a halt. He became conscious of a sharp pain at the top of his head and when he investigated, his fingers came away bloody.

Slowly, painfully, he rose to a sitting position and groaned. "God, I feel like someone just got after me with a bois d'arc fence post."

"What happened?" Julia asked in concern.

"Zeb Moss threw me down the stairs." Shawn tried to smile. "Now he owes me."

"Why are you here?"

"I've come to take you home, Julia," Shawn answered.

He rose to his feet and stretched, trying to work out the kinks, a movement that caused him so much pain he regretted it instantly and groaned. "Hell, I shouldn't have done that."

Julia shook her head. "You can't take me home, Shawn. Not ever. It's way too late for that now."

"I know this sounds strange coming from a man locked in a beer cellar by a bunch of shot-gun-toting hardcases," Shawn said. "But I'll find a way."

"There is no way." Julia's eyes were in shadow. "I'm being sold into slavery. Zeb Moss told me that."

Shawn's first reaction was to laugh, but he managed to keep a straight face. "Julia, slavery ended with the War Between the States, remember?"

"Not in Africa and the Arab countries. Zeb Moss says that's where I'm headed, me and other women."

Suddenly it was not a laughing matter. "How does he plan to get you there?"

"We'll be picked up on the Texas coast by an Arab ship, Zeb says, and taken to a place off the African mainland called Zanzibar where there are slave markets."

"When is he moving you out of here?"

"I don't know. Soon, I think."

Shawn hurt all over, but he tried to ignore the pain and think. Finally, coming up with little, he could say only, "We've got to get out of here."

"Shawn, that's impossible. All you can do now is to try to save yourself."

"That might be pretty impossible, too, the way

the hard times have come down recently." He picked up the lamp and took Julia by the arm to the rickety table and chairs near her cot.

After the woman sat, he said, "All right, I think I might have figured something." He saw hope flash briefly in Julia's eyes. "When do they bring you food and water?"

"They've brought nothing so far."

"I'm sure they will. If what you've told me is true and not just Moss spinning a windy to scare you, he must consider you a valuable commodity and he won't let you starve."

"I know what you're planning, Shawn, and it won't work. Even if you overcome the man, or men, who bring us food, you still have to get up the stairs and into the saloon. Zeb or one of his gunmen will kill you for sure."

"A body's got to try." Shawn sat in silence for a few moments, then said, "The saloon is still closed. I wonder if there's a guard?"

"Sure to be. I don't think Zeb would leave us alone."

"He might figure a locked trapdoor is enough."

"Would you?"

"No, I guess I wouldn't."

"Then there's your answer."

"Well, guard or not, I'm going to give it a whirl." Shawn stretched again, gauging the extent of his hurt, then reached into his pocket and produced the Smith & Wesson .32, passing it to

Julia. "The idiots didn't search me. If I get the trapdoor open and somebody tries to stop me, blow his fool head off."

"But it's locked."

"I know it's locked, but I'll get my back against it and push."

"Break it apart?"

"Yeah, either the door or my back."

But then a key rattled in the padlock, the trapdoor creaked open, and suddenly it was too late. Too late for everything.

# Chapter Thirteen

Shawn O'Brien reached out, grabbed the revolver from Julia's hand, and shoved it into his pocket.

Broadcloth-covered legs appeared on the stairs, then the barrel of a shotgun. Two other pairs of legs followed, the booted and spurred limbs of Zeb Moss's hired hardcases.

For a single wild moment, Shawn thought about drawing the .32 and shooting it out. But five rounds from a belly gun against three scatterguns were not good odds. He let the moment pass. Best to live to fight another day when the deck wasn't so stacked against him.

"You're out of here, O'Brien," Rance Bohan said, his prodding shotgun making more than a nodding acquaintance with Shawn's belly.

"I'm glad you came to your senses, Bohan,"

Shawn said. "And Trixie is coming with me, of course."

"Wrong on both counts," Bohan said, his smile ugly. "Trixie stays here and you come with us. We're going for a little ride. Not far. Just beyond the city limits where it's quiet-like."

"What are you planning, Bohan?" Shawn's eyes narrowed.

"You'll find out. Now get up them stairs or you get it in the belly right here and now. I don't care. It won't be me has to clean up the mess afterward."

"Bohan, you're a joy to be around," Shawn retorted.

"Yeah, ain't I though? But you haven't even seen the worst of me. Not by a long shot, you haven't."

"Shawn . . ." Julia tried to find words and failed. But the tears in her eyes spoke volumes.

"I'll be back for you, Julia," Shawn said. "I promise."

Bohan grinned. "Don't count on it, O'Brien. Now move!"

Shawn was roughly hustled up the stairs. Behind him he heard Julia's soft sobs and his fear for her and for him turned to a slow-burning anger.

He was surprised to see the dawn as he walked out of the saloon, Bohan and the two hardcases close behind him. His horse stood at the hitching rail with three others, saddled and ready for the trail

"Get up on the hoss, O'Brien," Bohan said. "I see a fancy move and you're a dead man."

"Where are we headed, Rance?" Shawn asked, knowing it would irritate the gunman.

"Damn you, I told you that you'll find out," Bohan exclaimed. "And don't call me Rance. The only people I allow to call me by my given name are my friends."

"Well, don't that beat all," Shawn drawled. "I didn't think you had any."

Bohan's smile was thin as the edge of a knife. "Keep it up, O'Brien. I'll soon cut you down to size."

Shawn swung into the saddle under the watchful cold eyes of shotgun muzzles. There was no snow, but frost crackled in the air and black clouds hung low over the city.

Bohan led the way east along the north bank of the Santa Fe River, timbered, snow-covered mountain peaks rising on all sides. He kept close to the bank, riding through heavy stands of cottonwood, wild oak, and willow.

Shawn tried to guess where they were headed, and why. Only Rance Bohan knew the answer, but he sat thin and dry on his horse and said nothing.

After an hour of making their way through rough country where every rock they passed was covered in a slick of ice and the wind bit like a snake, one of the hardcases figured it was time to complain. "How much farther, Rance? I say we gun him here and have done. Hell, I ain't even had breakfast yet."

Bohan drew rein and looked around him. "How far can a man with a bullet in his belly crawl? Anybody know?"

A second hardcase, older, grimmer, and maybe wiser, said, "One time down in the Texas Badlands I seen the body of a ranny who'd crawled three miles across desert country with a Comanche bullet in his gut. Seems to me this cold would ice a man's belly and he could drag hisself a sight farther."

"Damn you fer a talkin' man, Cletus," the younger hardcase said, his eyes ugly.

"Man asked a question an' I answered it," Cletus said.

"Cletus is right," Bohan said. "We'll ride a piece longer. I want O'Brien to know he's dying, but I don't want him to crawl back to Santa Fe and leave us with a heap of questions to answer."

Shawn felt a mix of fear and anger and the savage desire to rip Bohan's heart out with his bare hands. He felt the solid weight of the .32 in his pocket, but it was not the time to use it. Bohan and his hardcases were on edge and they'd be alert to his every move. Better to bide his time and strike when they least expected it.

It was thin, mighty thin, but it was all Shawn had and he was determined to make the best of it when the time came and things turned ugly.

Rance Bohan drew rein. Ahead of him, through a tattered veil of falling snow, he scanned a low ridge, the rocky slope studded with piñon and juniper. Snow lay here and there like discarded hotel sheets and the tops of the taller rock spires had a crest of white, making them look like wise old men who had come down from the mountains.

"There," Bohan said, pointing. "We'll take O'Brien to the top of the ridge and put a bullet in his belly. A gut shot man isn't going to crawl down from there."

The younger hardcase dashed a drip from the end of his nose with a gloved hand. "Gun him here, Rance. Then I'll dab a loop on him and drag him up among them piñons."

Bohan turned to Shawn. "If you got any prayers, O'Brien, say them now. In a few minutes you'll be hurting too bad for anything but screaming."

"You damned tinhorn, Bohan. You go to hell."

The gunman smiled. "O'Brien, it's going to be a real pleasure putting a bullet into you." He brushed back his caped greatcoat and drew his

Colt. His voice was flat, hard, and hollow, the voice of death. "Git off the horse."

The time had come for Shawn O'Brien to make his play.

His hand dropped to the pocket of his sheepskin and closed on the little revolver.

Rance Bohan sat his saddle, dead for two seconds before the sound of the rifle shot crashed among the surrounding peaks. A bloody hole appeared between the man's eyes, but he stayed where he was, straight-backed and upright in the saddle.

The young hardcase, his eyes wild, leveled his shotgun at Shawn. A second rifle shot blew the man out of the saddle. He triggered his scattergun as he fell, and his horse took both barrels of buckshot in the belly. The animal screamed and dropped on top of him.

"Mister, I don't know what the hell is happening here, but I'm out of it," the older man named Sam said, raising his hands high. Terror showed in a face suddenly drained of color.

"The hell you are." The fear Shawn had felt had destroyed any inclination of mercy in him. He triggered the .32 dry into the hardcase's chest. The man tumbled from the saddle, dead when he hit the ground.

* * *

Shawn watched a drift of gunsmoke from the ridge catch in the wind. Then a buckskinned figure rose from behind a shelf of rock and stood watching him. The man raised his hand in greeting and climbed the ridge to the crest, then disappeared from view.

Shawn was puzzled. Because of snow and distance he couldn't make out his savior's face. He looked like Luther Ironside, but was too short. Apart from Luther, no one else he knew wore buckskins.

Unless . . .

He shook his head. No, it couldn't be him.

But it was.

A few minutes later, Uriah Tweedy rode along a thin trail between the drop of the rise and the river, the butt of his old Henry rifle on his right thigh. When he got close enough, Tweedy smiled under his beard. "Howdy, young feller."

"Tweedy, what the hell are you doing here?" Shawn looked at the man in wonder.

"Savin' your damned fool skin, last I looked."

"But you're shot through and through. You should be in bed."

"Yeah, I should be, but I ain't."

"You rode all the way here with a broken shoulder to help me?"

"The hell I did. I'm here to save the woman I plan to marry up with."

"Who?"

"Who? You mean you don't know? Why Miss Trixie, you danged fool."

Shawn was taken aback. "She's . . . I mean . . . damn it, Uriah, you're an old coot."

"And she's a young woman. That's why I plan to wed her. She'll be a sweet consolation to me in my old age." Tweedy looked around him. "An' speakin' of sich, where is she?"

"It's a long story, and none of it makes for agreeable listening."

"Then I'd better hear it. But not here. Weather's closing in. I say we head for Santa Fe afore it gets dark." Tweedy's eyes roamed over the dead men. "These rannies part of the story?"

"Yes, they are." Shawn looked at Tweedy as though he could scarcely believe the man was real. "How come you were here just when I needed you, Uriah? It's . . . well, it's like a miracle."

"Miracle my ass, sonny. Soon as I heard where you was headed I pulled out and followed you, figuring you'd lead me to Miss Trixie." Tweedy shook his head. "You ain't exactly a hard man to track. Just as well the Apaches are all in Florida or you'd be a goner fer sure."

Shawn let that go, and said, "How did you find me here?"

Tweedy sighed, as though he was talking with

a none-too-bright child. "Wasn't I in Santa Fe and didn't I keep an eye on the Lucky Lady saloon? When I seen them three hardcases lead you out of there by the nose and you lookin' as scared as a rabbit in a coyote's back pocket, I figured your goose was cooked. Lucky for you them rubes was riding slow, so I got ahead of them."

Tweedy was silent for a few moments, then feeling that further explanation was called for, he said, "Sonny, when a man hunts ol' Ephraim for a living, he knows when to stay out of sight and when to start shootin'. You catch my drift?"

"Uriah, I can't go back to Santa Fe. I'm a marked man."

"Of course you're a marked man, so you'll bed down in the livery stable like I done. The place is run by a broken-down old range cook by the name of Miles Marshwood. He knows how to keep his trap shut and there's not a hoss or wagon goes in and out of the city Miles don't know about. We can keep an eye on Zeb Moss and his men and find a way to free Miss Trixie."

"Damn, Uriah, it's thin," Shawn said. "And dangerous."

"Of course it's thin, unless you got a better idea."

"I don't."

"Then it's all we got, so we'll make the best of it." Tweedy motioned to the dead men. "Find yourself a rifle and a belt gun. Then we'll ride."

"How does your shoulder feel?" Shawn finally asked.

"How do you think it feels?" Tweedy demanded.

"I'd guess it hurts like hell."

"Then you'd be right."

"What about them?" Shawn pointed to the dead men.

"What about them?"

"Should we do something . . . cover them up, maybe?"

"Hell, sonny, we don't have time for that. Leave them for the coyotes." Tweedy thought about that, then added, "That is, if'n coyotes eat their own kind."

# Chapter Fourteen

The man who stood on the deck of the U.S. Navy's sloop of war *Kansas* was dressed in the coarse black robe of a Spanish priest. That he was highly agitated was obvious, the way he kept pressing the heels of his hands into his eyes as though trying to eliminate a vision that continued to haunt him.

Commander John Sherburne, just thirty-seven years old but with the lined, weathered face of the lifelong sailor, stood beside him. "Father Diaz, the villagers are sure it was slave traders and not common bandits?"

Father Oscar Diaz took his hands from his eyes, their sockets red from the pressure of his hands. "Those that are still alive say slave traders. They were all dark, bearded men and their leader wore Arab robes."

"Four young women taken, you say?"

"Yes, including a bride who was just married this morning."

Father Diaz, young and pleasant-faced, trembled all over, as though he stood in snow. But it was fear and shock that caused him to shiver uncontrollably, not cold.

A man with a measure of stern kindliness in him, Commander Sherburne called for a glass of rum and bade the priest drink hearty. "If ever a man needed a drink, it's you, Father."

The priest touched the glass to his lips, and then said, "Commander, what will you do?"

"I'll land and see the village for myself. If it is as you say, and I've no reason to doubt you, I'll pursue the pirate vessel."

"The ship is long gone, I fear," Father Diaz said.

Sherburne smiled. "This is the newest steam sloop in the United States Navy, Father. We'll catch her, never fear."

"A schooner," the priest mumbled.

"I beg your pardon?"

"One of the women said the ship was a schooner and it sailed away south. She is old, and may know these things."

Sherburne nodded. "A fast ship, no doubt, but she depends on the wind and can't outrun the *Kansas,* never fear." He turned to the lieutenant at his other side and said, "Lower the jolly boat and tell Sergeant Monroe I want him and two of his marines to accompany me onshore."

"I will go with you," Father Diaz said.

"You're welcome to remain on board," Sherburne said.

The priest shook his head. "My place is with my flock, Commander. Now more than ever." He tossed off his glass of rum and seemed glad of it.

White seagulls glided across a pale blue sky as Commander Sherburne and his men landed on the beach.

Sergeant Monroe, a profane man, cursed violently as he caught the smell of death. "Damn it. They're rotting already."

Sherburne heard the marine, but ignored his outburst. He jumped into the surf and walked toward the village, a couple sailors close behind him. Monroe and his men followed, their bayonets fixed and eyes wary.

The scene was as Father Diaz had described. The blacksmith's body lay on the beach and the village was strewn with corpses, a few shot, the majority hacked with swords. There was blood everywhere, and fat, black flies gorged on open wounds. Higher than the seagulls, but gliding just as elegantly, buzzards waited and watched with their endless patience.

Women huddled in groups and wailed their

grief. A few kneeled silently by the corpses of their menfolk, the restless rustle of the surging surf and the yodel of the gulls their only requiem.

Father Diaz, his face a mask of pain, said almost apologetically to Sherburne, "The women can't bury the dead, Commander."

For his part the captain of the *Kansas* was infused with a white-hot anger and, for the first time since he'd entered the service as a boy, the desire to kill the enemy. His ship carried twenty carronades, powerful, close-range weapons, and he made a vow to reduce the slaver schooner to matchwood and its crew to smears of blood and guts on the deck.

More seamen and the remaining marines were ferried from the sloop to bury the dead, a melancholy task that took until dark to complete.

Before he left for his ship, Commander Sherburne spoke to the priest. "I've done all I can for you, Father, and God knows it was little enough."

"To bury the dead is a holy and honorable thing," Father Diaz said. "And it is much appreciated."

"I know you'll do what you can for the women, Father. Tell them I'll bring back the girls who were taken." He tried to offer more words of consolation, but could find none. Finally he said. "Just . . . tell them that."

Father Diaz bowed his head, and then said, "The village is gone and it will never come back. I'll take the women somewhere else, inland, where they'll feel safe."

The commander nodded, but said nothing more.

The priest raised his hand and made the sign of the cross over Sherburne. "Go with God. And may holy Saint Brendan the Navigator protect you and all who sail with you."

# Chapter Fifteen

It was dark when Shawn O'Brien and Uriah Tweedy rode into Santa Fe. The old man led the way to the livery stable, a rectangular timber building with a flat roof, a wide door, and a sign outside.

LIVERY & FEED STABLE
~*M. Marshwood*, PROP.

M. Marshwood, prop. was a sour-faced, stringy old man who wore a tattered mackinaw and a scowl as though he'd never been pleased to see anybody or anything in his life. "Oh, it's you again, Uriah. I reckoned you was gone fer a spell."

"Came back with this young feller in tow," Tweedy said. "His name's Shawn O'Brien, one o' them Glorieta Mesa O'Briens."

"Colonel Shamus O'Brien your paw, boy?" Marshwood asked.

"He is," Tweedy answered before Shawn could say a word.

"Can't he talk for hisself, or is he a little simple in the braincase?" Marshwood wondered.

"Colonel O'Brien is my father," Shawn said. "And I can talk for myself."

"Thank God for that," Marshwood said. "I never could abide a silent man. Never could abide a talkin' one, either." The oldster glared at Shawn from under the brim of his frayed Johnny Reb kepi. "Colonel O'Brien is a fine man and a gallant soldier." He looked Shawn over from the toes of his boots to the top of his hat. "I cain't say you favor him."

"Miles," Tweedy said quickly, "we need to stay here for a couple days. Can you feed us and bring us some liquor?"

"Yes to both them things," Marshwood answered. "Cost you, though."

"Don't worry. We'll settle up when we leave," Shawn offered.

"Damn right you will," Marshwood growled. "If'n you don't, I've got a Greener scattergun that acts as my lawyer an' does my talkin' fer me."

Shawn grinned. "Uriah told me you were a loveable old man, Marshwood."

"If he said that, he's a damned liar. I don't like anything or anybody but that old calico cat you see over there. She's got better manners than folks, an' that's a natural fact." He looked at Tweedy. "You sharp-set, Uriah?"

"Been living on grass fer a couple o' days, Miles."

"You?" Marshwood said to Shawn.

"I could eat."

"I'll bring you something."

"And a bottle of good bourbon," Shawn added.

"Show me your money, boy. Two things don't come cheap around these parts, good whiskey and fancy women."

Shawn handed Marshwood ten dollars. "Will that cover it?"

The old man studied the coin, then said, "I guess it will at that."

He threw a blanket over his shoulders, and then stopped at the door. "Stay out of my office while I'm gone, and don't touch nothing. If anything's missing or out of place I'll know it."

"We'll see to our horses, Miles," Tweedy said.

Marshwood nodded. "Sack of oats and hay back there. I got the oat sack marked, so don't take two scoops an' tell me you only took one."

After Marshwood walked into the wind-torn night, Shawn smiled. "Trusting sort of feller, isn't he?"

Tweedy said, "Don't underestimate that old man, sonny. He helped blaze the Goodnight Trail and he fit more'n his share o' Comanche an' Apaches. He killed a man in Wichita and another in Fort Worth and one time when he was marshalin' he put the crawl on Bill Bonney and that hard crowd."

"Something to remember," Shawn said. "I won't take two scoops of oats and pay for one."

"Miles is a good man to have on your side," Tweedy said.

Shawn smiled. "He doesn't like me much."

"Hell boy, he likes you just fine. If he didn't we'd be sleeping out in the snow tonight."

"So that's the story," Shawn said, using a piece of bread to wipe up the last of the gravy on his plate. "Right up until the time you came along and saved my life."

Tweedy nodded. "Maybe you could've done it your ownself with the belly gun."

"Yes, maybe. But I doubt it." Shawn laid the plate aside. "How's the shoulder holding up?"

"It's a bigger hurting than ol' Ephraim ever laid on me. I can tell you that."

"You should see a doctor."

Miles Marshwood scratched his hairy neck. "Let me take a look o' that wound, Uriah." He saw the doubt in Tweedy's face and went on. "I've patched up more gunshot punchers that you could shake a stick at. Now get them buckskins off an' let me take a look."

"Miles, don't you go a-proddin' an' a pokin' now, like that Luther Ironside feller at Dromore did," Tweedy said. "You could hurt a feller."

"All I'm doing is lookin' to make sure the wound ain't pizened. Damn it, Uriah, you're surely a complainin' man."

After a moment's hesitation, Tweedy pulled off his shirt. The wound in his shoulder was red, raw, and looked painful.

Shawn shook his head. "Uriah, you got yourself a misery there."

"And don't you think I know that?" Tweedy grumbled.

"It ain't bad," Marshwood said after his examination. "There's no pus and it don't smell bad." He turned his head and said to Shawn, "If I smelled that it was rotten I'd suspect the gangrene and have to cut it out of him. But even then, he'd probably give up the ghost. A man can't live through a deep cuttin' like that."

"I'm here, you danged fools, and I got ears," Tweedy protested. "And Miles, you ain't cuttin' at me with a bowie."

"Hell, didn't I just say I don't have to? Ain't that what I said, huh?" Marshwood rose to his feet. "Stay there. I'm gonna get a salve from the office."

"What kind of salve?" Tweedy asked, suspicion in his eyes.

"Well, if'n you must know, it's Dr. Gisborne's

surefire cure fer piles, pox, consumption, pimples, female problems, cancer, baldness, poor eyesight, the rheumatisms an' a dozen other miseries. Now if'n it can fix all them things, I reckon it will fix that shoulder."

"Good for Dr. Gisborne," Shawn said, grinning. "I guess his salve will fix most anything."

"That's what's printed right there on the box," Marshwood said. "An' the printed word never lies." He stepped into his office and returned with a box the size of a soup bowl and a strip of red cloth. He applied a liberal amount of the good doctor's cure-all to the cloth and then bound it around Tweedy's shoulder. "A few days an' you'll be right as rain, Uriah."

"Yeah, if it don't kill me first."

"Well, if'n it does, I'll write a sharp letter to Dr. Gisborne, I can tell you that," Marshwood said. "I'll let him know that his salve don't work a damn. Mind you, I used it on the cat one time when she got chewed up by Tom McMaster's hound dog and she healed up just fine."

Tweedy poured a liberal dash of whiskey into his tin cup, growled that the "damned snake oil is punishing me something terrible," and withdrew into an aggrieved silence.

But the quiet didn't last long. Venting his spleen on Shawn, he said, "You given any thought to how we'll scout the saloon? You bein' a walkin' gun target an' all."

"I figured that was down to you, Uriah," Shawn said.

"Not all day and all night I can't, sonny, with me bein' all shot up an' all."

Marshwood interrupted. "I have a solution to your problem, Uriah. His name is Willie Wide Awake an' he's a watching kind o' feller."

"Miles, I'm not catching your drift."

"Willie don't sleep," Marshwood said. "I mean never. Oh, there was a time he laid down to it, but he don't any longer. He says when he drops off he has scary dreams about his wife's mother, so he reckons to stay awake fer the rest of his days. He says it keeps a man sharp."

"You mean he could keep an eye on the Lucky Lady for us?" Shawn asked.

"Yes sir," Marshwood said, "all day an' all night, that's the intention. Nobody pays heed to what's goin' on around him like a sleepless man."

"How much will we have to pay him?" Tweedy said, his face sour.

"O'Brien here has change comin' from the whiskey an' grub. That will cover it just fine."

"Can we trust this wide awake feller?" Tweedy asked.

"Willie will keep his mouth shut, and if he did open it, nobody would pay any attention to what he had to say anyway."

"He'll need to start now," Shawn said. "And I mean right away."

Marshwood nodded, then threw his blanket around him. "I'll go talk to him."

"Miles," Tweedy said, "tell him about my intended. If he sees her leaving the saloon with Zeb Moss he's got to come a-runnin' to us right quick."

"I'll make that plain to him, Uriah. Just make sure you're ready to move when he gits here with news."

# Chapter Sixteen

"I don't much care for a night action, Mr. Wilson," Commander John Sherburne commented. "What does she have in hand?"

"Half a league, sir," Lieutenant Wilson answered. "She's a fast ship, like all damned slavers."

Sherburne slanted his second-in-command an irritated *don't tell me what I already know* look. "Then steady as she goes, Mr. Wilson," he said finally, his brass telescope to his eye. "We'll catch her soon enough."

"Sir, perhaps I could do something with the long gun forward." Wilson was young, eager, with a round, open face.

"We'll get a little closer, Mr. Wilson." Sherburne smiled. "And then you can have at it."

Apart from the helmsman, a stoical, weatherbeaten old hand, the two officers were alone on the quarterdeck. The sloop of war *Kansas* battled an oncoming sea, and great breaking waves crashed over her bow. The ten carronades on each side of the ship were lashed down tight, but their well-drilled gun crews could clear for action in less than two minutes.

Sherburne reached into the pocket of his peacoat and produced a silver flask. "A brandy with you, Mr. Wilson?"

The lieutenant shook his head. "Regrettably, I must refuse, Captain. Before I left for sea, Miss Edna Coffin, my betrothed, bade me promise that my lips would ne'er touch strong drink, nor would I indulge in the sinful pleasures of loose women."

"You weren't on the beach today, Mr. Wilson."

"No, sir. On your orders I remained on the ship."

"Trust me, if you'd seen what I saw, you'd want a drink."

"Yes, sir. Perhaps, sir."

Sherburne sighed and tilted the flask to his mouth. After a hearty swallow, he put the flask away and returned the ship's glass to his eye. "She has every scrap of sail set, Mr. Wilson, but God willing, we'll catch the rogues before nightfall."

"The long gun, Captain?"

"Soon, Mr. Wilson." Sherburne stroked his black, spade-shaped beard. "It won't be long now until we're in range."

\* \* \*

"She's a sloop of war, great lord," Hassan Najid said, his black eyes troubled. "An American steamship. Allah curse it to Hades."

Sheik Abdul-Basir Hakim glanced at the billowing sails and realized he could get no more speed out of his schooner.

"Ten carronades a side," Najid said as if his thoughts ran parallel to his master's. "She can stand off and blow us out of the water, damn her."

"Aye, and they'll have a long nine forward." Hakim studied the sloop through his glass and nodded. "She'll be in nine-pounder range soon."

Najid thought for a moment, then said, "We can throw the women overboard, lord. The sloop will stop and try to save them."

"Will they?"

"They're Americans. They won't sail past drowning women in a shark-infested sea."

Hakim nodded. "You've given me an idea."

"When do we toss them into the sea, lord?" Najid grinned.

"We don't, but bring the women on deck. I have other plans for them."

"But . . . but my lord . . ." Najid said hesitantly.

"You're right about Americans, a soft people. Will they loose a broadside on us with captive women lined along the deck?"

Najid's expression changed from doubt to glee. "A fine plan, great lord."

"Then let it be done." Hakim stared across a mile of churning gray sea to the oncoming sloop. "Hurry, Najid, there is no time to be lost."

Commander Sherburne put the speaking-trumpet to his mouth and yelled, "Belay the long gun, Mr. Wilson, and report to the quarterdeck."

Lieutenant Wilson arrived breathless and before the captain could speak he said, "The wind is dropping, sir. I believe I can hit her stern and disable her steering."

Sherburne passed his telescope to Wilson. "Look. On deck."

Wilson was not by nature a profane man, but he swore loud and long. "The fiends. No Christian man would do such a thing."

"Very effective though," Sherburne said. "Don't you think?"

"I still believe I can reach out to her with the long nine, Captain. If I disable her steering, she'll wallow like a sow."

"And if you miss, what then, Mr. Wilson? I rather fancy dead women all over the deck and questions to be answered when we get back to port."

"I await your orders, sir," Wilson said humbly.

"We'll overtake her and then you can try the long gun," Sherburne said. "We'll need to be close to avoid hitting the women."

Wilson saluted. "I understand, sir."

Sherburne glanced at the graying sky and the slowly dying light as the afternoon shaded into evening. "You may pipe the hands to dinner, Mr. Wilson. It will be yet a while before we can risk a shot with the nine."

"A most singular situation, Captain," Wilson replied.

"Indeed, Mr. Wilson, most singular," Sherburne agreed. "And I fear it will get even more so if darkness overtakes us."

"She's holding her fire, lord," Hassan Najid pointed out.

"Yes," Sheik Abdul Basir-Hakim murmured. Then after some thought, "Her captain wishes to get closer before he risks a shot."

"But he'd kill the women," Najid said.

"Perhaps." Hakim grabbed Najid's arm. "Put the woman in the bridal dress at the stern where she can be seen. The Americans might try to disable our rudder but with her there, they'll think twice."

Najid rushed off to carry out the sheik's order, and for the hundredth time that afternoon, Hakim stared at the sky. The wind was falling and the sloop was gaining fast. He needed the darkness. Why wouldn't it come?

\* \* \*

"Damn it, Captain, where did that come from?" Lieutenant Wilson pointed to the wall of blue-gray fog rolling toward the stern of the *Kansas* and her prey with the sullen persistence of a rainsquall.

Sherburne said nothing.

Wilson stepped to the rail and looked back to the stern, where the sloop's fast-spinning screws churned the water to a V of white foam. "The fog is closing in on us fast, Captain." His voice rose in agitation.

"Get for'ard to the long gun, Mr. Wilson. Try a shot across the schooner's bow. Maybe we can convince them that lowering sail would be a sociable thing to do."

Wilson saluted. "Aye, aye sir." He hurried forward, calling on the gun crew to ready the nine-pounder.

The port rail was lined with idlers who were watching the beautiful ship in the distance and exchanging opinions on how the captain would handle this latest crisis. The opinion of the majority was expressed by a red-bearded, Scottish seaman who said, "I say the cap'n should blow that slave scow into matchwood, women an' all, afore the haar gets here."

Mutters of agreement were drowned out by

the roar of the long nine. A moment later an exclamation point of sea and foam rose twenty yards off the schooner's port bow.

"Damn them," Sherburne said. "They're not slowing." As far as he could tell there were almost fifty women on deck, lined up along the starboard rail and one, the bride from the village, lonely and vulnerable at the stern.

Did the destruction of an Arab slaver justify the killing of their captives? Sherburne wrestled with the question while Mr. Wilson, for'ard at the long gun, looked back expectantly for an order.

The captain's orders were to engage and sink any foreign ship, boat, barge, or galley that posed a threat to the United States. A slave ship so close to the California coast was an obvious threat and his duty was clear—he must engage and sink the vessel. Sherburne was about to order Wilson to pound the schooner with the long gun and clear the carronades for action.

The fog bank took the matter out of his hands.

A thick gray mist enveloped the *Kansas* and within seconds, visibility was reduced to a dozen yards.

Sherburne cursed the vagaries of the Pacific weather, then left the quarterdeck and hurried forward. "Did you mark her last position, Mr. Wilson?"

The lieutenant's ruddy face was ashen behind the veil of the fog. "I did, captain."

"Lead her fifty yards and fire." Sherburne turned to the seamen around him. "Listen for the fall of shot, lads."

The breach loading long nine roared, belching flame and smoke, and its carriage recoiled back on the hooking ropes with mindless savagery.

Sherburne raised a hand for quiet, and he and the crew listened for the fall of shot. A faint splash sounded in the distance, no louder than a rock thrown into a pond. Then silence.

"Shall I try again, Captain?" Wilson said.

"No," Sherburne said. "We've lost her, by God." He looked around at his seaman. "But we'll find her, lads, never fear."

A few of the hands cheered. Then the only sound was the *thud-thud* of the sloop's engines, a small ship dwarfed into insignificance by the vastness of the lonely sea and sky.

# Chapter Seventeen

"I never in all my born days thought I'd be glad to see and talk to a hangman," Uriah Tweedy said. "We been stuck in this livery fer three days an' two nights."

"Seems longer," Shawn said, scratching the stubble on his chin.

"So," Tweedy said, "what brings you to town, Mr. Lowth?"

"Alas, a hanging, Mr. Tweedy."

"Anybody we know?" Shawn said.

"A chicken thief who stands five-foot-four-inches tall and weighs one-hundred-and-ten pounds." Thaddeus Lowth smiled. His teeth looked like yellowed piano keys. "In my profession, knowing the height and weight of the condemned is important to ensure a proper drop, you understand. As to the name of the condemned, the sheriff didn't put it out and I never inquire."

"Seems a hard justice to hang a man for stealing chickens," Shawn opined.

Lowth nodded. "An excellent observation, young man. But in reality, and here I quote Deputy Clark, 'He ain't getting' hung for chickens. He's gettin' hung for being a damned nuisance.'"

"I knowed a nuisance one time that got shot. Know who shot him?" Tweedy waited expectantly, got no takers, so he said, "Pat Garrett, that's who. The ranny who gunned poor Billy Bonney down Fort Sumner way."

"What did the miserable wretch do to deserve such a fate?" Lowth asked.

"Who? Billy or the nuisance?" Tweedy looked at the hangman in confusion.

"The nuisance, of course."

"Oh, well, it seems Garrett was doin' some tin-panning up Colorado way and every time he washed a shirt an' hung it out on a rope, the nuisance stole it."

"Not a real smart thing to do to Pat Garrett, I imagine," Shawn said.

"No, it was real dumb. Pat took it for as long as he could, then his patience broke and he cut loose. Put three bullets into the nuisance and that was the end of him." Tweedy looked at Lowth. "How come you ain't got a cozy berth in a hotel, Mr. Lowth?"

"Ah, mine is a much-maligned profession. Hotels say it's uncomfortable for their other guests to have a hangman in residence because it makes them think of death and Judgment Day. In short, the management always gives me the boot."

"That's too bad, Mr. Lowth," Tweedy said. "But ol' Miles Marshwood will make you an' your mule right welcome."

"Yeah. He's a real welcoming kind of feller." Shawn held up the bottle. "Drink?"

Lowth shook his head. "I never indulge in ardent spirits."

"Women?" Tweedy scrunched in nose in question.

"Oh dear no, Mr. Tweedy. My lady wife would never allow it." Lowth's smile looked like someone opening the lid of a piano. "Mrs. Lowth is very big in bloomer circles, you know."

"You don't say," Tweedy said, suddenly interested. "Because of the size of her ass?"

"Oh no. She makes silk bloomers for ladies of refinement. She employs a dozen cutters and sewers, bless her."

Lowth sat beside Shawn and Tweedy and stretched his long, skinny legs out in front of him. Then, as though he loved to expound on a topic of conversation that fascinated him, he said, "Mrs. Lowth tells me often that nothing is dearer to the female heart than her undergarments. She says, in her quiet way, 'That is why, while still retaining her maidenly modesty, the modern woman expects her drawers to fit closely without pinching or chafing that priceless treasure she guards so diligently against every onslaught of the rampant male sex.'"

"Wise woman, your wife," Tweedy said, nodding his approval. "A woman's got to guard that priceless treasure, I always say."

"Indeed," the hangman said. "Mrs. Lowth is so proud of her undergarments she will not sell them to ladies of questionable morals, if you catch my drift, Mr. Tweedy."

"Indeed I do, Mr. Lowth. Can't have whores wearing your wife's bloomers, can we? No sir, that would never do."

"I'm glad you agree, Mr. Tweedy. Mine is a lonely profession and it's seldom I meet anyone who values a thing I say." Lowth smiled. "Unless it's about a hanging, of course. Then they appreciate my professional opinion. All things considered, it's not the easiest task in the world to snap a man's neck clean, Mr. Tweedy. Snap it like a dry twig, one might say."

"You have stated the problem most clearly, Mr. Lowth. Yours is indeed a skilled occupation." Tweedy took a swig of whiskey, wiped off the neck, and passed the bottle back to Shawn. "Now tell me, what was the most interesting hangin' you ever done?"

Lowth sighed. "They're seldom interesting, Mr. Tweedy. Some men die well, others have to be dragged kicking and screaming to the gallows, but there's always a sad sameness to the affair. However I will tell you this. I always advise an indoor hanging whenever possible, even if it means I merely throw my rope over a barn beam." He pointed upward. "Like those."

"And why so, Mr. Lowth?" Tweedy said.

"Ah, it's because the ladies don't like to be out in the sun. Their delicate skin, you know." Lowth puffed up a little. "And speaking of the ladies—"

"God bless, 'em," Tweedy said affectionately.

"Indeed, Mr. Tweedy. Speaking of the ladies, I always try to get the condemned to give a little speech about how whiskey and loose women brought him to his present pass, even though he had a good mother."

Lowth removed his bowler hat and wiped the sweatband with knobby, arthritic fingers. "I assure you, the ladies love that speech and time after time I hear them say to their shrinking husbands, 'Just wait until I get you home.'"

Shawn laughed, then thumbed open his watch. It had just gone one in the morning, his fourth night in the livery. Would Zeb Moss ever make his move?

"Now, Mr. Lowth," he heard Tweedy say, "let's return to the subject of drawers. It's a real interestin' discussion an' one that I never had afore."

"And of the greatest moment, Mr. Tweedy," the hangman said. "Since all ladies, be their station in life high or low, wear them. Now, let's consider the material. I mean cotton or silk. Why, there's a case to be made for both and . . ."

Bored, Shawn rose to his feet and stepped to the door of the barn, ignoring the talk behind him.

The wind had dropped and the snow fell straight down in large flakes. The street was empty, but there was as yet life at the Lucky Lady. Laughter, both male and female, rose above a piano and banjo mourning the killing of Jesse James by the dirty little coward Bob Ford.

Shawn stepped away from the barn into shadow, his eyes searching through the darkness. Rectangles of orange light spilled from the saloon onto the snowy street, but the hitching rails were in darkness and he couldn't make out if horses were present.

He watched a man cross the street, a puncher by his awkward, high-heeled walk, and vanish into the Lucky Lady. Then the only movement was the fall of snow in the gloom.

To allay his boredom, Shawn had hit the whiskey heavily, and now he felt tiredness overcome him. Time to seek his blankets and sleep away yet another useless night.

But then, in an instant, he was wide awake.

\* \* \*

A solitary figure, hunched inside an old army greatcoat, made his way along the street toward the barn. The man had a quick, short-stepping walk and his head constantly swiveled on his neck as though he feared an enemy lurked in every shadow.

Shawn drew his gun and stepped into darkness again. The Colt up and ready, he waited.

Finally the man, smaller than he'd first appeared, did a quick right turn and walked with determination toward the barn. Shawn moved into yellow lamplight and said, "Hold it right there, mister. I can drill you real easy."

"Hell, it's only me," the man said.

"Who's you?"

"Willie Wide Awake, as ever was."

"Keep your hands away from your sides and step into the barn."

Willie did as he was told and his sudden appearance put a period at the end of the words on Thaddeus Lowth's lips. He stared at the visitor. "Good heavens, that man needs some rest."

"No sleep," Willie shook his head. "Nary a wink in years."

"If you'll forgive me for saying so, you look like a cadaver in a greatcoat," Lowth said.

"Alas, such is the sad lot of the sleepless." Willie looked at Tweedy. "Uriah, I have information on Zebulon Moss and his men."

"Then speak on, dread apparition," Tweedy said.

"Zeb's boys are saddling horses in his livery stable at t'other end of the street. Them rannies are pulling out of town, you ask me."

"Is there a woman with them?" Shawn asked quickly.

"No, I reckon she's still at the Lucky Lady." Willie looked fearfully over his shoulder. "Moss has a bunch of women in the saloon, been bringing them in for the past couple o' nights."

"What fer?" Tweedy wanted to know. "Ain't he got enough females already?"

"I don't know," Willie said. "But he's got plenty more, Uriah, an' that's a natural fact."

Shawn took charge. "Uriah, saddle up. Willie, get back down to the saloon and keep your eyes open. If you see Moss and his boys leaving town, hustle back here and tell us. I want to get a trail on him."

Willie touched his forehead with a crooked finger. "I'm on my way, cap'n." He turned and disappeared into the darkness.

As Shawn and Tweedy saddled their horses, Lowth looked on with growing interest. "Are you embarking on an adventure, Mr. Tweedy?"

"Seems like, Mr. Lowth."

"May I join you?"

"Hell, Mr. Lowth, you're all tied up. You've got a man to hang an' that's an important task."

"He's only a chicken thief. Of little account."

"And a nuisance."

"I don't want to hang him. The condemned has little appeal for me. I'd prefer to go with you."

"Can you use a gun?" Shawn quickly asked.

"Oh dear me, no. But I'm a dab hand with a rope."

"Mr. Lowth, we'll be shootin', not hangin'," Tweedy pointed out.

"I'd still like to follow along."

Tweedy looked at Shawn. "What do you say? Maybe he'll bring us luck."

"Hell, he can ride with us," Shawn said. "Could be we'll be saving the life of a chicken thief and damned nuisance."

Lowth needed no other invitation. He threw his saddle on his mule and said, "I will be a rock, Mr. Tweedy. There is no one calmer in a crisis than a hangman."

Tweedy nodded. "Just so, Mr. Lowth. My old ma told me that very thing the day they strung up my pa. Of course he wasn't a chicken thief, you understand. He killed a man with a wood ax."

"The murderer is always a better class of condemned, Mr. Tweedy. A real crowd-pleaser. Your late father is to be complimented." Lowth finished saddling his mule and loaded his packhorse with the tools of his trade, a dozen hemp ropes and a selection of black hoods.

Shortly thereafter, Willie returned. "Zebulon Moss is pulling out, heading south. Got six of his boys mounted and two up on a John Deere wagon with a canvas cover. The women are inside. I heard some weeping and wailing, that's fer sure."

"You did well, Willie." Shawn handed the man a double eagle. "Use that to see a doctor. Ask him for a sleeping draught."

"Or spend it on whiskey," Tweedy said, leading his horse to the front of the barn. "Damn rotgut they sell in this town will knock you out quick enough."

"It's been a real pleasure doing business with you gents," Willie said, tapping his forehead with the coin. "Now see you don't get yourselves shot. Silas Creeds is with them boys of Zeb's and he don't sit on his gun hand."

# Chapter Eighteen

"Shawn is out trying to save a maiden in distress, and as for Jacob, God alone knows where he is." Shamus O'Brien was distressed.

"Then I wish them well and I'll pray for their safe return to Dromore," Dr. James Glover said.

"Amen." Shamus stared hard at the physician. "You said you had something of the greatest import to discuss."

"Yes, I do. That's why I wished to talk to you alone, Shamus."

"Then talk, man. Don't sit there perched on the edge of your chair like a crow on a stick."

Glover smiled. A man with an Apache lance head in his back and worried about his sons had reason to be testy at times. He got to his reason for being there. "Dr. Conrad Jakobs is waiting in the library. I think you should listen to what he has to say."

"A Dutchman, you said in your letter."

"Yes. He's chief surgeon at Leiden University Hospital. He has a worldwide reputation, Shamus. He's a fine surgeon."

"I knew a Dutchman during the war," Shamus said, "a colonel of artillery. I didn't cotton to him much."

That comment brought another smile to Glover's thin lips. "Will you listen to him, Shamus?"

"He thinks he can get the lance head out?"

"Yes. That's what he thinks."

"And if he starts cutting, and can't? What then?"

"I'd prefer that Dr. Jakobs answers your questions."

Shamus pushed his wheelchair to the drinks table and lifted a decanter. "Bourbon?"

Glover shook his head.

"You still don't drink, doc, huh?"

"I never have, Shamus. You know that."

"What about what's-his-name, the Dutchman?"

"Dr. Jakobs does not imbibe, either."

Shamus poured himself whiskey. "Never did trust a man who doesn't drink." He smiled. "Except doctors. They don't know any better."

"Will you talk to Conrad?" Glover pressed.

"Hell, yes, if it pleases you. Bring him in."

"I want Samuel and Patrick here, and Lorena."

"Ganging up on me, huh?"

"In a word, Shamus, yes."

* * *

Shamus pulled down his shirt and glared irritably at Dr. Jakobs. "Well?"

"Colonel, the blade is wedged between two vertebrae and is pressing on your spinal column." Jakobs was a tall man in early middle age with a shock of unruly white hair and the face of a poet.

"Hell, doc, tell him something he don't already know." Luther Ironside had refused to be kept away from such an important occasion and Lorena had warned him to be on his best behavior. She gave him the brows-down, female stare that would scare any man.

But Ironside persisted. "Can you get it out? It's been there for nigh on twenty-five years."

Jakobs answered Ironside, but he looked at Shamus. "I can remove the blade, Colonel. But—"

"There's always a but," Shamus grumbled. He looked severely at Jakobs. "Unload it on me, doc."

"If the object is not removed with proper care it could shift and sever your spinal cord," Jakobs said.

Lorena gasped. "What then, Doctor?"

"At best, Colonel O'Brien could be completely paralyzed. At worst, he won't survive the operation."

"You're not making a good case for a cutting, doc," Shamus said.

Always one to consider all the options before making a decision, Lorena asked, "But if the surgery is successful, what then?"

"The patient will walk again."

"Chances?" Patrick asked.

"Fifty-fifty," Jakobs answered. "Maybe slightly less."

Shamus shook his head. "I don't like the odds, doc. I'd be bucking a stacked deck."

"Colonel, you're already living on borrowed time. The blade in your back could move at any time and kill you." The surgeon looked unhappy. "I don't like to tell this to any man, but if you don't elect for surgery, I give you no more than a year to live, two if you're content to lie in bed and move very little."

Ironside looked at Shamus. "Colonel, doctors don't know everything. Remember old General Grimes had a pistol ball lodged near his heart? The docs wanted to cut it out of him, but the general said no. Hell, I bet he's still living yet."

"This is much more serious," Jakobs said. "It's a matter of life or death."

Shamus nodded. "I'll study on it, doc."

"But not for too long," Jakobs warned. "I must leave for Leiden next week."

"Shamus, that gives you four days to make your decision," Dr. Glover said.

Samuel looked at his father's physician. "What do you think, Doctor?"

"I concur with everything Dr. Jakobs says. The lance head is dangerously close to the colonel's spinal cord and it could move at any time, day or night." He looked at his patient and smiled. "Let's not dwell on what might happen, Shamus. Dr. Jakobs is an excellent surgeon, the best in Europe, and he could have you walking again. Don't you want to be free of that wheelchair and your constant pain?"

Shamus looked around the room. "What do the rest of you think? Luther, you've got an opinion on everything. Give me your thoughts on the matter."

Ironside looked like a man in pain. "Colonel, there are some things a man has to decide for himself. I'm lost."

"Samuel?" Shamus said.

It took a while for Samuel to speak. "Pa, I don't have the words . . . or the wisdom."

"Patrick?"

"I want you out of that wheelchair, Colonel."

"Lorena?"

"I don't want to lose you, Shamus. And I want you to see your grandchildren grow up. I urge you to have the surgery."

"Is that what Saraid would have said?" Shamus asked, remembering his wife of so long ago.

"I'm sure she would," Lorena said.

A silence fell on the parlor, stretched, and grew tense. The doctors exchanged glances and Ironside, hunched and miserable, stared at the rug between his boots. Outside snow fell and children laughed and yelled in the distance.

Finally Shamus looked at Dr. Jakobs. "When can you do it?"

"With Dr. Glover assisting me, I can perform the surgery tonight."

Shamus looked at his old friend. "Luther, Grimes died a week after the war ended."

Ironside looked up, his face heavy with concern. "I didn't know that, Colonel."

"He should've had the surgery," Shamus said.

"Have you reached a decision, Shamus?" Glover asked.

Shamus nodded once. "Do it tonight."

"A wise decision, Colonel," Jakobs said. "And a brave one."

Shamus smiled. "Right now I'm so brave I need another drink."

Jakobs shook his head. "No more alcohol until after the surgery, Colonel, if you please."

"Then be damned to ye for a sober-sided Dutchman," Shamus argued.

But his voice was weak and his words carried no conviction.

# Chapter Nineteen

The schooner *Nawfal* had tacked against the prevailing wind and sailed north through the Gulf of California, heading for an inlet on the Sonora coast south of Mexicali. But as darkness crowded close and the danger of running aground increased, the ship dropped anchor in the Sea of Cortes and waited for the dawn.

Sheik Abdul-Basir Hakim was well pleased. He'd slipped away from the American sloop in the fog and then turned back for Sonora, where he'd meet Zebulon Moss and the women he'd promised.

Not that he'd the slightest intention of paying Moss. The whisper of honed steel would be the unbeliever's only reward.

The night was a cave of darkness, moonless, and the north wind chill. Hakim heard the call of night birds from the shore rise above the rush of the surf and farther off a coyote yipped once, then fell silent. He considered having a Chinese girl sent up for his amusement, but dismissed the idea. These were dangerous waters and he'd need all his strength and cunning should the sloop reappear out of the gloom. Lying with a woman would rob him of both.

A seaman brought the sheik coffee and dates and then vanished forward into the dark. The schooner swayed on her anchor. Her boards creaked, the wind harped through the rigging, and the current murmured along her sides.

Sheik Hakim drank his spiced coffee and wished for morning.

Dawn had barely touched the sky above the Sierra Madres with violet light when the *Nawfal* raised anchor and sailed north.

During the mid-afternoon, the schooner passed Tiburon and Guardian Angel islands, then steered into an inlet two miles south of the estuary where three great rivers, the Colorado, Salt, and Gila, emptied into the gulf. It was narrow, hemmed in on two sides by steep, brush-covered bluffs. Tangles of wild oak and smoke trees grew on the flat, effectively shielding the mouth of the fiord from the casual observer. Any warship scouting from the south would scout ahead with telescopes and observe nothing but empty sea. It was also a lost, lonely place where few humans ever visited.

To Hakim's irritation, there were interlopers present.

Five men stood on the south bank, Mexican peons by the look of them, and stared at the beautiful ship as it moored in the inlet, its deck and rigging swarming with swarthy, bearded sailors.

Two small fishing boats had been pulled up onto shore and a pregnant woman with a baby in her arms squatted near them, stirring something in a pot over a small, smoky fire.

"Fishermen, lord," Hassan Najid said. "They will leave soon."

"Yes, and perhaps they'll meet the American sloop and tell them what they saw at this place," Hakim said irritably.

Najid bowed his head. "God be praised, your wisdom is great, lord." He looked at his master. "Is it your wish that I kill them?"

"It is my wish, Hassan. But the woman might bring something at the slave market."

Najid looked to shore. "She has the sullen, stupid face of a peasant, her breasts are slack, and she's with child again. Who would want her?"

Hakim sighed. "Yes, what you say is true. She is worthless. Kill her with the rest."

"And her baby?"

"Give it to my women. It might amuse them."

\* \* \*

Sheik Hakim watched the massacre from his ship.

The fishermen died like dogs and his lip curled in contempt. He had no taste for killing Mexican peons unless they were brave and showed fight like the blacksmith at the village. They screamed like women when the steel hit them and offered no defense but pleas for mercy. Their woman died better, quietly, along with her baby, the result of a careless stroke of the sword. Perhaps she was relieved that death was about to free her from a life of miserable poverty and grinding bondage.

Najid held a severed head high and grinned at Hakim. The sheik condescended to bow, acknowledging his second-in-command's prowess with the blade, though he thought it a small matter to kill an unarmed man.

# Chapter Twenty

"I never did cotton to night riding," Uriah Tweedy said. "It worries a man."

Beside him, Thaddeus Lowth, his head bent into wind and snow, smiled. His breath smoked as he said, "Worry is like a rocking horse, Mr. Tweedy. It's something to do that doesn't get you anywhere."

"Truer words were never spoke, Mr. Lowth. But I worry just the same." Tweedy turned to Shawn. "How about you, young feller? You've been mighty quiet."

"Worries me that we aren't able to free Julia Davenport before Zeb Moss reaches Old Mexico and the slave ship."

"Hell, boy, we got four, maybe five days," Tweedy said. "We'll come up with somethin'. Hell, I'm gonna marry that little gal and I'll see no harm comes to her."

Shawn and his two companions looked like

three old men. Frost and snow whitened their eyebrows and mustaches and they rode bent over in the saddle, making themselves small to the cutting wind.

Tweedy was an excellent tracker and he read Moss's trail south with ease. The heavy John Deere left deep ruts in the snowy mud and the four mounted men made no attempt to scout their back trail.

For a while Shawn and the others rode in silence, each busy with his own thoughts. For his part Shawn wondered if he'd taken on a job he couldn't handle. The way to Mexico was long and hard and ahead of him rode half a dozen of the most dangerous gunmen in the west. With him he had an old, half-crazy bear hunter and a hangman who knew more about ladies' bloomers than gunfighting. The odds were stacked against them and they weren't going to get any better.

He decided he'd have to pick his fights, shoot and run, and try to wear down Moss and his men. No matter how the pickle squirted, it was a tall order and the prospect didn't fill him with confidence.

One thought led to another and Shawn raised his voice against the black wind. "Uriah, why is Moss making a five-hundred-mile trip to Old Mexico across some of the roughest country west of the Mississippi?"

Tweedy shook his head. "I ain't catching your drift, boy."

"He could've sent Creeds and the rest of his boys. He'd no call to go in person."

"Don't know." Tweedy rubbed life into his frozen lips with his gloved hand. "It bears some studyin', I guess."

"If I may interject, Mr. O'Brien?" Lowth asked.

"Interject away, Mr. Lowth," Tweedy answered for Shawn.

"One might suppose that Mr. Moss is undertaking such an arduous journey because there's something he covets waiting for him at his destination."

"When a wise man is talkin', let your ears hang down an' listen, boy," Tweedy said to Shawn. "Them's words of wisdom."

"I'm listening," Shawn said. "Moss covets money, but he could trust Creeds to bring it back to him."

"Then there's something else," Lowth said. "A thing of much more value."

"Like what?" Shawn was intrigued.

"Like a slave ship, Mr. O'Brien. I'm not an expert on such matters, but I believe such a craft would be of great value. Certainly valuable enough for an avaricious gentleman like Mr. Moss to think it's worth a trip of five hundred miles."

Shawn considered that, then said, more to himself than Lowth, "Kill the captain, take over the ship and crew, and go into the slave trade as a profitable sideline." He tried to meet Lowth's eyes through the darkness and spinning snow. "It's thin, Thaddeus. I never pegged Zeb Moss as a sailor."

"He doesn't need to sail the ship, Mr. O'Brien. His gunmen will. I imagine they can keep a crew in order. Hang one or two of the more mutinous, if you'll forgive me making a reference to my profession, and the rest will fall in line very quickly."

"If Moss plans to take the ship, he'd want to be there in person to make sure it's done right, huh?" Shawn gave some thought to the idea.

Lowth's icy wool muffler had ridden up over his mouth. He pulled it down and said, "My sentiments exactly."

"Moss could make a fortune in the slave trade," Shawn said. "It's only a small step from owning a brothel to operating a slave ship."

"And much more profitable," Lowth pointed out. "It takes a long time to amass a fortune off the backs, for want of a better word, of two-dollar whores."

"It's a thought—" Shawn grimaced and arched his back. "Oh my God!" he yelled, slumping forward in the saddle, his face a mask of pain.

"Damn it, boy, what ails ye?" Tweedy cried.

"My back," Shawn said through gritted teeth. "Low down. It hurts like hell."

Tweedy drew rein and put his arm around the

younger man. "Didn't you say you was pushed down stone steps at the Lucky Lady?"

Shawn hunched his shoulders, his head tilted in pain. "Yeah, I fell down stairs. I thought I'd broken every bone in my body. Damn, this feels like a knife cutting into me deep."

Tweedy's eyes searched a distance that looked like white streaks of paint flung across a black canvas. "Over there," he said finally, pointing. "Into the trees."

Still supporting Shawn, he led the way. For a moment Tweedy's horse floundered in a deep snowdrift, its knees kicking high, but the animal recovered and reached the shelter of the pines, pulling Shawn's horse after him.

Lowth followed the path cleared for him, but his mule balked and the packhorse shied, unsure of its footing. Tweedy left Shawn and went back and helped Lowth get his animals into shelter.

"A parlous path, Mr. Tweedy," Lowth said, breathing hard as he clambered down from the saddle.

"To be sure, Mr. Lowth. But the young feller is in a bad way and what must be done must be done."

In the copse of pines, Shawn sat erect on his horse, his shoulders no longer raised against pain. "It's gone. It went as suddenly as it came. One minute the knife was there, cutting me, then it was gone."

"Boy, you gave us a scare," Tweedy said. "You tellin' me you don't have the misery no more?"

"I feel fine," Shawn said. "What the hell causes a pain like that?"

"Maybe," Tweedy said after some consideration, "you've got a touch of the rheumatisms, boy. They can nip at a man, fer sure."

Shawn nodded. "Maybe so. Let's get back on the trail."

"Not yet," Tweedy said. "You rest up for a spell. The trail will still be there."

"I have coffee and sugar on the packhorse, and a pot of course," Lowth offered. "Perhaps we should have a cup if a sufficient quantity of dry wood can be obtained for a fire."

"Bound to be some around here, Mr. Lowth," Tweedy said. "Unhitch that pot and I'll get something goin' to put under it."

Shawn fretted about losing time, but the pain had drained him, and hot coffee and a cigar would be welcome.

Besides, it was a long, long way to Mexico . . . a lot of long-riding miles . . . a lot of time.

# Chapter Twenty-one

"How is he, Doctor?" Lorena O'Brien asked anxiously. Samuel stood next to her, his face a mask of anxiety. Behind them, Ironside was gray as a ghost and as menacing as the wrath of God.

"He's resting quietly," Dr. James Glover said. "The chloroform takes a little time to wear off. Dr. Jakobs is with him."

"Did he get it?" Ironside said. "Did he get the lance head out?"

Glover reached into a pocket of his frock coat, produced a piece of metal the size and shape of an arrowhead, and dropped it into Ironside's hand. "It's wrought iron and was slowly lodging in Colonel O'Brien's spine, hence the pressure on his spinal cord and the almost constant pain."

"The lance head was made from a Mexican saber blade," Ironside said. "This is the tip. It was hurting him bad, huh?"

"Worse than the colonel would ever care to admit."

Conversation faltered. Three people stood teetering on the edge of a precipice, afraid of the answer to the question they had to ask.

Finally Lorena spoke for them all. "Will the colonel recover, Doctor?"

Glover shook his head. "I'm afraid only time will answer that question."

"Hell, doc, you must have some idea," Ironside said. "Tell us something, anything."

"I'm sorry. We'll have to wait and see."

"Damn it, there is no *we*," Ironside protested. "The Dutchman left and soon so will you. Who's gonna be here for the waitin' and seein'?"

Glover smiled. "I'll be here, Luther. Mrs. O'Brien has kindly prepared a room for me and I'll attend the colonel until he's on his feet again."

"Just as well . . ." The rest of what Ironside had to say trailed off into an ill-tempered growl.

Lorena glared at him. "Luther, Doctor Glover will do his best for the colonel. Do you have nothing to do? If not, the ladies need firewood in the kitchen."

"I got plenty to do, ma'am," Ironside stiffened his back and walked away, muttering to himself. "Wood for the kitchen . . . I'm the only one who does anything around here . . . damned doctors . . . kill a man faster than scat . . . woman giving orders . . . never heard the like . . ."

Glover watched Ironside go. "I fear we've upset your segundo, Samuel."

"Luther is easily upset. But he's very worried about the colonel."

"We're all very worried about the colonel," Glover acknowledged.

"What time is it?" Shamus O'Brien croaked.

Lorena stepped closer to the bed. "One o'clock, Colonel."

"Day or night?"

"It's one in the morning. How do you feel?"

"It's dark outside."

"Yes, it's dark. And it's still snowing. Drifting a little in the hills."

"Has anybody checked on the herd?"

"Yes. Luther and Patrick are out with the vaqueros."

"Good," Shamus mumbled. "That's good."

"Shamus, how do you feel?" Lorena asked again.

"Nothing."

"What do you mean?"

"From the neck down I can't feel my body. It's as though it's no longer part of me."

"Dr. Glover says your recovery will take time."

"I'm paralyzed, Lorena, like a puppet with its strings cut."

"I'll get the doctor."

"Wait, Lorena." Shamus turned his head slowly and with effort to look at her. "You will soon be mistress of Dromore, as my wife Saraid once was. Samuel will take my place and you must give him all the support you can."

Lorena opened her mouth to speak, but Shamus talked over her. "Samuel is a good son and a good man, but he lets his heart rule his head. So do Shawn and Patrick. You'll have to show them the way, not Jacob's way, but the middle road. Do you understand?"

Lorena fought back sudden tears. "You'll get well again, Colonel. You'll stand on Saraid's pink hearthstone on your own two feet. I just know you will."

"The middle road, Lorena. Always the middle road . . ." Shamus's words drifted away as he fell into sleep.

Lorena brushed a wisp of gray hair from the colonel's forehead, her heart heavy as lead. He looked shrunken somehow, and vulnerable.

# Chapter Twenty-two

Shawn O'Brien huddled close to the hatful of fire he shared with Uriah Tweedy and Thaddeus Lowth. They were protected from the worst of the wind by an upthrust of limestone rock higher than a man.

Tweedy accepted the communal coffee cup from Shawn and looked over the rim at the shivering hangman. "You starting to regret taggin' along, Mr. Lowth?"

"Gracious me, no. I've never before embarked on an adventure and I must admit I'm quite excited." Lowth hugged his skinny knees to his chest and smiled. "This is a quest, just like those the knights of old rode forth on."

For a moment Tweedy was puzzled, then he said, "Here, are you talkin' about them McKnight brothers down to the Texas Trinity River country that got hung fer hoss stealin' a few years back?"

"Uriah, he's talking about"—Shawn searched his mind for an explanation that would make sense to the old bear hunter—"old-time cavalry that went looking for stuff."

"Oh, like scouts, you mean?"

"Yes. Something like that."

Tweedy looked at Lowth. "We're scouts all right. But scoutin' Zeb Moss's back trail ain't exactly a healthy occupation."

"And hence the adventure," Lowth said. "Without danger, there is no quest."

Random snowflakes filtered through the pine canopy and sizzled on the hot coals. Beyond the orange circle of the firelight, there was only darkness and the restless rustle of the trees.

"Uriah, you reckon Moss is holed up like us?" Shawn asked, talking behind a blue drift of cigar smoke.

"Bet on it, sonny. This is good country fer men and dogs but it's hell on women and horses. Ol' Zeb can't push them females too hard and get them all used up, not if he plans to sell 'em, he can't."

Tweedy looked hard at Shawn. "What's on your mind?"

"We have to hit him hard and real soon. We can't fall behind."

"We won't. Zeb's got a wagon slowin' him down, remember?" Tweedy took time to light his pipe, and then said, "Hit him hard how?"

"Ride in shooting, drop a couple, then hightail it out of there."

"Easier said than done, sonny."

"I know that," Shawn said. Then irritably, "Don't you think I already know that?"

"No offense," Tweedy said. "It's just that sometimes it's easier to pull your freight than your gun."

"You mean quit?" Shawn exclaimed. "Give it up?"

"Hell no. I'm not quittin' on Trixie. She's my intended, you recollect?" Tweedy studied the glowing coal in the pipe bowl. "What I say is we shadow 'em for a spell before we go to shootin'. Bide our time, like."

"Then strike while the iron is hot, in other words," Lowth said.

"Exactly, Mr. Lowth," Tweedy said. "Your grasp of the situation does you credit, sir."

"The hangman sometimes must assess the facts and make up his mind quickly, Mr. Tweedy. He can't dilly-dally when a trap must be sprung."

"No indeed, Mr. Lowth. True words, every single one of them."

Shawn accepted the cup from Lowth and refilled it from the pot. "We'll pull out at first light and press Moss close. As you said, Uriah, bide our time and hit him when he least expects it."

"Trouble is, Zeb always expects it," Tweedy pointed out.

"He can be fooled, like any other man," Shawn said.

Tweedy nodded. "Maybe so."

Suddenly Lowth was alert. "Anybody hear that?" He straightened up, listening into the night.

"I didn't hear nothin'." Tweedy looked into the darkness.

"I thought I heard a gunshot," Lowth said softly.

Shawn shook his head. "I didn't hear it."

"You gettin' spooked, Mr. Lowth?" Tweedy whispered.

"Not at all, Mr. Tweedy, but I do have very acute hearing, something Mrs. Lowth has often commented on. She says it's a most singular gift and would be eminently useful should I ever decide to enter the detective profession."

"It's getting colder and there's a frost coming down," Shawn said. "Maybe you heard a pine snap."

"Perhaps, Mr. O'Brien, but it did sound like gunfire."

"Zeb and his boys, you think?" Tweedy said to Shawn.

"I don't know, Uriah."

"Interestin', though," Tweedy nodded.

"Yeah, real interesting," Shawn agreed.

* * *

After a night of fitful sleep under the thin wool of his blanket and the thinner warmth of the feeble fire, Shawn rose at first light and stretched the frost out of his joints.

Thaddeus Lowth was already awake. He had coffee going and was frying salt pork in a small pan. "Good morning, Mr. O'Brien. Did you sleep well?"

"Hell no," Shawn said, in little mood for pleasantries.

Snow was falling again and the morning was crisp and cold as frozen glass, as though it would shatter into a million pieces and drop to earth as ice crystals if someone even spoke too loud.

Lowth kneeled by the fire and stirred the brown pork slices with a fork. Without looking at Shawn, he said, "That was a gunshot I heard last night. I have considered it, and there is no doubt in my mind."

"Then I guess we'll come upon a body today," Shawn said.

"Someone shooting at a deer, perhaps," Lowth said.

"This is high country, Thaddeus, above the aspen line. The deer head down to the flatlands in winter."

Lowth permitted himself a rare smile. "Then they are more sapient than humans."

"I reckon," Shawn mumbled, reminding himself to ask Patrick what the hell *sapient* meant.

Gray land, gray sky, and ahead of them appeared nothing but bitter cold and distance. The horses slowed their pace as the footing under their hooves grew more slick and treacherous with every passing mile.

Tweedy read the muddy trail as a scholar reads a book and his face grew more and more puzzled. "He's swung southwest, O'Brien. If I didn't know better, I'd swear he's headed for Albuquerque."

"Heading wide around Dromore range, maybe," Shawn said.

"No need to make a loop this wide." Tweedy shook his head. "Damn it, boy. I reckon he's gonna head south along the Rio Grande."

"Take him right into Albuquerque all right," Lowth said. "I hung a couple rustlers there a while back."

Snow flurried in the air like sea foam and the breath of the three riders smoked in the cold. The canopies of the pines on the surrounding hills looked like arrowheads of white marble.

Suddenly Zeb Moss's intentions became clear to Shawn. "He's not taking the wagon all the way to Old Mexico. He'll take the Santa Fe railroad and ride the cushions in comfort."

"With all them captive females?" Tweedy said. "Folks will talk, ask questions."

"Moss is a rich man who wants to be richer," Shawn said. "He can afford a private Pullman, away from prying eyes."

"Well, where do we go from here, Mr. O'Brien?" Lowth questioned.

"Do as we're doing. Follow him."

"And then what?" Tweedy wasn't so sure of Shawn's plan.

"We take the same train, ride the cushions with Moss, and bide our time, like you said, Uriah."

"O'Brien," Tweedy said, "if'n my intended wasn't with ol' Zeb, I'd quit on you just about now."

Shawn grinned and waved Tweedy on. "Find me the trail, Uriah."

Thirty minutes later they came on an old stage station and a dead man.


"Looks like he was trying to farm bedrock," Tweedy said. "I never figured grangers were long on smarts, but this'n beats all."

The dead man lay on his back. Snow had gathered in the hollows of his eyes and turned his black beard white. He lay close to the house and when Lowth scraped scarlet snow off the man's chest he found a single bullet wound. "Right through the heart."

"That's the gunshot you heard last night, Mr. Lowth," Tweedy said.

"Indeed it is, Mr. Tweedy. I wish it were otherwise." Lowth shook his head. "Poor man."

The stage station had been abandoned years before after one too many Apache raids on the horse corral. It seemed that the dead man had moved in and tried to establish a farm, an impossible dream in the high country.

"You reckon this is Zeb Moss's work?" Tweedy asked Shawn.

"Who else?" Shawn shrugged his shoulders.

"Fer why, you reckon?"

"For the sheer hell of it," Shawn said angrily.

But when he and Tweedy went inside they found evidence of a woman, young, judging by the cut and slimness of her clothes. A brush on the dresser in the bedroom showed evidence of long red hair.

"Moss wanted the woman," Shawn said. "And when her husband tried to intervene, he killed him. That's how I piece it together."

"Looks like," Tweedy agreed. "Another female for the slave block, and a slim young redhead at that."

"You still feel like quitting, Uriah?" Shawn said.

"I ain't quitting, sonny. Not until I get my own woman back."

"Then so be it." Shawn stepped to the bedroom door. "Look around, see if we can find some grub and extra blankets."

Then he heard the cry of a baby from a crib behind the bed and froze in the doorway. A baby meant big trouble coming down fast.

His thought was echoed by an anguished yelp from Tweedy. "Mr. Lowth, I reckon your quest has just gone to hell in a handbasket."

# Chapter Twenty-three

"There's a milk cow out back," Uriah Tweedy said as he came back into the bedroom after scouting outside. "Babies drink milk, don't they?"

"I reckon," Shawn said. "I seem to recollect that they live on milk."

"Then go out there and fill a bucket," Tweedy boomed.

"Hell, I don't know how to milk a damned cow," Shawn argued, worry making him testy.

"You're a puncher, ain't you?" Tweedy growled.

"A puncher punches beeves, not milk cows."

"Well, we need milk. Somebody's got to do it afore that screaming younker drives us all crazy."

"Then you go fill a bucket."

"I hunt bears. What do I know about milk?" Tweedy scowled, the baby's shrieks scrambling his brains. "What variety of kid is that anyhow?"

"I don't know," Shawn snapped back at Tweedy.

"Then take a look, damn it."

"You take a look. I don't know a thing about babies."

"You can tell a girl baby from a boy baby, can't you?" Tweedy taunted.

"So can you."

"Gentlemen, gentlemen. She's a little girl and she badly needs . . . um . . . a change of garments," Lowth interrupted the argument.

"You do it," Shawn and Tweedy said in unison.

"Do either of you know anything about caring for an infant?" Lowth asked as he scouted around the bedroom, the screaming child in his left arm.

"I've seen my sister-in-law do it and it's damned complicated," Shawn said, his irritation growing. "You have to be trained for that kind of thing."

"Well, some milk would be a start." Lowth held up a stack of white cloths. "Look!"

"What's them?" Tweedy frowned. "Some kind of loincloths?"

Lowth smiled. "It's what you tie around the baby to catch . . . well, whatever it catches."

"Damn it, Thaddeus, you're married," Shawn said. "Haven't you ever had a baby before?"

"Oh dear no, Mr. O'Brien. Mrs. Lowth doesn't

believe in them. Messy little creatures, she always says."

"Hell, it can't be that complicated," Tweedy said. "We prop the kid up somewhere and pour milk down her. The milk goes in one end and comes out the other. What's so all-fired difficult about that?"

"Thaddeus, you clean the kid good," Shawn instructed. Then, his face became grim, like a man about to face a firing squad, and he muttered, "I'll go milk the cow. Is there a bucket out there?"

"No, but there's a water jug in the kitchen," Lowth said. "I think that will hold enough for a baby."

"Then we've got to get back on Moss's trail," Shawn said. "We can't miss the train."

"What about the kid?" Tweedy asked apprehensively.

"We'll take her with us," Shawn answered. "We can't leave her here to starve."

Tweedy groaned. "I knew it. Now we're all gonna die."

"I filled the jug," Shawn said. "Milking is not so bad when you get the hang of it."

"How do we feed it to her?" Tweedy grumbled.

"The fastest way possible," Shawn said. "Maybe then she'll quit her caterwauling."

"Prop her up, Mr. Lowth. Get her to open her

mouth an' I'll pour that jug o' milk into her."
Obviously, Tweedy had no idea how to feed
a baby.

"I found this, Mr. Tweedy." Lowth held up a
small ceramic dish that looked like a gravy boat
with a spout at one end. "I believe we put the
milk in here and feed it to her."

"Looks like you may be right, Thaddeus. But
do it fast." Shawn held his hands over his ears.

Lowth did as he was told. As soon as he put the
spout to the baby's lips, she drank greedily and a
blessed silence descended on the cabin.

"A baby gettin' wet-nursed by a hangman."
Tweedy shook his head in disbelief. "I never in all
my born days seen the like."

"Mr. O'Brien," Lowth whispered, "look around
the kitchen and see if you can find a jar with a lid.
We'll need to carry milk with us, and this feeding
thing. And we'll also need a warm blanket and a
sack to tote the loincloths."

"Damn it. Does a baby need all that stuff?"
Shawn questioned.

"I'm afraid so." Lowth nodded his head.

"And we'll need a woman's dress and a hat,"
Tweedy added to the list.

"What the hell for?" Shawn muttered.

"To get you on the train without attracting Zeb
Moss's lead," Tweedy answered.

"Tweedy, am I thinking what you're thinking?"

"There's no other way. It has to be done."

"Well, I ain't doing it," Shawn declared. "No way am I dressing up like a woman.

Tweedy smiled. "Young feller, don't be such a caterwauling baby."

Thaddeus Lowth held the baby in his arms when they took to the trail again and Shawn led the hangman's packhorse.

Uriah Tweedy scouted ahead, but he had no doubt Albuquerque was Zeb Moss's destination.

By the time they reached the Sandia Mountains the wagon tracks were so fresh Shawn and Lowth slowed to a walk. They kept pace but were careful not to dog Moss's back trail too closely.

Tweedy returned and drew rein beside Shawn and glanced up at the sky. "If'n the snow holds off, I reckon we'll reach the city by nightfall."

Shawn nodded. "I reckon."

"You'll change into your woman's fixins afore we ride into town, Mrs. Lowth," Tweedy looked like a mischievous leprechaun from the pages of one of Shawn's childhood books. "I found a black veil in the cabin that will cover your face. I mean, I've seen women with mustaches before, but nary a one with a dead mouse hanging under her nose."

Shawn grimaced. "Enjoying this, aren't you, Tweedy?"

"Hell boy, ol' Zeb doesn't know me or Mr.

Lowth on sight, but he'd sure as hell recognize you, so you're the one's got to wear the dress. Oh, an' you'll carry the baby. Make you look real harmless, like, bein' sickly Mrs. Lowth an' all."

Shawn glared at the old bear hunter, blue ice in his eyes. "Tweedy, when this is all over, remind me to put a bullet in your belly."

Tweedy thought this uproariously funny. He slapped his buckskinned thigh and roared, "Damn it, Mrs. Lowth, maybe you ain't as harmless as I figured."

"Don't listen to him, Mr. O'Brien," Lowth put in. "I'm quite sure you'll make a charming wife."

He said it to be kind, but all he managed to do was add fuel to the fires of rage already smoldering in Shawn's belly.

# Chapter Twenty-four

Later that morning, Dr. James Glover stepped into Shamus O'Brien's curtained bedroom and nodded to Lorena. "How is he?"

"The colonel says he's paralyzed from the neck down, Doctor. He thinks he's not likely to recover."

"Colonel, can you hear me?" Glover leaned over the bed, his thin face shadowed by the lamplight.

"Damn it, man, of course I can hear you," Shamus snapped. "I'm all frozen over, not deaf."

"You mean you can't move?"

"Jesus, Mary, and Joseph, of course that's what I mean. I'm paralyzed, damn it."

"Your spinal cord is intact, Colonel," Glover said quietly.

"Then why can't I move?"

"Because you're afraid to move."

"I'm afraid of nothing. I wasn't even afraid of the Apache who shoved his lance into me in the first place."

"You're afraid to move because you fear that you cannot. Is that not so, Colonel?"

"Are you saying I'm a coward, you damned pill wrangler?"

"If you're afraid to move, then yes, you're a yellow belly."

Shamus roared in anger. "Lorena, get me my gun!"

"Look at you!" Lorena yelled, pointing her shaking finger at her father-in-law.

"What the hell?" Shamus glared at her.

"You're sitting up!" Glover rushed to the bed and supported Shamus. "Not too much too fast, Colonel."

"I can move!" Shamus cried. "Damn it, doc, I can move my legs!"

"All it took was a little motivation," Glover said. "Calling you a yellow belly worked wonders, but I do apologize for that."

"Thank God and his Blessed Mother," Shamus shouted. "This is a miracle!"

"Dr. Jakobs deserves some of the credit, Colonel," Glover remarked dryly.

"Yes he does, and God bless him, too."

Overcome by emotion, Lorena covered her

face and ran sobbing from the room, calling out for Samuel.

Luther Ironside was the first to dash inside.

Shamus was still sitting up. "I can move my legs, Luther. Hell, I can even wiggle my toes." He demonstrated, even though his legs were covered by a sheet.

"Good, now get on up out of that there bed and we'll put you on a hoss right away, Colonel," Ironside said, beaming.

Glover shook his head. "Easy does it, Luther. The colonel can toddle around the house for a few weeks to get the feel of his feet under him. Then we'll talk about riding horses." The doctor glanced at the bedroom window. "Besides, it's dark and snowing outside."

"Then the colonel can have a drink, huh, doc?" Ironside pushed.

"I suppose one won't hurt him, if that's what he wants."

"Brandy, Luther," Shamus ordered.

Samuel, Patrick, and Lorena bustled into the bedroom.

"You heard?" Shamus grinned.

"I sure did, Pa," Samuel grinned back.

"Look." Shamus moved his legs. "It's a miracle."

"Of modern medicine," Lorena added.

"Maybe so," Shamus said, "but I'm sure the good Lord had something to do with it."

"I can't discount that, Colonel," Glover said. "No man of science can."

"I only wish Shawn and Jacob were here to see this," Shamus said quietly.

"So do I, Colonel," Patrick agreed.

Shamus shook his head. "Two of a kind. Reckless. Feckless."

"A pair of knights errant, off tilting at windmills," Patrick quoted.

Shamus gave his son a blank look.

"*Don Quixote* by Miguel de Cervantes, Pa." Patrick pushed his eyeglasses higher on his nose. "Remember when Don Quixote attacked a windmill, thinking it was a giant?"

"Son, you say some powerful strange things." Shamus shook his head slightly.

"I didn't beat him enough when he was a boy, Colonel," Ironside said, handing Shamus his drink. "That's why he has all these strange notions by times."

Shamus drained his brandy in a gulp, then said, "Lorena, avert your eyes. I'm going to get up and take a stroll around the room."

Glover put a hand on the man's shoulder. "Colonel, I don't advise it. You need to recover for a few days."

"Do as the doctor says, Colonel," Lorena agreed. "You need to regain the strength in your legs."

"Daughter-in-law, I'm strong enough right

now," Shamus argued. "Now clear away there and give me the road."

He swung his legs over the bed, pulled down his nightshirt, and got to his feet. "Nothing to it." Taking a step, he tottered, waved his arms with despair in his eyes, and fell flat on his face.

Ironside rushed to the colonel and lifted him in his strong arms. "I'll put you back in bed, Colonel."

"I can't walk, Luther," Shamus said, his face ashen. "I'm just like I was before."

Glover helped settle his patient back in bed. "It's too early. You've sat in a wheelchair for years and you need to regain the strength in your legs."

"Damn you. You heard what I said," Shamus yelled. "I can't walk."

"Someone will help you at first, then you'll use a cane for a while," Glover explained. "You'll walk again, Colonel, but it will take time."

"You'll walk with me, Colonel," Ironside urged. "Come morning, we'll take a . . . what does Pat call it? A promenade."

"It's impossible, Luther," Shamus argued. "My legs won't move."

"They'll move," Ironside said adamantly. "I'll make them move."

"Listen to Luther, Pa," Samuel coaxed. "He'll help you."

Shamus groaned deep in his chest, then lay back on his pillow and closed his eyes.

One by one the others crept out of the room until Ironside stood alone. "Colonel, if'n I could, I'd give you my own legs to walk on."

Shamus seemed to be asleep, and Ironside didn't know if he heard or not.

His hat and shoulders covered with snow, Jacob O'Brien rode toward Dromore, leading a dun horse with a dead man draped over its saddle.

# Chapter Twenty-five

"Is all prepared?" Sheik Abdul Basir-Hakim asked.

"Yes, great lord," Hassan Najid said. "The man is drugged and has six naked Chinese girls attending him."

"A foretaste of paradise," Hakim predicted. "He will die all the more willingly to taste the real thing."

"He says he is eager to destroy the infidels and fly to his reward."

"Where will the bomb be placed?"

"Abdullah will light the fuse and then charge into the infidels, the holy name of Allah on his lips," Najid said. "The bomb will detonate very quickly."

"Allah be praised. Will it kill them all? We must be sure that none survive."

"The device is loaded with musket balls and iron nails. It will kill every living thing within twenty paces of the blast."

Hakim laid a hand on Najid's sweaty shoulder, disliking the task. "You have done well, Hassan. Once back in our own land you will be richly rewarded. You are indeed a holy warrior."

"Thank you, great lord. It is Allah's will to destroy infidels wherever they can be found. One of the Chinese girls, the prettiest, will accompany Abdullah. She will put Zebulon Moss's men at their ease and they will suspect nothing." Najid smiled, his breath rotten in his mouth. He pushed his hands upward in a V shape. "Then boom!"

Both men laughed, standing alone in the moonlight. "Pity about the Chinese girl, is it not?" Hakim grinned, causing more mirth.

"Lord, since she's going to be killed anyway, may I use the wench for my amusement?"

Hakim nodded. "I give her to you, Hassan. She is yours until she sacrifices herself."

Najid leered. "She might well seek her death as eagerly as Abdullah after I'm finished with her."

The sheik waved a dismissive hand. "A woman is nothing. Do with her what you will."

The two men retired to Hakim's silk tent pitched on the sand, small by Arab standards. A slave schooner had little room to store luxuries. The crew of the Nawfal slept outdoors on the sand, the women confined to the ship under guard. A smaller shelter made from a tent covered with palm leaves, called by the Bedouin an *Al Arish*, housed the pampered suicide warrior and his Chinese girls.

The sheik and his second-in-command shared a dish of mild, salty cheese and dried dates washed down with green tea and mint.

"Once we kill Moss and the other infidels, we will take his women and set sail at once," Hakim said. "It all has to be done quickly."

"What of the American sloop of war, great lord?" Najid asked, remembering the blasts fired on them earlier.

"What of it?"

"Does she lie in wait?"

"The Americans are stupid and impatient," Hakim said. "The warship is long gone, to some dunghill of a port where the crew can find rum and whores."

"Is this so, lord?"

"Of course it is so. Listen to me, Hassan, and remember—the Americans are cowards. That is why they were happy to let us slip away in the fog. They feared to board us and face our Arab steel."

"Aye, death to the American infidel," Najid said, raising his cup.

"And may Allah curse their vile ship." Hakim lifted his cup in agreement.

* * *

"Damn your eyes, Mr. Wilson, don't tell me that again," Commander John Sherburne raged at his first lieutenant. "I don't want to hear it."

Wilson's young, round face flushed, but he was a dogged officer, not an overly intelligent one. "But it remains a possibility, sir."

Sherburne bit off the sharp retort on his lips, and said, "Yes, Mr. Wilson, of course it is. But the schooner is here in the Gulf, not in the Pacific. I can feel her, smell her stench."

Wilson ventured a small, "Where?"

"Mr. Wilson, if I knew that, would we be swinging on our anchor off a pissant island that isn't even on our charts?"

"No, sir."

"I'll find him," Sherburne affirmed. "I'll steam the *Kansas* up and down the length of the gulf and find him, even if it takes me till doomsday. Then so help me I'll gut that Arab like a hog."

The two officers stood on the bridge under a bright moon, veiled now and then by scudding, silver-rimmed clouds. From the crew's quarters a man with a fine tenor voice sang, "There's a New Coon in Town," then eight bells chimed the last dog watch as he finished a song that was currently all the rage in the eastern cities.

"We'll commence the search again when we

have daylight on our side, Mr. Wilson," Sherburne said.

"Very good, sir. I'll post extra lookouts."

"You look a bit peaked, Lieutenant. Missing your betrothed?"

"Alas, Captain, that is not the case. Miss Coffin forbade me to think of her too often lest my imagination stray into carnal matters. She often reminds me of the sinfulness of sexuality and of the extreme sinfulness of the sexual organs. 'William,' she once told me, 'those who feel the lusts of the flesh are the living citadels of Satan. A respectable married woman should consider intercourse with her spouse as a duty, not a pleasure. In other words, my dear, she must lie still and suffer.'"

Sherburne concealed a smile by coughing into his fist. Finally he managed, "She sounds like a re-markable woman."

"Indeed, Captain, she's a frail, chaste creature, is Miss Coffin."

"Too bad."

"Sir?"

"I said, 'Good lad.' I mean for getting betrothed to such a fine lady."

"Yes, I count myself blessed that she will soon become my helpmeet."

Sherburne, a man with a vast appetite for wine, women, and song, stared at the moon and decided that his first lieutenant was a sanctimonious little prig. He and Miss Coffin of the Locked Knees deserved each other.

"I'm retiring to my cabin, Mr. Wilson. Pipe the crew to an early breakfast and then double the watch. Roust me out of my bunk at daybreak."

"Aye, aye, sir."

"We'll catch him, by God." Sherburne slapped the bridge rail with the flat of his hand. "We'll catch him and rip his heathen guts out."

# Chapter Twenty-six

"I paid for the three of us to ride the cushions and for the horses to ride with the livestock. The train is headed south, but the ticket clerk is a right talkative feller and he says the private car is scheduled to be coupled to another train at Rincon and then it'll head east for Sonora." Tweedy looked at Shawn. "It's an expensive trip and you don't have any change comin' back, Mrs. Lowth."

"Damn you, Uriah. I've never done anything less dignified in my life."

"Oh I don't know, sonny," Tweedy said. "I reckon you make a handsome woman in that dress an' all. Does he not, Mr. Lowth?"

"Well, my real wife, though large in girth, is a fragile creature, much given to those ill humors that afflict only the female sex. I'm afraid Mr.

O'Brien does not match that description in any way."

"And this baby I'm holding is wet," Shawn complained. "I know this baby is wet, damn it."

"You can't change her until we board the train, Mrs. Lowth." Tweedy grinned, having fun.

"Uriah, I swear. Call me Mrs. Lowth again and I'll gun you first chance I get." Shawn was not having fun.

"I'll keep that in mind, Mrs. Lowth," Tweedy responded with a bigger grin.

They stood on the station platform under a cone of pale orange light from an overhead lamp. The night was cold, but the snow had stopped, replaced by a thin mist and a raw hoarfrost.

The locomotive hissed and vented steam like an angry dragon, the fireman and engineer agleam with scarlet light from the firebox as though stoking the furnaces of hell.

Zebulon Moss's reserved Pullman was hitched behind the tender, and he and the women had already boarded. Two gunmen, Silas Creeds easily recognized by his top hat and ankle-length coat, stood on guard at the door, their breaths steaming.

It had been Shawn's idea to give Moss's men a good look, figuring a veiled woman with her baby, an old geezer in buckskins, and a man who looked like a seedy office clerk would not alarm them. And he'd been right. Creeds had briefly glanced at the party under the lamp and then looked away, dismissing them as no account.

Thaddeus Lowth put his arm around Shawn's waist and spoke in a voice loud enough to be heard by the Moss gunmen. "Do you care to board now, my dear?"

Enraged, Shawn bit his tongue . . . but he nodded his agreement. He had a role to play, a bitter cup he must drain to the last humiliating drop. Besides that, he was anxious to get on the train where it was warm. Stripped down to his boots and long johns under the thin cotton dress, he was freezing to death.

His pants, shirt, and sheepskin were in what Lowth grandly called his "portmanteau," and he wouldn't be reunited with them again until they reached Sonora—unless Moss planned an unscheduled stop along the way.

The train consisted of three cars and a dining car. Bringing up the rear was a boxcar and caboose. The locomotive was named The General Lee and that made Shawn more favorably inclined toward the Santa Fe railroad company. But as he and the others entered their carriage he knew he faced hours of jolting, sooty misery in a woman's dress that was bursting at the seams as it failed to contain his wide shoulders.

"Take the window seat, my love." Lowth's voice pitched soft like a doting husband.

Only a few passengers were in the car and Shawn growled, "Don't say that again, Thaddeus. Not ever again."

"He's right though," Tweedy hissed. "Git in the corner by the window, pull your veil down, and for God's sake look small and frail."

The train, lost in a vast land, hammered through the darkness on a narrow ribbon of frosted steel. The locomotive's great headlamp picked out random flakes of snow fluttering like moths around a flame. Iron wheels rattled like castanets and the passenger cars rocked on a track that was never quite level. The chimney spewed sparks into the air and belched smoke that found its way into every nook and cranny of the carriages.

Hunched and miserable, and holding the wet, hungry baby in his arms, Shawn was so relieved when Lowth said, "Give her to me, my dear, it's time I changed and fed her," that he didn't get angry.

She stopped crying instantly when Lowth took her, as though babies and hangmen had a natural affinity, one for the other.

Shawn watched as Lowth fed the child and displayed gentleness that he figured must be unique in a man who broke necks for a living. He was about to mention it to Tweedy, but the words died on his lips as the car door slammed open and Silas Creeds, all hostility and arrogance, stepped inside and made his way along the passageway.

As part of his disguise Shawn carried a tapestry handbag on his lap. He slid his hand inside and his fingers closed on the Colt he'd taken from Rance Bohan's body. The revolver was short-barreled and handy and had been tuned by a gunsmith who knew his craft. Somewhere along the way Shawn had lost his .32, otherwise both revolvers would've been in the bag.

Creeds, his top hat at a jaunty angle that suggested the man had been drinking, made his jolting, swaying way toward the dining car. He had time to register the alarm in Tweedy's eyes and lurched to a halt, staring at Shawn for a moment. "Where you headed, little lady?"

Shawn kept his head bowed, the veil over his face. He kept his hand on the Colt, aware that a close-range gunfight in a railroad car was a recipe for disaster. There were only a dozen other passengers, but most of them would be in the line of fire and some would be hit.

Lowth answered quickly. "My lady wife is unwell, and dare not show her face."

"She's got the pox," Tweedy added.

"Is that so?" Creeds pushed his right hand into the pocket of his coat. "Well, I still want to see her face. It could be I have a place for her in my present business enterprise. You savvy?"

Lowth shook his head. "My dear sir, I'm afraid that is impossible. My wife is not feeling well and she has no head for business."

"Pox or no, I want to see her. Now!" Creeds' eyes hardened to nail heads as he drew his Colt self-cocker and shoved the muzzle against the baby's head. "Now, or I scatter the brat's brains."

"Damn you." Tweedy gritted his teeth. "You're picking on a sick woman and a helpless child."

"Shut your trap, pops," Creeds ordered. "Well, does the kid get it?"

At that moment, a middle-aged respectable-looking man in a black wool coat lurched along the aisle, holding on to the back of seats for support. "Here," he yelled at Creeds, "that won't do."

Creeds waited unto the man was almost on top of him, then, without turning, he swung his arm and slammed the Colt against the side of the would-be rescuer's head. The respectable man went down hard and a moment later his hysterical wife kneeled beside him, his bleeding gray head in her lap.

"Creeds, damn you for a yellow-bellied coward!" Shawn cried, jumping to his feet, still wearing his flowered hat and veil. But there was nothing feminine about the blue Colt in his fist.

Creeds immediately thumbed back the hammer

of the Lightning. "Drop the gun or I kill the kid, then his pa."

"She's a girl, you know," Lowth said, trying to defuse the situation a little.

"You, shut your trap." Creeds ordered the hangman again while staring at Shawn. He nodded. "Well, make your choice or make your play."

Shawn had only an instant to make up his mind. He knew with certainty that Creeds would kill the baby, then swing his gun and start shooting, but the appearance of two more Moss gunmen took the decision out of his hands. He saw them pick up the respectable man and throw him into a seat, followed by his wife.

"Drop it," Creeds said, reading defeat in Shawn's slumped shoulders.

Shawn dropped the Colt onto the seat opposite him and Creeds said, "Now, take off the veil."

Shawn tore off the hat, and Creeds' eyes widened in surprise. "Well, well, if'n it ain't Shawn O'Brien. You took to wearin' women's fixins?"

The other gunmen laughed and Shawn's anger flared. "Damn you, Creeds. If I'd had an even break with you, you'd be dead now."

"Big talk comin' from a man dressed like a woman," Creeds sneered. "And an ugly one at that." He rammed a stiff finger into Tweedy's chest. "What the hell are you, old-timer?"

Tweedy lifted his hat an inch above his head.

"Uriah Tweedy's the name, Silas, as ever was. I'm a bear hunter."

"How did you get tied up with O'Brien?"

"Ol' Ephraim is sleeping away the winter, Silas, so young O'Brien hired me as a scout."

"Not much scoutin' to be done on a train," Creeds remarked dryly, swaying with the rhythm of the car.

"A truer word was never spoke, Silas," Tweedy said. "But a hired man does what he's told."

Shawn mentally cursed him for a traitorous dog.

"Who's he?" Creeds nodded at Lowth.

Tweedy opened his mouth to speak, but Creeds said, "Let him talk for himself."

"My name is Thaddeus Lowth, a hangman by profession."

"A hangman?" Creeds said, surprised.

"Yes indeed, and an honorable and ancient profession it is."

"Hell, if you say so." Creeds looked at Shawn and grinned. "The baby yours, ma'am?"

The two late-arriving gunman sat on opposite sides of the aisle, guns in their hands and smiles on their faces, enjoying the fun.

"You should know, Creeds," Shawn said. "She belongs to the man you murdered along the trail."

"Oh, him? He was damned uppity, tried to stop us taking his wife, pretty little thing that she is." The gunman frowned. "I didn't see no kid back at the cabin."

"She was there," Shawn said. "You missed her."

Creeds pulled down the baby's blanket with his gun and looked at her face. "Lucky, wasn't you, little girl? If Uncle Silas had found you, you'd be a dead baby right now."

Shawn looked hard at the gunman. "Take the baby to her mother, Creeds."

"Of course, O'Brien," Creeds replied, his face ugly. "We're all going to see the baby's mother . . . and Uncle Zeb." His thin lips pulled away from his yellow teeth. "We'll all have such fun."

Then, through the silence that fell on the group, Creeds spoke again. "I'm going to kill you, O'Brien. Somewhere between here and Sonora I'll put a bullet in your head." He grinned like a ravenous wolf. "Now you study on that."

"You go to hell," Shawn answered. But despite his defiance he knew he was in mortal danger.

# Chapter Twenty-seven

"What the hell, Jake?" Ironside stood in front of the youngest O'Brien brother. "I know you bring live folks back to Dromore all the time, but this is your first dead 'un."

"Anybody recognize him?" Jacob O'Brien said to the men gathered around his horse.

Samuel grabbed the dead man's hair, lifted his head, and stared at the dead, bearded face for a moment. "He's nobody I recognize."

The man wore buckskins and a bear claw necklace. His beard and hair, shaggy and unkempt, gave him a look more animal than human.

"What happened, Jake?" Patrick asked.

"He took a pot at me in the high timber country an hour north of here," Jacob said. "I fired into his smoke, and he fell out of the brush. He was dead when I got to him."

"Wolfer by the look of him," Ironside said. "Since the Apaches were cleared out by the army the deer moved back and the lobos are gettin' fat an' sleek. There's money to be made from prime pelts these days and the ranchers pay a ten-dollar bounty on a dead wolf."

"He saw you and wanted your horse and guns, Jake," Samuel guessed. "You were lucky."

"Seems like." Jacob looked around him. "Where's Shawn? He out sparking some girl?"

"It's a long story, Jake," Patrick said.

"How's the colonel?"

"Another long story," Samuel said.

"Then I'd better hear them." Jacob thumbed over his shoulder. "But I need to see him buried, first."

"Seems to me that ain't going to be necessary." Ironside's far-seeing eyes fixed on the snowy distance. "Two riders, following tracks."

Jacob let go of the dead man's horse and turned his own mount to face the oncoming men. As they rode closer at a walk, Jacob saw they were big, bearded men bundled up in bearskin coats, both wearing battered top hats adorned with an eagle feather stuck into the brim.

Samuel and Patrick were unarmed, but being a careful man, Ironside was always heeled. "I'll take the one on the right, Jake."

Jacob nodded, his eyes fixed on the oncoming

riders. His great beak of a nose tested the wind as though he smelled something amiss.

"Wolfers," Ironside said through his teeth, glancing at Jacob. "I guess the man you gunned had kin."

"Seems like." Jacob acknowledged and cleared his ragged mackinaw away from his gun.

When the two riders were close enough, Ironside said, "Howdy, gents. Ain't much of a day fer ridin', is it now?"

The two men drew rein and their eyes moved from Ironside to Jacob, but they sat their saddles in silence.

Jacob noted that both riders had a booted rifle under their knees, but he saw no sign of belt guns.

The man on the left, bigger and older than his companion, rode forward and gathered up the reins of the dead man's horse. The younger man kneed his mount closer and silently stared hard into Jacob's face, as though he was committing his every feature to memory.

For his part, Jacob was repelled by the man. At some time in the past, a bullet had destroyed his left cheekbone then ranged upward, taking out his eye. A mass of scar tissue cobwebbed from the corner of his mouth to his eyebrow as though the skin had become molten, then hardened like lava. Whoever he was, the man was a walking nightmare.

"Sorry about your friend," Jacob said, tense and ready. "He didn't give me any choice."

Finally the man spoke. "Sorry don't cut it, mister." He swung his horse away and his companion followed, riding into the tumbling snow, leading the dead man.

"Seems like you made yourself enemies, Jake," Ironside said, rubbing his stubbly jaw.

Jacob smiled slightly. "Luther, I've got so many of those two more won't make a difference."

"So the bottom line is that we don't know where Shawn is," Jacob said from his chair in the parlor.

"Maybe Santa Fe," Samuel speculated. "Maybe some other place." He shrugged his shoulders.

"I came through there with stage line money burning a hole in my pocket. If he'd been there, I'd have seen him."

"Then your guess is as good as mine, brother," Samuel said.

Jacob looked at Lorena and changed the subject. "Why can't the colonel walk?"

"Maybe you should ask, 'Why *won't* the colonel walk?'" Lorena explained.

Jacob said nothing, waiting in silence.

Lorena sighed. "He's afraid, Jacob. He tried and he failed, and he's a proud man who fears he'll fail a second time."

"Luther, did you try to get him out of bed?" Jacob asked the segundo.

"I gave her a whirl, Jake. But the colonel ain't a man to be railroaded into doing a thing he don't want to do. He's got his gun up there on the table next to him and he'll kill any man who prods him too hard."

"So what is he doing now?"

"Nothing. Lying in bed, staring at the ceiling," Lorena said. "Sometimes he sleeps, but I don't know if he really is asleep or if he's just faking it because he doesn't want to talk to anyone."

Jacob glanced out the window. "Hey, Luther, the snow isn't coming down too hard. How about you and me taking a walk?"

For a moment Ironside looked puzzled, then his face cleared into a wide grin. "Sounds like a plan to me, Jake. Sure as shootin'."

Samuel laid his coffee cup on the table, clattering in the saucer. "Jake, I don't advise it. Pa's as mean as a wounded bull buffalo, and his Colt isn't for show."

Patrick pushed his glasses higher on his nose. "He told me to get the hell out of his bedroom and not to let the door hit me on the ass on my way out. He never spoke to me like that before. Well, that I can remember anyhow."

"You were always the colonel's favorite, Pat," Luther said. Then, with bland insincerity, "And mine."

Jacob grinned. "Luther, you still got the old battle flag?"

"Sure do."

"Then get it. We'll need it on our walk."

"Ain't much of it left, Jake. It was all shot up at Five Forks, mind, and it hasn't fared well since."

"It'll do. Go get it and meet me outside the colonel's room."

Samuel shook his head. "Jake, I sure hope you know what you're doing. Pa isn't in a talking frame of mind. Hell, you and Luther could get shot."

Lorena smiled. "The colonel talks tough, but he won't shoot at Jacob and Luther."

"Has your mind taken a set on that, Lorena?" Patrick asked grimly.

"No." Lorena shook her head. "No, it hasn't."


Jacob tapped on Shamus's door.

"Go away!" the colonel bellowed.

"It's me, Pa, Jacob."

"Where the hell have you been?"

"Here and there, Pa."

"Then go away and come back later for the wake. Let a man die in peace."

Jake smiled, but when he opened the door and stepped inside his face was empty. Luther was right behind him, moving carefully as though he was walking on eggshells.

"Hell, boy, what are you doing with the battle flag?" Shamus barked.

"I'd answer that, Colonel," Jacob said, "but Lorena says you're not in a talking frame of mind."

"And she's damn right. Now get out of here and put that flag away properly."

"Pa doesn't want to talk, so we'll be quiet as mice, Luther," Jacob whispered. "He keeps a bearskin coat in the wardrobe. Bring it here."

"What are you doing, boy?" Shamus yelled. "Luther, put that damned garment back."

Jacob continued whispering. "Hang it over the chair there, Luther. Now help me get the colonel on his feet."

"Jesus, Mary, and Joseph, Saint Peter and Saint Paul, and all the saints in Heaven help me," Shamus roared as he was hauled to a standing position. "You're trying to kill me."

"Get the coat on him, Luther," Jacob said.

"Luther Ironside, don't you dare," Shamus bellowed.

Ironside ignored the colonel and wrapped him in the huge coat.

"Now his boots, Luther. They're by the fireplace."

"Damn you, Luther," Shamus yelled. "May the curse of Mary Malone and her nine blind children chase you so far over the Hills of Damnation that the Lord Himself can't find you with a telescope."

"Mad, isn't he?" Jacob grinned at Ironside.

"And getting madder. Who's Mary Malone?"

"I've no idea." Jacob shook his head.

"Both of you will find out soon enough," the colonel yelled. "Now put me back in bed and the pair of ye be damned."

"Right. Luther, shove the colonel's hat on his head and we'll carry him downstairs."

Despite Shamus's angry protests Jacob and Ironside manhandled him down the stairs and out the front door, into a keening wind and falling snow.

"Set him on his feet, Luther," Jacob instructed.

Shamus continued his rant. "What are you doing to me? You're trying to murder me!"

"We're taking a walk, Pa," Jacob said calmly.

"I can't walk!" Shamus insisted. Then, "Luther, you're fired. Jacob, you're disinherited."

"And you're walking," Jacob said, maintaining his calm demeanor.

"Where to, damn you?"

"To the far corner of the house and back."

"I can't walk that far."

"But you will," Jacob pressed, raising the Confederate battle flag.

Torn by shot and shell, ragged as the Rebs who once marched behind it, the flag snapped bravely in the wind with the same tattered dignity as the soldiers who fought and died for it.

"Walk, Colonel," Jacob ordered. Snow whitened his mustache and eyebrows.

"Damn you, boy, I can't," Shamus insisted. "Take me back to bed."

"Pa, you served honorably under this flag and today you have another battle to fight. Will you shame your banner now?"

Ironside stood next to his commanding officer. "Follow the flag, Colonel. I'll be at your side as I always was."

Shamus stared at the Stars and Bars for long moments, then straightened his shoulders and stood tall. He looked frail inside the huge bearskin coat, but his voice was as commanding as ever. "Unhand me, you rogues."

Ironside and Jacob let their hands drop to their sides, but stayed one on each side of the colonel.

Standing without support, Shamus gave the

orders. "Jacob, lead on. You won't see me dishonor my flag, not this day and not any day."

"Colonel, it's just another march," Ironside said. "We done plenty of those with nothing but parched corn in our bellies and no boots on our feet."

His eyes fixed on the streaming flag, Shamus took one tottering step. Then another. He stopped. "My legs hurt. They hurt real bad."

"They'll get stronger with every step you take, Colonel," Ironside said.

An incongruous figure in an ankle-length fur coat, carpet slippers on his feet, and a battered Stetson on his head, Shamus staggered forward. Despite the numbing cold, sweat popped on his forehead as he forced himself to put one foot in front of the other.

Jacob looked to see how the colonel was progressing, then raised his voice in song.

> "We are a band of brothers,
>   And native to the soil,
>   Fighting for the property
>   We gained by honest toil.
>   And when our rights were threatened,
>   The cry rose near and far—
>   'Hurrah for the Bonnie Blue Flag
>   That bears a single star.'"

Ironside's rusty baritone joined in on the chorus and Shamus's lips moved, whispering the great song that he remembered so well.

> "Hurrah! Hurrah!
>    For Southern rights hurrah!
>    Hurrah for the Bonnie Blue Flag
>    That bears a single star."

Finally they reached the far corner of Dromore, a tall, rangy old-timer wearing chaps and a sheepskin coat, a raggedy man whose entire wardrobe was probably worth fifty cents, and between them, Shamus. Though his mouth was grim from pain, he never took his eyes off the snapping flag.

Jacob said, "Now we'll help you back, Pa."

"I'll do it myself," Shamus declared boldly. "Step away from me, son." He turned and stumbled forward again.

Led by Samuel and Lorena, the entire staff of Dromore, from butler to scullery maid, stood outside in the snow and watched Shamus's struggle.

"I'll help him," Patrick said, stepping toward his father.

Samuel put out an arm and stopped him. "No, you won't. Pa has to do this himself."

Lorena was alarmed. "Samuel, he could get hurt."

"That's a chance he'll have to take."

The crowd around the door watched in silence. No one cheered Shamus on, but two dozen people willed him to make it. A couple vaqueros in from the range sat their horses and watched. Like everyone else, they remained silent.

Finally Shamus made it to the door and Lorena moved quickly to his side. To her husband she said, "Help me get him into bed,"

The colonel grinned, his teeth chattering. "No bed, daughter-in-law. Get me into my chair and bring me a brandy."

"Somebody bring the colonel's wheelchair," Lorena said.

"The hell with that, woman," Shamus roared. "Help me to my chair beside Saraid's pink hearthstone." He turned and looked at Jacob. "We'll walk again tomorrow."

"That we will, Colonel. And the next day."

Shamus turned to his longtime friend. "Sergeant Ironside, put our flag away with honor. We won't need it again."

"Yes, sir, Colonel," Ironside said, giving the old, palm-forward salute of the Confederate cavalry.

Shamus looked from Ironside to Jacob. "Well done, you scoundrels. Well done, both of you."

"Well done your ownself, Colonel," Ironside said.

Shamus smiled. "All in all, I did pretty well, didn't I?"

"Damn right you did." Ironside's eyes were moist. "Damn right you did, Colonel O'Brien."

# Chapter Twenty-eight

"What the hell are you, O'Brien?" Zebulon Moss grinned. "I never took you for a fancy boy." The gang boss sat behind a huge desk in the main compartment of the Pullman, its red velvet and shining brass décor reflecting his taste. A bed was recessed in one corner and a fully appointed bar stood in another.

"He was following us, boss," Silas Creeds said. "Him and these two. The old-timer is Uriah Tweedy, a bear hunter and crazy as a loon."

"Right pleased to meet you, Mr. Moss," Tweedy said. "Yes, I'm ol' Uriah Tweedy, friend to all, especially your good self."

"And him?" Moss jerked a thumb toward the man standing next to Tweedy.

Before Creeds could answer, Lowth said, "My

name is Thaddeus Lowth, a hangman by profession, and I have friends in high places."

"I'd imagine all your friends in high places are still swinging." Moss smiled. "Well, we may have need of your skills before this little escapade is over."

"Quest," Lowth corrected.

"Huh?" Moss asked, confused.

"It's a quest, Mr. Moss. We're on a quest."

"Yeah, whatever you say." Moss pointed his glowing cigar at Shawn. "Why the getup?"

"It's a disguise." Shawn grimaced. "Or it was supposed to be."

"Didn't fool Creeds for long, did it?"

Shawn made no answer and Moss said, "Still trying to rescue Trixie, huh?"

"That was the general idea," Shawn muttered.

Moss gestured to the partition behind him. "She's back there along with five other women."

The compartment was so huge Shawn reckoned the captive women and Moss's hired guns must be cramped for space behind the divider. "You plan to sell them as slaves?"

Moss smiled and repeated Shawn's statement. "That's the general idea."

"I'm going to stop you, Moss," Shawn said.

"And how do you aim to do that?"

"I don't know, but I will."

"Hell, I could shoot all three of you right

now, and nobody would be the wiser. But I tell you what, O'Brien. I can use another gun. Throw in with me and I'll forget everything that happened before." Moss looked around at Creeds and his other gunmen. "Boys, you heard what I said. Tell me, can I say fairer than that?"

"You sure can't, boss," Creeds said and the other gunmen mumbled their agreement.

"Never a fairer word was spoke, Mr. Moss." Tweedy looked at Lowth. "Is that not so, Mr. Lowth?"

Reading some kind of telegraphed message in Tweedy's eyes, he responded, "Indeed, Mr. Tweedy, as fair and true blue as ever was."

"There, O'Brien, your friends think I'm on the square." Moss's smile was a bit wicked.

It was in Shawn's mind to tell him to go to hell, but it was not the time for pride. If he were to rescue Julia Davenport it would be easier if he were a member of Moss's inner circle.

"Well?" Moss prodded.

"Do I have a choice?" Shawn replied, allowing his shoulders to slump in apparent defeat.

"In life there is always a choice, O'Brien," Moss said. "You can choose to join me or you can choose to die. It's quite simple, really."

"You've got yourself a man," Shawn said, the taste of dirt in his mouth.

"Wise choice. The whore hasn't been born yet that's worth dying for."

"What about these two?" Shawn inclined his head toward Tweedy and Lowth.

"Do you want them?" Moss asked.

"Tweedy's good with a rifle . . . and Lowth is a—"

"I want Lowth," Moss quickly interrupted. "Where we're headed, a hangman will come in real handy." He turned to his head gunman. "Creeds, a drink for Mr. O'Brien and his friends." He looked at Shawn. "Where are your duds?"

"I have them in safekeeping," Lowth said. "Yes, they're safe and sound."

"Then go get them," Moss said, a little annoyed. "I don't want one of my men looking like a pansy."

Lowth held up the baby in his arms, his climbing eyebrows asking a question.

"You, Higgins," Moss ordered. "Take the kid to its mother. If the woman can keep it alive it might increase her price on the slave block."

Although dressed in his own clothes, with a Colt once more strapped at his waist, Shawn felt dirty. And every time he looked into Moss's face his skin crawled. The man had the cold, staring eyes of a reptile.

"I need to fill my cartridge belt," he said to Creeds as he accepted a glass of bourbon from the man.

"Your revolver is also empty," Creeds said. "You'll get all the cartridges you need when we get to where we're going."

Shawn looked at Moss. "You don't trust me?"

"I trust nobody," Moss said. "Listen to Creeds. When we reach Sonora you'll get your ammunition. In the meantime, drink your whiskey, relax, and enjoy the train ride."

"Can I talk to Julia?" Shawn asked.

"To Trixie? No, you can't. Stay away from those women back there, O'Brien. They're valuable merchandise and I don't want them handled."

"Who are you selling them to, Moss?"

"You're working for me now, O'Brien. From now on you address me as *Mister* Moss. As for whom I'm selling the women to, you'll find out in Sonora."

"I'll buy Julia from you," Shawn offered.

"Maybe. I'll decide on that after I speak to the interested parties. White women don't come cheap in the West African slave markets and my contact will bid high."

"I'll match it," Shawn bargained.

"We'll see. Of course by the time the bidding begins, you might be dead."

"Boss, O'Brien and me still have a score to settle," Creeds said.

Moss sighed. "See what I mean?"

# Chapter Twenty-nine

The rabbit hunt had not gone well and Sheik Abdul Basir-Hakim was not at all pleased. He leaned on his Lebel Model 1886 rifle and considered the kills. "Only three, and scrawny at that. I did not get a shot, Hassan."

"A thousand pardons, great lord." Hassan Najid shrugged as he spread his hands. "We are surrounded by wilderness and game is scarce."

"Not a good day's hunting," Hakim said. "I have wasted my time, it seems."

Najid feared the sheik's wrath. "There are still a couple hours before darkness falls. Perhaps . . ."

Hakim shook his head and shouldered his French rifle. "I am no longer in the mood for rabbits." He looked around him at the desert brush flats that stretched as far as the eye could see. "You are right, Hassan. This is not rabbit country, too dry and no timber. Did you kill one, Hassan?"

Najid sighed. "The littlest one."

"A kill is a kill when one hunts for sport," Hakim said. "My congratulations to you. And the others?"

"Two crewmen, lord. They shot one each."

"See that their marksmanship is rewarded."

"Your wish is my command, lord."

Hakim took one last glance at the three dead Mexican peons sprawled and bloody on the sand and spat. "Poor hunting indeed."

As he and Najid walked back toward the schooner and their encampment, Hakim said, "Tell me now about the black woman."

"Ah, the light-fingered one," Najid replied. "Her name is Katie Shore and she is one of the San Francisco whores."

"And? Tell me what happened?"

"The Shore woman stole a hair comb from a Chinese girl. When the girl confronted her, she slapped her and said, 'Yes, bitch, I stole the comb and I'm keeping it.'"

"There were witnesses? To those words?"

"Indeed, lord, and not only other Chinese. Other women heard and saw it."

"Then this Katie person must be punished according to our law."

"We await your judgment," Najid said

"I will make my decision on the woman's fate before the evening meal. A thief is not to be tolerated. The Holy Quran says, male or female, the hands of the thief must be cut off as an example to others."

"Allah is just," Najid said.

"Then you will bring the woman to me and a man with block and sword, should I decide in that direction. But no matter how I decide, tonight, Hassan, you will see justice done according to the laws of Islam."

Katie Shore was high yaller and beautiful. Her honey-colored skin, glossy black hair, and voluptuous curves had made her one of the Barbary Coast's most popular whores—until the night she was drugged, kidnapped, and carried onto the slave schooner. Gone was the woman's professional finery. She stood before Sheik Hakim with her hair unbound, dressed only in a plain cotton shift.

Hakim sat in a folding chair outside his tent and the captive women had been herded to the spot to witness the proceedings.

In the lilac light of the fading day Katie Shore stood in isolation. The woman looked terrified and her black eyes kept darting to the huge corsair standing behind a beheading block, a massive scimitar across his naked chest.

"Do you know why you are here, woman?" Hakim spoke in English, a barbaric tongue he despised, but knew well. Beside him, his eyes eager, Najid grinned like a vulture.

Katie shook her head. "I don't know why."

"You deny that you stole a comb off another woman?"

Scared as she was, it took the woman a while before she could form her words. "I borrowed the comb. I was going to return it."

"Bring forth this woman's accuser," Hakim ordered.

A young, pretty Chinese girl was pushed before the sheik.

"Is this the woman who stole your comb?" Hakim asked, pointing to the black woman.

The girl's eyes moved to Katie. She nodded, her gaze fixed on the ground at her feet.

"Did she return it?"

The Chinese girl had been forced to work as a whore, but her English was limited, horny men not being long on conversation. She said nothing.

Hakim gaze swept over the assembled women. "Do any of you Chinese speak English?"

A woman stepped forward. "I do."

"Ask her if the comb was returned," Hakim instructed.

The woman spoke to the young whore in Chinese, and after some hesitation, the girl replied.

"Well?" Hakim asked impatiently. "What did she say?"

"The black woman refused to return the comb."

"Then it was theft." Hakim stared hard at Katie. "Do you know how a thief is punished?"

"Please don't whip me," Katie begged. "I'll give the comb back."

"I will not whip you," Hakim promised.

"Thank you, oh, thank you," Katie said, hope bright in her eyes.

"The punishment for theft is to have both your hands cut off," Hakim informed.

Katie screamed and threw herself at the sheik's feet. She looked up at him, her cheeks streaming tears. "Please, not that. I couldn't bear that."

Hakim kicked the woman away from him. "Though you are nothing but a common thief, I am not without mercy."

"Thank you . . . thank you . . ." Katie sobbed. "I'll never steal again. I promise."

"That is well." Hakim's eyes were cruel, his mouth a tight, hard line. "You shall lose only one hand, the left that does no work in bed or out."

Katie screamed and again clung to Hakim's legs and begged for mercy.

The faces of the other captive women were masks of horror, confused, as though they couldn't believe what was happening or that such barbarism existed.

Suddenly Hakim seemed bored and he waved an indolent hand. "Take her to the block and let justice be done."

Still screaming, the woman called Katie was dragged to the block and made to kneel. A burly sailor looped a rope around her left wrist. Sitting down, he pulled on the rope so her forearm was forced onto the block. A second man pushed on her back, rendering her immobile.

The swordsman, a huge brute with the broken face of a prizefighter, looked over at Hakim. Katie continued to call out for mercy to men that had none.

The sheik nodded and the sword fell in a flashing arc.

Women crowded around Kate, who no longer screamed, but stared at the bloody stump of her wrist the way a gut-shot man stares at his belly, a mix of disbelief and horror in her eyes.

"Hassan, see to it that the physician attends to

the woman," Hakim ordered. "If she dies I stand to lose money."

Najid hurried away, and the sheik rose to his feet, glancing at Katie, his face expressionless. He saw her only as female flesh for the slave auctions, a commodity, not as a human being.

Hakim stepped to his tent, then stopped and looked behind him at the sea. The strange, uneasy feeling that had been with him since the end of the rabbit hunt was stronger, disturbing his tranquility of mind. He turned and walked down to the beach. The gulf was calm but rose and fell in rounded swells as though hungry sea monsters swam just under the surface, watching, biding their time.

Kneeling, Hakim lifted a handful of water from the silent surf and let it trickle through his fingers. Then he tasted it. It was salty, bitter on his tongue, and with the tang of iron, like blood.

He rose to his feet and his eyes searched the dark waters.

It was out there, the thing that disturbed him so much.

Hunting him.

He glanced at the tent where his suicide bomber wallowed with his well-worn whores, all the while dreaming of virgins. Anxiously, Hakim wondered when Zebulon Moss would come with his women. It must be soon.

Hakim looked at the sea again, swollen and full of menace. Somewhere out there in the purple darkness was a thing that wanted to tear his guts out. Suddenly Sheik Abdul Hakim-Basir, the mightiest warrior in all of Islam, was afraid.

# Chapter Thirty

Agraciana Morenos chided her husband, who sat by the fire toasting his toes. "Maria Gomez has a husband who would walk with her to the big house in the snow."

"Juan Gomez is a rotten vaquero. Everybody knows that."

"But a good husband. Everybody knows that also."

Agraciana's husband shrugged, his eyes on the flames of the burning log. "You baked the *churros* for the patron. You should deliver them."

"Ach. It is a trial and a tribulation to have such a husband." She took her battered hat from the rack on the wall near the door and shrugged into her husband's sheepskin many times too big for her. Stepping into the kitchen, she retrieved the colonel's churros, the sweet Mexican doughnuts he loved to dip into his morning coffee.

Many times the patron had told her she made the best bear sign he'd ever tasted and Agraciana had made a habit of taking a batch to him two or three times a week.

After one last, frowning glance at her husband, the woman stepped outside. The morning was cold and snow tossed around in a whipping wind. The walk from her house to Dromore was not such a long one, but in the freezing weather she decided it was quite far enough, especially for one who was quick with child.

The snow crumped under her booted feet as she drew nearer to the house. A sullen sky grayed the crest of Glorieta Mesa and the stiff breeze stirred the branches of the pines.

Agraciana reached the door of the house and rapped the brass knocker, the *rat-tat-tat* loud in the morning quiet.

But louder still was the flat statement of the rifle shot that slammed a large-caliber bullet into her slender body.

Drinking coffee in the kitchen when he heard the shots, Jacob leaped to his feet and grabbed his holstered Colt from the gun rack by the front door on his way outside. Behind him, he heard people running.

Once outside, he glanced at the wounded,

groaning woman, then to the drift of smoke lifting from the trees on the rise fifty yards from the house. The range was too great for a revolver. To Samuel and Lorena at the door, he yelled, "See to her!" and headed toward the stable, buckling his gun belt as he ran.

"Jake!" Samuel shouted, but Jacob ignored him.

He saddled his black, swung into the leather, and left the barn at a gallop, sparing a quick glance at Agraciana. Lorena knelt in the snow beside her, and for a second time Jacob ignored Samuel's yell to stop. Wearing neither coat nor hat, he headed for the rise at a run, the Colt in his upraised hand.

The bitterest of cold and freezing snow was borne on an icy wind. Jacob, dressed only in shirt, jeans, and boots, knew he would need to find the bushwhackers quickly. He could not survive long in such weather.

The black slowed to a canter for the last few yards to the trees, then Jacob reined him back to a trot. He rode into the pines, his eyes wary. There were tracks aplenty—two different sets of boot prints in the snow, one large, the other smaller—but no sign of the men who made them.

Beyond the ridge the ground sloped to a large meadow and the dirt beneath the black's hooves was iron-hard as he galloped down the rise onto the flat. A few white-faced cattle foraged for grass along creeks fringed with ice and in the distance dull gray clouds hung so low there was no delineation between earth and sky.

Two pairs of parallel horse tracks angled across the meadow's virgin snow, the riders seemingly in no hurry, riding at a walk. That irritated Jacob. Had those two such a low opinion of Dromore that they didn't fear a pursuit?

It seemed that way—unless they rode toward a place where others of their kind waited.

Then another possibility occurred to him. It could be the bushwhackers had mistaken the Mexican woman for a man, dressed as she was in masculine clothing. They were in no hurry to leave because they planned other killings . . .

To avenge their brother killed by Jacob O'Brien.

The more Jacob thought about it, the more he decided that was the case. It was no random act. It was the start of the wolfers' campaign of vengeance.

Anxious to get out of the cold wind for a few moments, Jacob angled toward the stand of mixed spruce and ponderosa pine trees a hundred yards to the right of the tracks. Shivering in the thin shelter, he pulled a sack of tobacco from his pocket and managed to build himself a cigarette, but half of it spilled on the ground. His forehead felt like a chunk of frozen steel and he couldn't feel his toes in his boots. Ice clung to his eyebrows and shaggy mustache and his breath smoked like damp firewood.

After only a short respite, he rode out of the trees and followed the trail again. His head bent against the wind, he urged his horse forward, figuring he was getting close.

But an hour later he still followed tracks that showed no sign of ending.

Stiff with cold, Jacob's head ached and his ungloved hands were frozen into claws. The long-legged black plodded on gamely and Jacob knew he would give out long before the horse. He began to dream about finding a spot out of the wind where he could build a fire and get warm.

And drink coffee, steaming hot, black as night and sweet as sin, poured from a sooty pot just off the fire . . .

Jacob jolted upright and lifted his great beak to the wind. Yes! He smelled it. Smoke. And close enough to be strong. Surely it was only a little farther now.

To Jacob's north rose the craggy bulk of Hurtado Mesa and around him in the timbered, broken country snow was piled in treacherous drifts, a trap for the unwary. The smell of smoke hung heavy in the thin air. He was close. Very close.

A man on a horse was a target and Jacob swung stiffly out of the saddle. He tethered his horse to a piñon and cleared snow away from a patch of grass. It wasn't much but the black seemed grateful as he lowered his nose and began to graze.

It was the last thing Jacob wanted to do, but it had to be done. He unbuttoned his shirt at the neck and shoved the frozen fingers of his right hand under his armpit. The shock took his breath away.

After a few moments, Jacob withdrew his hand, bent and stretched his fingers, and buttoned up his shirt again. He worked his fingers again and decided they were flexible enough—if he moved fast.

He left the shelter of the piñon and, within minutes, picked up fresh tracks. The smell of smoke grew stronger. Gun in hand, he topped a shallow rise between two massive boulders and almost stepped onto the wood-shingled roof of a lean-to.

Crouching, his frozen knees aching, he took the lie of the land. The lean-to had been built on the other side of the rise and backed up to a shelf of bare rock. The horse tracks angled twenty yards to his right, where they followed an eyebrow of game trail and ended at a graveled talus slope. A small pole corral was built next to the lean-to and held three horses, two of them saddled.

Jacob frowned. Three horses. Did that mean there were three men in the cabin?

Cold and stiff as he was, he didn't like those odds, but he was damned if after all he'd been through he'd turn tail and run.

The talus slope was icy, but the gravel held as Jacob walked down to the flat on stiff knees. His gun hand was cramping again and he knew he had only a short while to get the job done.

The lean-to had no windows to the front and he stood three yards from its sagging pine door.

Never a man to study too hard on the right or wrong of a thing, Jacob cut loose. Three fast shots slammed through the door, splintering wood, and then he ran for the corral and took cover behind a fence post.

Outraged cries followed the racket of the shots and two men ran outside. One was the man with the horribly bullet-scarred face he'd seen at Dromore, the other was an old-timer in a ragged plaid shirt and miner's boots.

Scarface spotted Jacob instantly and the rifle in his hands came up fast. He fired . . . too quickly . . . but close enough to scratch Jacob's left arm. Jacob stepped away from the fence post and fired. Scarface took the bullet square in the chest and dropped to one knee, working his rifle. Aware that it was his last round, Jacob fired again. Another hit. The man stared at Jacob for an instant, showing his shock at the time and manner of his death, then pitched forward and lay still.

Jacob swung his empty Colt on the miner.

The old man wore a belt gun, but Jacob hoped he wouldn't make a play.

He didn't. "I ain't in this, mister. Just lookin' fer a place to hole up fer the winter."

"Drop the hardware," Jacob ordered. "Where's the other one?"

The old man unbuckled his belt and it thudded to his feet. "Inside. Maybe gut shot. Maybe dead." The miner looked into Jacob's eyes. "Mister, you're pure pizen with Doobie Colt's gun, ain't you?"

Jacob ignored that. With fumbling, cold, rigid fingers, he reloaded his revolver, filling all six chambers. If the old-timer was a tad disappointed he didn't let it show.

Jacob said, "I didn't catch your name."

"That's because I didn't put it out. But it's Lem Cook of the Parker County, Texas, Cooks. Yours?"

"It doesn't matter." Jacob answered and smiled. "Now Lem, walk into the cabin and I'll follow you."

"I wouldn't want to do that, mister."

"Figured that." Jacob, his left hand flexing, picked up the dead man's revolver. "Stand away from your gun, pops."

Lem scuttled backward as though he'd just stepped on a rattlesnake nest as Jacob hammered shot after shot through the thin walls of the lean-to. Despite his frozen hands the shots sounded as one, and he was rewarded by a scream from inside, followed by a string of curses.

Jacob reloaded as quickly as his stiff, fumbling fingers would allow. His guns up and ready, he charged inside the lean-to. A dying man lay on his back on a bunk, his face and chest bloody.

"You've done for me, damn you," the man said. "I'm shot all to pieces."

"Things are hard all over," Jacob said, feeling no sympathy at all. He stepped to the potbellied stove where a coffeepot smoked, found a tin cup, filled it, and took a drink. "Good coffee."

"Where's my brother?" the man croaked out.

"Outside."

"Is he dead?"

"As he'll ever be."

"Your name is O'Brien, ain't it?"

"Yeah, and the woman you shot today is no relation."

"I thought she was a man."

"You thought wrong."

The cabin was warm and Jacob felt the frost melt in his joints. The coffee was good and hot and his fingers were finally supple enough to build a cigarette.

The wounded man groaned. "You got brothers, O'Brien, just like I had."

"They're nothing like you had."

"Don't you want to know my name?"

Jacob shook his head. "Mister, I don't give a damn."

"Then listen to this, O'Brien"—the wounded man grimaced as a shock of pain hit him—"your brothers will die, all of them, just like mine did." He spat blood at Jacob's feet. "A dying man's curse on you and yours."

Jacob hurriedly crossed himself then raised his Colt. But he looked into the eyes of a dead man and lowered it again.

Lem Cook stood at the door, his face stricken. "A dead man's curse is a terrible thing, young feller."

"So I've heard," Jacob acknowledged.

"I mind a tinpan by the name of Deacon Mac-Gyver up Denver way. He stabbed his partner one day an' the dying man cursed him. Tole Deke he'd die soon. The very next day ol' Deke was killed by a rockfall. An' that's a natural fact."

"You don't say?"

"I do say, young feller, so you watch your step."

Jacob poured himself coffee, thinking. Worrying. He wondered where Shawn was and what had happened to him. Suddenly he had a bad feeling about his brother.

And he knew that what his Irish mother had called his sixth sense would give him no peace.

# Chapter Thirty-one

"No matter what happens, O'Brien, I'll kill you," Silas Creeds said.

"You've told me that," Shawn said. "Maybe two or three times already."

"Just enjoy keeping you appraised of the situation." Creeds grinned. "I like to see the expression on your face. It's funny, all scared an' stuff."

They stood on the train platform at the Rincon rail junction watching Zebulon Moss's private car being shunted onto the rear of a westbound cannonball that would head straight through to Sonora, Mexico. Behind them was an imposing two-story depot and an adjoining single-story freight and storage addition. Miles of scrub desert stretched around the wooden structure where nothing moved except a dust devil stirred up by a silent wind.

Seeing that he couldn't get another rise out of

Shawn, Creeds set his battered top hat at a jaunty angle and strolled away.

Uriah Tweedy stepped beside Shawn. "You're gonna have to kill that feller, O'Brien."

Shawn nodded. "Seems like."

"Hell, boy, it won't be easy. He's a demon on the draw an' shoot."

"With his kind it never is easy."

Tweedy looked around him at the dusty platform shadowed under an overcast sky. Seeing that no one was paying any particular attention, he held out his hand. "Got something for you."

"What?"

"Open your hand. But don't let anybody see you, especially ol' Silas."

Shawn did as he was told and Tweedy dropped two .45 rounds into his open palm.

Before Shawn could speak, the old man said, "Found them in the bottom of my ditty bag. I reckon I must have tossed them in there at one time or another. Or somebody else did."

Shawn smiled as he pocketed the rounds. "Uriah, you may have saved my life."

"Yeah, well, don't think too much of it, sonny. I'm only tryin' to save the life of my intended."

The captive women were locked inside the Pullman, curtains drawn across the windows. Moss and his gunmen were also on board. Only Creeds and a murderous snake of a man by the name of Whitey Ford were hanging around the platform.

Shawn lit a cigar, idly watching the private car clank onto the rear of another passenger carriage until his attention was drawn to Ford. The gunman, dressed for the city in a long black coat and bowler hat, had walked to the edge of the platform and then his body stiffened, his gaze intent on something Shawn couldn't see.

A young woman ran into Shawn's line of vision. Her skirts hiked to her knees, she bolted from the rear of the Pullman, heading into the desert country.

Ford let out a whoop, jumped from the platform to the rails, and went after the escapee.

Creeds stood on the platform and hollered, "Go get 'er, Whitey." He slapped his thigh and roared with laughter. It promised to be an interesting diversion.

With Creeds intent on the fleeing woman, Shawn quickly loaded the two rounds into his Colt, jumped onto the rails, and ran.

Behind him, Creeds yelled out, then cut loose with a shot, missing by a couple yards. He was an up-close draw fighter, not a marksman.

Shawn recognized the escaping woman as Julia Davenport, and fear for her safety gave length to his stride, widening the gap between himself and the gunman. Cactus and brush tore at his legs as he pounded after her.

Ahead of him, Whitey Ford yelled something like, "I'm gonna git you, Trixie, darlin'!" With his attention fixed on the woman, he was unaware of Shawn, gun in hand, just fifty yards behind him.

Ford whooped and fired a shot, kicking up a plume of dust in front of Julia.

As she swerved to avoid a clump of vicious cat claw, the high heel of her lace-up boot buckled, and down she went, sprawling on her face.

Ford was on her like a cougar on a doe and dragged her to her feet. He backhanded her hard across the face, knocking her down. Grinning, he bent to pick her up again.

Shawn skidded to a halt, yellow dust kicking around his boots. "Leave her be, Whitey."

The gunman turned as fast as a striking rattler, his gun leveling fast.

Shawn fired. Ford took the shot high in the chest and staggered back a step, his face suddenly ashen. The gunman fired, missed, fired again. The bullet burned across Shawn's right thigh, drawing blood. Aware that he had only one shot left, Shawn two-handed his Colt to eye level and fired again. A red rose appeared in the middle of Ford's forehead, just under his hat brim. The gunman gave Shawn a quick, startled look, then fell, thudding dead onto the parched ground.

"Julia, it's me. Shawn."

The woman scrambled to her feet and ran into Shawn's arms. He felt the rise and fall of her breasts against his chest as she sobbed her relief. She lifted her eyes to Shawn's face and he saw then widen in alarm. He began to turn. . . .

Way too late!

Something hard crashed into the back of Shawn's head and suddenly he was falling. The ground rushed up to meet him and then there was only blackness.

When O'Brien awoke he was aware of softness underneath him, and imagined for a moment he was back in his bed at Dromore. But the pain in his ribs and face and the racketing motion of the railcar soon convinced him otherwise. He tried to open his eyes, but his right was swollen shut and stubbornly refused to budge. As it was, his vision was blurred, like a man swimming under-water in a muddy creek.

He moved his legs, then his arms and felt a carpet under him.

"Ah, Mr. O'Brien awakes." The voice seemed to come from a long distance, but it unmistakably belonged to Zeb Moss.

Shawn struggled to a sitting position, the pain in his ribs and wounded thigh spiking at him. His mouth was full of blood and his head rang like a gong.

"How are you feeling, O'Brien?" the voice said again. "Quite well enough to hang, I hope."

Shawn tried to clear his head and focus with his good eye. The words falling out broken he said, "What . . . happened . . . to me?"

"Good question! Excellent question!" Moss's words came as if he was at the end of a tunnel. "Mr. Creeds hit you over the head with his gun, then proceeded to put the boot into you. Harsh? Yes, you might say that, but then Mr. Creeds set store by the late, lamented Whitey Ford."

"Damn right I did. He was true blue, was ol' Whitey, when he was sober." Creeds' voice came from far off.

Slowly, Shawn's vision cleared a little. His grotesquely swollen right eye remained firmly shut.

Moss, broad, blond, and handsome, sat behind his desk, resplendent in a red smoking jacket with a black shawl collar. He held a snifter of brandy in his ringed left hand, a fat, gold-colored cigar in his right. Six of his gunmen sat around the compartment, staring at Shawn, hostile but mildly amused.

"What did you do to Julia?" Shawn asked. "Where is she?"

Moss smiled. "Ah yes, dear Trixie. She gave me her beautiful body, but, alas, she was born without a heart, so that she could not give."

"Where is she? Did Creeds hurt her?"

"No. She is well and none the worse for her run across the desert." Moss said. "But what of you, O'Brien? How do you fare?" He waited a moment, then said, "Not well, I see."

"Boss, let me hang him," Creeds put in. "Hell, we got an expert right here."

"Did you attend to that, O'Brien? There speaks evil. I love evil, you know, it's so varied in its forms."

Shawn glared as best he could with only one eye open. "You're trash, Moss. A damned murderer and pimp masquerading as a gentleman. If you're going to kill me, get it the hell over with."

"Oh, don't worry, I'll kill you all right," Moss offered. "The question is when."

"Hell, boss, I'll do it right now," Creeds said, getting to his feet. "I can kick him to death right where he's at."

"The thought is indeed tempting, Mr. Creeds," Moss agreed, "but you know what we have planned. When the dangerous times come down we could use his gun."

"O'Brien can't be trusted with a gun," Creeds cried, appalled. "He's already proved that. He killed poor ol' Whitey, didn't he?"

"Yes, and the young gentleman will be sadly missed." Moss was silent for a while, his face frowning in thought, then he smiled at Creeds. "My decision is not to make a decision until later. The chances are you'll hang him, but until then I want to keep O'Brien alive."

"Boss, I—"

Moss waved a hand over his gunman's objections. "Take O'Brien away and put him with the other two. I've made my decision, Mr. Creeds. Now carry out my orders."

Creeds and another man hauled Shawn to his feet. They took time to pick up a length of rope before dragging him outside to the car's platform. Tweedy and Lowth were already bound to the rail, their hands tied behind them. After trussing up Shawn in a similar manner, Creeds grinned wickedly. "I hope you'll be comfortable out here, O'Brien."

"Go to hell."

Creeds rewarded him with a kick to the ribs that hurt so badly Shawn almost passed out. Then the door closed and he was left with Tweedy and Lowth on the rocking steel platform in a cutting wind.

# Chapter Thirty-two

Jacob O'Brien returned to Dromore wearing a dead man's bearskin coat so odiferous Lorena made him leave it outside.

"And take a bath at the earliest opportunity," she said. "You've probably picked up fleas."

Samuel stood aside in the hallway as his wife flounced past him. "Lorena chiding you again, brother Jake?"

"She didn't like my coat. It does smell bad, but it's warm."

"What happened out there? You left before I knew what was happening."

Jacob told him and then asked, "How is the woman?"

"She's hurt badly, but she'll live."

"The colonel?"

"Walking. He's still stiff and sore, but he wants

to walk everywhere. Luther is at his wit's end trying to slow him down."

"Pa is game."

"He's all of that."

"I'm hungry." Jacob rubbed his belly.

"I'll ask the kitchen to send a meal to your room, let you get cleaned up first."

Jacob shook his head. "No, just have them sack up some grub. I need a fresh horse and then I'm headed for Santa Fe to try and get a lead on Shawn."

"Jake, that's a wild-goose chase. He could be anywhere by now."

"Maybe so, but I'm going to try."

"You sound flat," Samuel said, his face concerned. "The black dog stalking you again?"

Jake nodded. "Yeah, I guess so. Killing a man always depresses me, seems like."

"A killing weighs heavy on any man."

"I guess so." Jacob turned to the door. "Bring the grub, Sam, and my mackinaw."

"Don't you want to talk to the colonel first?"

"No. Just tell him where I'm headed."

Before Samuel could speak again, Jacob stepped outside into cold and snow.

In the barn, he saddled a yellow mustang, a mean, ugly little horse that would carry a man all day and into the next. He turned when he heard footsteps behind him.

"You're leaving us again, Jacob," Shamus was alone and carried a sack of supplies and a ragged mackinaw.

"I'm going after Shawn, Pa."

"It's a cold trail, son."

"I know it. But I reckon I'll try." Jacob smiled. "You're getting around, Colonel."

"Like my grandson, I toddle here and there. We run races, you know, him and me. Do you have money?"

"Enough, I reckon."

Shamus reached into the pocket of his sheepskin and produced five double eagles. "Take this. You may need it."

Jacob knew better than to argue and took the money. "Thank you, Colonel." He hesitated, then said, "A dying man cursed me, Pa. Me and my brothers."

"And this troubles you?"

"Considerably."

"Then I will pray to Our Lady for his poor soul," Shamus said, crossing himself.

"You don't fear a curse?"

"No, I don't. The good Lord protects us from such things, though He expects us to pray for those who cursed us."

Shamus reached into his pocket again. "Take this. Remove your hat so I may put it around your neck."

Jacob bent his head and Shamus placed the rosary around his neck. "These were your sainted mother's beads and they will protect you. Put your trust in them."

Jacob nodded. "I sure will, Pa." He tied the sack of supplies to the saddle, then mounted. After the mustang tried to buck him off a few times he settled down and Jacob rode to the barn door.

"Jacob," Shamus called after him. "Bring me back my son."


The dark day was shading into darker evening when Jacob rode into Santa Fe, a town with plenty of snap. People, bundled up for the most part, thronged the street. Vendors were doing a good business, especially those who sold hot food. Corn tortillas wrapped around beef or chicken seasoned with peppers that scorched the tongue and could make a strong man break out in tears were particularly popular.

The saloons and dance halls were booming and tinpanny pianos, their notes all tangled together in knots, competed one with another for the chance to be heard in the street.

Cold, with snow on his shoulders and hat from a hard trail, Jacob badly wanted a whiskey, but postponed that pleasure until he put up his horse. He stopped a passerby and asked where the livery stable was, learning there were two. One was farther up the street, the other closer, but around the corner.

Jacob chose the closer one and led the mustang inside.

A stringy, sour-faced old man wearing a battered Reb kepi and a mackinaw even more ragged than Jacob's stepped out of his office and greeted him warmly. "Two bits for hay, two bits for a scoop of oats, an' I count the scoops in the sack, mind. Anybody I catch cheatin' gets shot."

"Then I guess I'll want two," Jacob said, grinning. "This here hoss is mighty hungry."

"Then I'll charge you extry an' if you can't pay is when I introduce you to a Greener scattergun that's both wife and child to me." The old man stared at Jacob. "What you got in your poke?"

"Grub."

"Hell boy, there's plenty grub in Santa Fe." The oldster gave Jacob a measuring look. "Unless you're dead broke."

"I plan to ride on at first light. Figured I might need the grub."

"Is that a fact?"

"Sure is." Jacob gave the hostler some coins. "I figure that will cover the hay and the oats."

"Two scoops, mind."

"I'm not likely to forget."

"That there's a grain-fed hoss," the old man said. "I figure you an' him has seen better days."

Jacob smiled. "Yup, old-timer, you might be right about that."

Jacob forked hay for the mustang and added oats and got a painful kick in the shin for his troubles.

When he returned to the front of the barn, the old-timer said, "Got coffee on the bile, if'n you're interested, young feller. If you ain't, the best place for whiskey and women is the Lucky Lady Saloon just down the street a piece."

"Coffee sounds good," Jacob said. "Then whiskey. As for the women, some other time I guess."

"Then pour yourself a cup." The old man motioned with his head. "In the office there."

When Jacob came back the oldster pushed a wooden box close to him with his foot. "Set, if you've a mind to."

"Don't mind if I do. I'm inclined to take a load off." Grateful, Jacob sat down on the box.

"Name's Miles Marshwood. I'm the proprietor of this establishment."

"And a fine one it is, too," Jacob said, lighting a cigarette.

"What brings you to Santa Fe? If it ain't any of my business, just say. By times I'm a talking man, you understand."

"I'm looking for a man."

Marshwood nodded. "Figured you fer some kind of lawman. Seems that every lawman I ever knowed had a big beak like your'n. Helps 'em smell out badmen, I guess."

Jacob smiled and shook his head. "I'm not a lawman. I'm looking for my brother. His name's Shawn O'Brien."

The oldster was surprised. "Here now, is he a well setup young feller, smiles a lot, and rides with crazy old Uriah Tweedy the bear hunter?"

"I don't know Tweedy, but it sounds like Shawn."

"How come neither of you favor your pa?"

"I don't know. My brother Pat does, but I'm the ugly one of the family."

Marshwood nodded. "Saw that right off my ownself."

"Do you know where Shawn is?" Jacob asked.

The old man's eyes darted to the door, then he said, "You didn't hear this from me, understand?"

"I didn't hear you say a word." Jacob waited for Marshwood to gather his thoughts and speak again.

"The feller who owns the Lucky Lady saloon goes by the name of Zeb Moss. Now it seems like he had your brother's woman, a gal named Trixie Lee who oncet worked for Zeb at the Lucky Lady."

Jacob waited a few moments for more. When it didn't come, he asked impatiently, "Well?"

"Well, Zeb took off with her, or so Willie Wide Awake says."

"Who the hell is he?"

"Willie never sleeps, stays awake the whole time. That is he did, until your brother gave him money to go see a doctor about his problem. The doc gave Willie sleeping powders, and now he sleeps all the time." The old man sighed. "We don't call him Willie Wide Awake no more."

"Where did he go, this Moss?" Jacob said.

"South, that's all I know. Willie said Zeb pulled out of town with a wagon and half a dozen hired toughs. Includin' Silas Creeds, an' he's a bad one."

"Heard of him," Jacob said. "Did Willie have any idea where Moss was headed?"

"No. South was all he knew."

"Why would Moss leave his saloon and light a shuck with Shawn's woman?"

"I don't know. But he surely did."

"How long ago?"

"A week, I guess. It's hard to keep track of time around here."

"Would anyone at the Lucky Lady know where Moss was headed?"

"Maybe. But a man could sure get hisself shot fer askin'."

Jacob rose to his feet. "I'm asking."

"Suit yourself, young feller. Is there anybody I can send your hoss an' traps to when you don't come back?"

"Keep them," Jacob said. "They're yours, on account of how you're such a sweet-natured old cuss and make such lousy coffee."

"Hell, boy, coffee always tastes good when it's free."

Jacob settled his gun belt in place and stepped to the door.

"One thing, young feller," Marshwood added "I hear that a ranny from Arabia visited the Lucky Lady pretty frequent before Zeb left."

"Arabia!" Jacob exclaimed. "Where the hell is Arabia?"

"Overseas, boy. It's a foreign country where them Arabs an' their camels live." The old man shrugged. "Thought I'd tell you fer what it's worth."

"It isn't worth much," Jacob said.

"No, I reckon not, but I figgered I'd tell you anyhow."

\* \* \*

Jacob bought a drink at the Lucky Lady and then, as casually as he could, asked after the whereabouts of Zeb Moss. Coming from a tall, hard-featured man wearing shotgun chaps and a mackinaw open to reveal a high-carried gun, the question was not easy to take. He was met with blank faces or calculating, silent stares of men who looked mean enough to have been up a dozen outlaw trails and back.

After an hour, Jacob realized he was deadheading on a track to nowhere.

He decided to go with the prevailing wind and said, friendly like, to one of the four bartenders on duty, "No piano player tonight?"

"Sick. Seems like he's always down with something."

"Mind if I tickle the ivories?"

"Why not? Everybody else does."

Realizing there were some mighty hard eyes on him, Jacob sat at the piano, played a riff, and was pleasantly surprised the ornate Chickering grand was in tune. It had been a while, and he took sensual pleasure in the silken feel of the keys under his fingertips as though he was caressing the neck of a beautiful woman. With his black depression weighing on him like a damp cloak, he began to play Chopin's Nocturne in C-sharp minor, a beautiful piece initially clouded by the same darkness and inner tension possessing him.

Western men and women, even the hardcases in the Lucky Lady, had an appreciation for music, and a quiet settled on the saloon, broken only by the clink of glasses and the *thud-thud* of the saloon girls' high heels on the timber floor.

When Jacob reached the middle passage of the nocturne leading into a more exultant mood before the chordal section expanded into a moment of fleeting happiness, a slim, pretty Mexican woman in a yellow silk dress stood by the piano, her eyes fixed on his long-fingered hands.

The piece ended and with it Jacob's depression fled and he glanced up at the woman. Her face was enraptured, captivated by the soul of the composer. Jacob expected her to say something, but to his surprise she threw herself into his arms and hugged him close. He felt her hand slip into the top pocket of his mackinaw, and then she was gone.

The bartender ambled over to the piano and handed Jacob a glass of deep amber whiskey. "You can play here anytime, mister. This one's on the house."

Jacob returned to the bar with his drink, uncomfortably aware that he was the center of attention, men and women staring at him as they tried to figure who and what manner of man he was.

After a decent interval, he left the saloon and took to the boardwalk. Halfway to the livery stable, when he was walking past a darkened dry goods store, a rifle shot hammered through the night. The bullet plowed into the brim of his hat, kept on going, and punched a small circle in the store window.

Jacob sprinted to the end of the boardwalk just a few yards beyond the store and dived for the shadows in the alley. He rolled away from the entrance as two more probing shots buzzed over him like angry hornets.

People were yelling and feet pounded in the street. Somewhere a man yelled, "Here, that won't do!" and another voice cried, "Get the sheriff!"

Jacob had a deep distrust of lawmen and the last thing he wanted was to answer a bunch of fool questions. He rose to his feet and was relieved to see that no one was looking in his direction as overly excited people ran around like headless chickens.

Keeping to the shadows he made his way back to the livery and left the hubbub behind him.

Miles Marshwood stood at the stable door. "What's all the shooting about?"

"Beats me." Jacob shrugged his shoulders.

"You got mud on you."

"I tripped. Drank too much, I guess."

Under his ragged mustache, Marshwood's mouth pruned in disapproval. "Sonny, in my time I seen more drunk men than I care to remember. You're not drunk or even close."

"All right then. Somebody took a shot at me."

"Who?"

"Hell if I know. It's dark out there."

"Was you askin' too many questions at the Lucky Lady?"

"Just one too many, about Zeb Moss. So, yeah, I guess I did."

"I warned you, didn't I? Did you get any answers?"

"No. But a gal in the saloon tried to pick my pocket."

"She get your poke?"

"I don't keep money here." Jacob's fingers strayed to the pocket of his mackinaw. He heard a brief crinkle of paper. "Hey, maybe she gave me money."

But it wasn't a banknote. The wrinkled scrap of paper had a single word written on it. *SONORA.*

Marshwood looked over Jacob's shoulder. "Hell, boy, that's in Old Mexico. Why would she write that?"

"Maybe it's where Zeb Moss was headed . . . and probably my brother."

"I'd guess that little gal at the saloon likes you."

"I doubt it." Jacob said. "More likely she doesn't like what Moss does to women."

"Well, I can tell you this, young feller, Zeb Moss had no reason to head fer Sonora, no reason at all. Hell, boy, there's nothing there but mountains and deserts. Seen it with my own eyes years ago, and I doubt if the place has improved since."

"It's the only lead I've got," Jacob said. "And the woman risked her life to give me this paper. That means something."

"Unless she wanted to throw you off the track."

"Then why be so secretive about it? All she needed to say was that Zeb Moss is headed for Sonora and I would've believed her."

"You're rolling the dice, O'Brien. But hell, take the chance. You sure as hell ain't going to get anywhere pokin' around here. And next time the ranny who tries to bushwhack you won't miss."

Jacob stuck the note back in his pocket. "Where do I get a train for Sonora?"

The older man glanced at his watch. "There's a flier leaves here for Albuquerque in an hour. From there you can catch a southbound on the Santa Fe line. I don't know any better than that."

"It's enough. I'm beholden to you." Jacob shook the hostler's hand.

"Hell, you didn't stay long."

"Maybe too long."

# Chapter Thirty-three

Frozen stiff by a cutting wind, his face black with soot from the locomotive's belching chimney, Shawn O'Brien was relieved when the train clanked to a halt at a water tower a mile south of the Texas border. A couple of minutes later the Pullman's door opened and Zeb Moss stepped onto the platform with Silas Creeds.

Moss smiled. "Good morning, gentlemen, and how was your trip?"

Shawn's jaw felt as though it was frozen in place, but he managed to say, "What do you think, Moss?"

"Uncomfortable, were we? Well, we will be at our destination soon." Moss nodded to where the track made a V with another. "The rails that swing to the left head due south along the Magdalena River, and that's the route we'll take."

Shawn worked his jaw a few moments, then asked, "What's your game, Moss?"

"Game? Mr. O'Brien, it's no game. There's money at stake. Oh, and your life, too. But then you already know that."

"Why Sonora? What's in Sonora that you want so badly?

"You'll learn the answer to that question soon. If you live that long, of course."

"Zeb, cut me loose," Uriah Tweedy suggested. "I'm no part of this."

Moss shook his head. "Tweedy, Mr. Creeds informs me that you're a nasty old man and as mean as a teased rattler. I'm sorry, but I believe you're in cahoots with O'Brien, no matter how much you deny it."

"I'm a prisoner of circumstances, Mr. Moss," Tweedy complained. "Yup, that's what I am, a prisoner of circumstances."

"And a hostage to fortune, no doubt," Moss said.

"Whatever that means, Mr. Moss, no truer words have ever been spoke. At least in this part of the country."

Moss laughed. "You amuse me, Tweedy, so maybe I'll let you live." He slapped his hands together. "Now for some good news. I've ordered coffee for all three of you and one of my ladies will be here directly to serve it. Your hands will be unbound for a while. How is that for a magnanimous gesture?"

"Mag . . . magin . . . just what you said, Mr. Moss,"

Tweedy said. "It's true blue as ever was. Can I call you Zeb?"

"No."

"Magnanimous means generous, Mr. Tweedy," Uriah Lowth explained.

"Yeah, it was that, too," Tweedy added.

Moss laughed again and stepped back into his private car.


An older man who seemed affable enough untied Shawn's hands. "They say there are still some renegade Apaches down this way, but I don't put any store in that talk. I fit Apaches one time, but I didn't make a go of it and they stole my mule right out from under my nose. Those savages are right partial to mule meat and they must've dined well that night."

Shawn had the Irishman's love of a good story and fine-sounding words and under normal circumstances he would've wanted to hear the gray-haired man's tale, but he contented himself with saying, "You're lucky you still have your hair."

The man nodded. "Well, what's left of it, anyway."

His companion was of a different breed. Barely out of his teens, he was trying to grow a man's mustache, but only a downy shadow covered his top lip. His green eyes were older and carried the scars of ancient wounds, and he wore a two-gun rig, seldom seen at that time in the West. Shawn guessed he'd be a Kid of some kind—plenty of those around—and he'd be mighty sudden with the iron . . . and merciless.

As though confirming Shawn's thoughts, the affable man introduced him. "This here is the Topock Kid and he'll be your chaperone." He smiled. "Don't let that baby face fool you, he's pure pizen. Killed his own pa with a wood ax when he was barely out of knee britches. Didn't you, Kid?"

"Keep it up old man, and you'll join him," the Topock Kid growled.

"See what I mean." The affable man stepped into the Pullman car. He seemed glad to leave.

"You drink your coffee and Masters will come back to tie you up again," the Kid said. "I see any fancy moves and I'll shoot you in the belly."

"Hey Kid," Tweedy said, "did you really take an ax to your pa?"

"No. It was a mattock. I bashed his skull in with the flat end."

"I guess you didn't like him much, huh?" Shawn assumed.

"No, I didn't, and I don't like you, either, O'Brien, so shut your damned trap."

"Ah, Mr. Topock, I think you meant to say the adze end," Lowth put in. "A mattock is a farm tool, right?"

"Hangman, are you trying to be funny?" the Kid said, his eyes ugly.

Lowth was spared having to answer. The car door opened and Julia Davenport stepped onto the platform, a tray in her hands. Deep shadows appeared under her eyes and she looked thinner. The dress she wore was stained and torn and the cups on the cheap tin tray rattled as her hands shook.

Shawn tried to rise, but the Kid snarled at him to stay the hell where he was.

"How are you, Julia?" Shawn asked carefully.

The woman angled a short, fearful look at the Moss gunman before replying, "I'm just fine, Shawn."

"No you're not," Shawn said. "You look tired."

"I'm fine," Julia said again.

Tweedy smiled. "I'm right happy to see you again, Trixie."

Julia managed a slight smile in return. "How are you, Uriah?"

"Never better."

Julia handed Tweedy a cup and poured coffee for him. "I'm glad to hear it."

"That's enough talk," the Kid ordered. "Pour the coffee, woman, then light a shuck."

"Trixie, have they done something bad to you?" Tweedy said, ignoring the youngster. "Have you been abused by Zeb Moss?"

"No, Uriah, nothing bad has happened to me, nothing at all."

"If they did—"

"If they did, what would you do abut it, pops?" the Kid said, sneering.

"Something real mean, sonny," Tweedy snarled. "Something I done a few times afore when I felt that way."

"Uriah," Julia said, "I'm fine, honestly. Look out for yourself."

"Listen to the little lady, old man." The Kid grinned and slammed a boot into Tweedy's thigh.

It was a bad mistake.

Moving faster than an old man with the rheumatisms should, Tweedy grabbed the Kid's leg and sank his teeth into the gunman's shin.

Like the others, the Topock Kid conformed to Moss's dress code and affected the elegant broadcloth and elastic-sided boots of a prosperous city businessman. There was no leather between the Kid's shin and Tweedy's strong teeth, and the old man bit deep. The Kid tried to kick him off as he would a cur dog, but Tweedy held on tight and gnawed . . . and gnawed. . . .

Screaming, the Kid's hand flashed for one of his holstered guns.

Shawn anticipated the move and sprang at the man. He grabbed the youngster's lapels and smashed his forehead down on the bridge of the Kid's nose. It was a move Luther Ironside called a "Johnny Reb Kiss," and it dropped the man real quick.

Splattered with the Kid's blood, bone, and snot, Shawn felt the gunman go limp as his eyes rolled back in his head. "Uriah, let go of his leg!"

Tweedy released the Kid's shin like a rabid hound, his mouth and mustache crimson with blood.

"Move an inch, and by God I'll scatter your brains."

The Colt muzzle pressed against his temple and the tone of the affable man's voice convinced Shawn that it was not a good time to make a play. He opened his fingers and let the Topock Kid drop to the platform floor.

The affable man stared into Shawn's eyes. "I'm not a threatening man by nature,"—his gun didn't waver—"but right now, O'Brien, you're just a holler and a half from death."

"What happened here?" Zeb Moss said, stepping onto the platform. He looked down at the moaning Kid and back up. "Mr. Masters, who did this?"

"Your man O'Brien did the nose breaking. The old-timer was the leg chewer."

Moss glared at Julia. "Did you have any part in this, Trixie?"

Shawn spoke before she could. "She had no part in it, Moss. We were trying to escape."

Moss's face was black with anger. "I regret

keeping you alive, O'Brien. I regret it deeply." He looked down at the Kid again. His head rolled on his shoulders and both his eyes were black and swollen shut. "Get him to his feet, Mr. Masters. When the hell can he handle a gun again?"

"Two, three days," Masters said. "Maybe longer. He's pretty bust up, Mr. Moss."

"Damn it. We meet up with the Arabs tomorrow morning. I can't afford to lose men now."

"We're getting thin on the ground, right enough," Masters agreed. "The Kid is one of the best there is."

"Then see that he's well enough to gun fight by tomorrow, damn it. I don't give a damn how you do it, but get it done."

Silas Creeds had stepped outside, crowding the platform. He'd heard the last of the conversation. "What about him?" He nodded in Shawn's direction.

Moss scowled, a man torn by indecision. Finally he said, "We need his gun."

"He won't fight for us, boss," Creeds pointed out.

"No, he won't. But he'll fight to save his own skin." Moss took Julia by the arm and pushed her toward the door. "Get inside, you." To Creeds he said, "Tell the engineer to get this damned train moving. We've tarried here long enough."

"What about O'Brien and them?" Masters asked.

"Tie them up again. We'll release them when we get to the end of the line."

Creeds stood at the top of car's iron steps, then turned his head and for the first time expressed doubt about what they were facing. "Boss, can we do the job with what we have?"

"We'll need to, Mr. Creeds. If we can't, by this time tomorrow we'll all be dead."

# Chapter Thirty-four

"All is ready to welcome the Christian devils?" Sheik Abdul-Basir Hakim asked.

Hassan Najid nodded. "As soon as they arrive, a table of salted beef and sweetmeats will be laid out for them, great lord."

"And rum? I want the infidels to get drunk as hogs."

"Two casks." Najid smiled. "Rum enough for ten times their number."

Hakim smiled. "And what of Abdullah, our brave warrior of Islam? He does not falter in his resolve?"

"No, sir. He eagerly looks forward to paradise and the company of many virgins."

"Then all is well." In a giving mood, Hakim said, "The Chinese girl I gave you, the one who will assist our holy martyr, did you enjoy her?"

"She amused me for an hour or two, lord," Najid replied. "I will use her again."

"Good, good. Then that pleases me."

Hakim turned, stared out at the Gulf, and a frown gathered between his eyebrows.

Attuned to his master's slightest swings in mood, Najid bent at the waist in question. "Something troubles you, lord?"

It took a few moments before the sheik answered. With some reluctance, he admitted, "The sea troubles me, Hassan."

Najid was perplexed. "But, sire, you are the finest sailor in all of Islam." The man's voice rose into a shout. "You are the Sea Falcon, scourge of all the oceans of the world."

As Najid knew they would, the sailors lounging nearby wildly cheered their captain.

After the noise died away, Hakim stood in thought, then said, "Here is a story, Najid. Once I met an old man in Jeddah who years before had lost both his legs to a shark. He told me that his fishing boat sank and, being a fine swimmer, he struck out for a distant shore. Now here is the interesting part—he told me he knew there was a shark in the water stalking him long before the beast attacked. He said he couldn't see the shark or smell it, but he knew it was there, lurking unseen. Is that not strange, Hassan?"

"Indeed, lord, but what unseen thing troubles you so? Is it the American warship?"

Hakim waved a dismissive hand. "Pah. I do not fear the American carrion dogs. They are women."

"Then what, sire?"

"I do not know. But it is out there in the deep and it stares at me with white, shining eyes as big as food platters."

"Aye, my lord is indeed troubled in his soul. But once we kill the Americans and take their women, all will be well."

Hakim nodded. "Perhaps you are right, Hassan. Allah willing, this will pass."


Commander John Sherburne watched with approval as sailors polished the lenses of the two huge searchlights on either side of the bridge. The *Kansas* now had eyes to see in the dark.

"We'll give then a try tonight, Mr. Wilson," Sherburne said. "I suspect that's when the rats come out of their holes."

"Indeed, Captain," Lieutenant Wilson agreed.

"I thought those lights were just so much damned ballast when I saw them loaded. Now they may prove their worth."

"Indeed, Captain."

The commander smiled. "You are still of the opinion that the Arab scow has left the gulf."

Wilson took the smile to mean that he could

be frank. "Sir, I believe she's halfway to the East African coast by this time."

"Then we'll agree to disagree, Mr. Wilson." Sherburne took a flask from his pocket. "You still don't indulge?"

"No, sir. I promised my betrothed that my lips—"

"Yes. You told me that already." Sherburne took a swig and wiped off his mouth with the back of his hand. "Give Sergeant Monroe my compliments and tell him I want his marines on deck tonight with full equipment. If we light up the enemy, the marines get a chance to land. I'll command the marine detachment myself."

"You, sir?"

"Me, sir."

"I'm sorry, I just meant . . . well, you're the captain and—"

"If I fall in the battle, Mr. Wilson, you are quite competent to take over command."

"Thank you, sir. But I'd rather hoped to command the marines myself."

"Why, Mr. Wilson? Glory? Promotion? Your name in the newspapers?"

His earnest round face flushed, Wilson said, "All of those things, sir."

Sherburne pretended an anger he didn't feel. "Be damned to you, sir. You're trying to usurp my command."

Wilson was flustered. "No, sir. Not at all, sir. I mean—"

"Go relay my order to Sergeant Monroe."

"Aye, aye, sir. At once, sir." Wilson hurried away as fast as his stocky legs could carry him, but Sherburne's voice stopped him. "Oh, and Mr. Wilson . . ."

"Yes, sir?"

"Tell Sergeant Monroe that you will lead the marine detachment should it land."

A grin split Wilson's face. "Yes, indeed, sir."

# Chapter Thirty-five

The railroad line to the Sonora coast headed straight as a string due south, skirting the timbered foothills of the Sierra Nevada.

Shawn and the others remained bound on the Pullman's platform throughout the dark night, red hot cinders stinging them like hornets. No more coffee—or water, either—was forthcoming. Shawn's mouth was dry and he was wishful for an ice-cold beer and maybe a steak burned black as charcoal to go with it.

"Hey, O'Brien," Uriah Tweedy raised his voice above the racketing roar of the train. He waited until he saw the white blur of Shawn's face turn in his direction and said, "I hope you didn't think I was turning yeller on you."

"It has occurred to me," Shawn replied "More than once, I'd say."

"Hell, boy, one of us had to be on the loose if

we was to have any chance of escape. I figured ol' Zeb would trust me."

"You thought wrong, Mr. Tweedy," Thaddeus Lowth pointed out. "And that was most unfortunate."

"Was it foolish of me to think otherwise, Mr. Lowth?" Tweedy asked. "Under the circumstances, like?"

"A drowning man will clutch at a straw, Mr. Tweedy. There's no blame in that."

"True spoken words as always, Mr. Lowth," Tweedy said.

Lowth directed his attention to Shawn. "What will become of us, Mr. O'Brien?"

"I don't know."

"But I think you have a good idea."

"So do you, Thaddeus."

Lowth hesitated a moment, then said aloud what he'd been thinking. "After Moss trades his women to the Arabs, he has no need to keep us alive."

"That pretty much nails it," Shawn agreed.

"But Zeb keeps saying he needs your gun, O'Brien," Tweedy said. "How do you explain that?"

"Maybe he thinks the slavers will try to cheat him and take his women by force." Shawn's voice was reduced to a dry croak.

"Whatever happens, I'll save Miss Trixie Lee,"

Tweedy said. "Even if I got to use my teeth on some other gunman."

Shawn smiled. "Bide your time, Uriah. We may come to that pass."

The car door opened and Masters stepped onto the platform carrying a jug. "I brought you men water."

"About time," Tweedy complained. "We're dyin' here."

Masters smiled under his mustache. "Chawin' a man's leg off give you a thirst, old-timer?"

"Hell yeah. I'm thirsty enough to suckle a she cougar."

Masters looked at him in amazement. "You ever done that?"

"Only a couple times up in the high Teton country. I never did cotton to it as steady grub, like."

Masters put the spout of the jug to Tweedy's mouth and the old man drank deep. He nodded to Masters. "Thankee, kindly."

As Shawn drank in turn, Masters made a bit of conversation. "We'll be near the Gulf of California coast soon. It's rugged, dry country, or so they tell me."

"How do we get there?" Shawn asked as Lowth took his turn. "All the way on this train?"

"No, just part of the way. The boss says there'll be a welcoming committee camped out by the rails waiting for us. They'll lead us to the slavers' camp."

"Doesn't it bother you, trading in human flesh?" Lowth wondered.

Masters shook his head. "I can't say that it does. Man pays me well for my gun, I go with the flow and mind my own business."

"It's a way, I suppose," Shawn said. "It's not my way, but it's a way."

"In my profession, it's the only way. And before you ask, I sleep just fine o' nights." Masters held up the jug. "All right, gentlemen, one more go-round, then you're done."

The dragon hiss of venting steam and the clang of the locomotive's bell woke Shawn O'Brien from a shallow doze. To his surprise the night had shaded into dawn and a light rain fell, blowing off a frontal storm in the North Pacific. He lifted his face to the drizzle, enjoying its coolness.

The carriage door slammed open and Silas Creeds scowled. "All right, end of the line."

Using the Barlow in his hand, he cut Shawn and the others free. "On your feet."

It took only a fraction of a second for Creeds to reach into the pockets of his coat and come up with his Lightning revolvers. "Down the steps, then stand against the carriage with your hands where I can see them."

Shawn was stiff, Lowth stiffer, and Tweedy stiffer still. Prodded by Creeds' guns, the three men stumbled painfully down the steps, then backed against the Pullman.

Another gunman took Creeds' place, his cold eyes wary as he held his Winchester on Shawn and the others. Behind him, the Topock Kid watered a stunted legume tree. Finished, he buttoned up and turned, looking like he'd run face-first into a brick wall. Both eyes were closed almost shut and looked as though they'd been dabbed with black, blue, and yellow paint. His broken nose, swollen at the bridge, did nothing for his features.

Shawn reckoned the Kid's own mother—if he had one—wouldn't recognize him.

The young gunman stepped through the misting rain like an avenging demon. Stopping a foot from Shawn, he shoved his battered face into his. His breath smelled like blood as he spoke. "This is the last day of your life. Enjoy it."

By nature Shawn was not teased-rattlesnake mean like his brother Jacob, but that morning he was nursing a grouch and was in no mood for sass, especially from a two-bit gunman. He drew back his right foot and kicked out hard. The toe of his boot slammed into the part of the Kid's shin that had been chewed by Uriah Tweedy . . . and caused an immediate uproar.

The Kid's face went from anger to agony. He grabbed his tormented shin and hopped on one leg, shrieking like a wounded cougar.

But only for a moment. Rage overcoming his pain, the Kid clawed for his guns.

"Kid, try it and I'll blow your guts out." The cold-eyed guard jammed his rifle into the youngster's belly and the tone of his voice assured the Kid that he'd pull the trigger.

"What the hell is it now?" Silas Creeds yelled as he hurried toward the frozen tableau of the rifleman and the Topock Kid.

"This boy just don't learn, Silas," the rifleman said, prodding the Winchester into the Kid's belly.

Suddenly Creeds was enraged. "Kid, stay the hell away from O'Brien! He has fancy moves and if he sees a chance, he'll kill you for sure."

"Let me kill him!" the Kid screamed.

"No! Now you git," Creeds ordered. "The boss wants him alive, at least for a spell." He thumbed over his shoulder. "Them boys by the track, or whatever the hell they are, have rum. Go get yourself a drink."

The Kid angled a hating glance as Shawn. "I'm gonna kill you, O'Brien. I swear to God, I'm gonna kill you before sundown."

"Be sure to bring some friends, Kid," Shawn

sassed. "Judging by what I've seen of you, you'll need them."

"O'Brien, you shut your damned face," Creeds cried. "You're nothing but trouble and I don't know why Moss keeps you alive."

"Because those nigras, as you call them, are going to turn on you, Silas," Shawn said. "Depend on it."

Creeds shook his head and smiled. "You got it the wrong way around, O'Brien. And you can depend on *that*." He swung on the guard. "Denver, keep everybody away from these three until the boss decides what he wants done with them."

Turning, Creeds stomped toward the front of the locomotive.

Shawn let out a quick breath. "I could sure use some of that Arab rum right about now."

"The Kid aims to kill you, O'Brien. Don't take him lightly," the guard advised.

"I never take cowards with a gun lightly," Shawn answered.

# Chapter Thirty-six

The storm front moved through and on to the thorny scrub desert country to the east, where the rain hit the ground and dried up in a matter of minutes. A weak sun rose in the sky and the morning grew warmer.

Fifteen minutes after his run-in with the Kid, Shawn saw three Arab seamen walk away from the tracks and head out in the direction of the coast. Moss and his riders showed up shortly thereafter, leading the horses of Shawn, Tweedy, and Lowth.

Behind Moss, Julia Davenport and five other women were roped together on foot. One of the women had flaming red hair and carried a baby in her arms, the mother of the child Shawn had found in the cabin. He recognized the two white women as girls who'd worked in the Lucky Lady.

Used and abused by men, they seemed resigned to their fate, ready to make the best of whatever came their way.

But the two Mexican girls, both young and pretty, were frightened and clung to each other as though each was trying to gain courage from the other. They were not saloon girls, but young woman kidnapped off the street because of their glossy hair and flashing eyes.

Zeb Moss kneed his horse closer to the Pullman and removed a gun belt from the saddle horn—all the cartridge loops filled—and passed it to Shawn. "Heel yourself, O'Brien. You'll need this before too long."

"What's on your mind, Moss?" Shawn asked, buckling the belt around his waist.

"You'll find out. When the shooting starts, just make sure your gun is pointed in the right direction."

Shawn smiled. "And what direction might that be?"

Moss smiled in return, but without humor. "If you don't find out real quick, you'll be dead."

Shawn gazed across the flats. The Arabs had stopped and were looking back at the train, waiting for Moss and his men to catch up.

Suddenly Shawn put it all together. "Hell,

Moss, you're going to gun the Arabs and take their women."

Moss nodded. "And their ship. A man can get rich in the slave trade if he plays his cards right."

"Half the navies in the world are out looking for slave ships, Moss. You ever think about that?"

"I reckon I'll take my chances. In for a couple years, then out a rich man. You can be a part of it, O'Brien."

Shawn shook his head. "I wouldn't allow myself to sink that low, Moss."

Stung, Moss leaned from the saddle and stared into Shawn's face. "Get on your damned horse. You try to make a run for it, I kill Trixie. Understand?"

"I hear you loud and clear, Moss."

"Good. Then we're reading from the same page of the book."


The desert brush country stretched ahead of them all the way to the shore. Scattered clumps of paloverde, ocotillo, ironwood, and skeletal limber bush stood in silent testimony that it was a rain-starved land. Tweedy was armed with his rifle and belt gun. Lowth carried only a rope over his shoulder. Shawn rode between them, behind Moss and Creeds.

"You plannin' to hang some poor feller with that there hemp, Mr. Lowth?" Tweedy asked, making conversation.

"In my line of work it always pays to be prepared," Lowth answered.

"Here, I've been meanin' to ask you something."

"Ask away, Mr. Tweedy."

"It's about them fancy drawers your wife makes."

"I'm listening to you, Mr. Tweedy."

Tweedy leaned across Shawn and whispered, "Would she make a pair for Trixie? Right fancy, mind, with that there lacy stuff an' all."

"Why, I'm sure she would. That is, if the young lady is of good character and of gentle breeding."

"Well, she's all of that now, a schoolma'am by profession." Tweedy leaned back in the saddle as though he'd fairly stated his case.

Thinking of something else, he leaned across Shawn again. "The drawers are for her to wear on our honeymoon, like."

"Of course you're talking about Miss Davenport," Lowth said.

"None other."

"Then I will consult with Mrs. Lowth at the earliest opportunity and she will give me her opinion on this rather, ah . . . delicate matter."

"Spoke like a true gent," Tweedy said, smiling. "And that's the truth of it."

"Uriah," Shawn interrupted as Tweedy once again sat back in the saddle. "Has it occurred to you that all three of us could be dead in a few hours?"

"What's that got to do with it?" Tweedy said, suddenly belligerent.

"It seems to be that if the slavers don't do for us, Moss will," Shawn said.

"Listen, sonny. Ol' Ephraim has been trying to put his claws into me for nigh on twenty year and he ain't kilt me yet. If he can't corral Uriah, a snake like Zeb Moss ain't likely to succeed, is he? An' afore you answer that, a bunch of black pirates with beards down to their belly buttons like them as is leading us ain't going to do me in, either." Tweedy spat over the side of his horse. "Hell, I haven't made a speech that long since I was a youngster an' first learned how to talk American."

Shawn grinned. "I sure wish I had your confidence."

"If it comes to a fight, boy, shoot an' move, shoot an' move. That's all there is to it. It's something ol' Ephraim taught me."

"I'll keep it in mind," Shawn said.

"You do that, sonny. Live longer if you listen to your elders."

As the riders neared the gulf, the water came in sight, glittering under the climbing sun. Shawn saw that a couple tents had been erected near the beach and the topmast of a sailing ship was just visible in a well-camouflaged inlet. A table had been set out, groaning under the weight of joints of salt beef, fruit, and stacks of flatbread. A large keg of Jamaican rum surrounded by glasses took up the middle of the table.

Behind the feast stood two dozen white, black, and Oriental girls, all smiling steadily as though they'd been ordered on pain of death to look welcoming. And behind them was a score of swarthy, bearded sailors. They showed no arms but for the cutlasses at their sides.

Catching Shawn's attention were the two men who stepped purposely toward Moss's cavalcade. One was immensely tall, dressed in flowing Arab robes of blue and white, his hand on the hilt of a scimitar in a scabbard studded with pearls and rubies. Beside him, in less elaborate robes, was a scar-faced rogue with shifty, rodent eyes lingering on nothing but seeing everything.

Grinning, Moss swung out of the saddle and stepped toward the tall Arab, guessing, correctly that he was the boss.

Sheik Abdul Basir-Hakim made a deep salaam, straightened, and deftly sidestepped Moss's embrace, leaving the man to drop his arms and look confused.

"Welcome to my humble encampment," Hakim greeted, teeth flashing white in his dusky face.

"It is an honor to be here, my friend," Moss replied.

"Please. There is food and drink for you and your men, Mr. Moss, though I fear my poor table does you no honor."

"Hell," Moss said, "it looks just fine to me . . . mister . . ."

"You may call me Sheik," Hakim offered smugly.

Moss clapped his hand on Hakim's shoulder, causing him to wince. "And Sheik it is." He turned to his men and yelled. "Light and set, boys. There's grub and rum for all of ye."

A cheer went up from the gunmen. They dismounted and crowded around the rum keg, handing glasses to each other.

Hakim glanced at Hassan Najid and smiled. It was going just as he'd hoped. Soon the American pigs would be drunk and easy to kill.

Shawn remained mounted, as did Tweedy and the fastidious Lowth, who frowned as he watched

Moss's gunmen among the women, swigging down rum with one hand, exploring with the other.

Or were they drinking rum?

It was Tweedy who noticed it first. He leaned over in the saddle and whispered to Shawn, "Them Texas boys ain't drinkin'. A man doesn't drink like that, real dainty from a glass like your maiden aunt sippin' sherry at a funeral."

Shawn studied the gunmen. They seemed rowdy and loud, drinking heartily as they pawed the girls, but no matter how many times they put a glass to their lips, the level of the rum stayed the same. And to a man, they tried to keep their gun hands untangled.

"What do you reckon, O'Brien?" Tweedy asked quietly.

"They're only pretending to drink and they're not sitting on their gun hands," Shawn said. "Moss is getting ready to make his move and take over the whole shebang."

"Lookee." Tweedy nodded toward the gulf. "Over yonder by the shoreline."

Shawn glanced toward the beach. Arab seamen drifted toward their stacked rifles, and a dozen had already armed themselves.

He glanced to where Hakim and Moss were standing together, examining the female merchandise. Julia looked lost and forlorn, keeping her eyes downcast at the sand under her feet.

Moss and the tall Arab were engaged in a deep, hand-waving discussion.

Haggling over prices, Shawn guessed. He eased his hand closer to his holstered Colt.

Didn't Zeb Moss know the danger they were all in?

# Chapter Thirty-seven

"O'Brien, get off that hoss, and that goes for you two as well." Silas Creeds motioned with his glass at Tweedy and Lowth.

Shawn swung out of the saddle and stood holding the reins of his mount. "Looks like the ball is about to open, Creeds."

"Soon. But not yet. The boss wants to look over the ship."

"He may not have time," Shawn pointed out.

"He's got the Arab in gun range. Zeb knows it and the Arab knows it. The ball will open when Zeb Moss decides to open it and it ain't yet." Creeds waved toward the table. "Go get yourself some grub, but stay clear of the rum."

Shawn looked around him. "I count thirty seamen, and most of them are already armed. You plan to take them on with six men?"

"Nine, including you and them two with you, and ten, counting Mr. Moss. The boss should count for two or three, just like me and maybe the Topock Kid, if he's well enough."

"It's getting a little too tense for comfort around here, Creeds," Shawn said. "When will the shooting start?"

Creeds gave his yellow smile. "When I put a bullet in you, O'Brien, you'll know when it *ends.* Until then, be ready."

After Creeds strolled away, Shawn and the others stepped to the table. Shawn was hungry. He wrapped some salt beef in a flatbread and discovered it made a tasty sandwich. He stayed away from the rum, though Tweedy helped himself to a glass.

"Know what I feel like, Mr. Lowth?" Tweedy said, after sampling the rum.

"Do tell, Mr. Tweedy." Like Shawn, Lowth was munching on a sandwich.

"It's like when I'm stupid enough to get myself downwind of ol' Ephraim an' he's as mad as hell and comes after me. I know I've got a fight on my hands and the only question is . . . when? And the answer is that Ephraim's smart an' won't brace me until he figgers he's got an edge. But as to when that will come about, only he knows." Tweedy looked at Shawn. "You take my meanin'?"

Shawn looked to where Moss and the Arab

were walking toward the sailing ship, unhurried, talking like two old friends out for a morning stroll.

"You mean hard times are coming down sometime soon, Uriah." Shawn smiled. "I hope you're loaded for bear."

Tweedy made a face. "Lousy rum. Damn furriners."

Shawn studied the terrain around the camp. There was no cover, no place to hide for miles, only desert brush on flat ground that stretched to the Sierra Madres. What he had in mind was impossible.

Tweedy winked. "Been thinking that my ownself, sonny. They'd ride us down afore we covered a quarter mile. Or they'd just stay right where they're at an' shoot us down."

Shawn nodded. "I know. And we'd have women along with us."

"It seems to me, Mr. O'Brien," Lowth put in, "that all we can do is wait and then react to whatever situation manifests itself."

"Fine words, Mr. Lowth," Tweedy said. "I don't know what the hell you're talking about, but them was high-sounding words."

"We wait and see, Uriah," Shawn explained. "That's what he means."

Tweedy took a swig of rum. "Hell, boy, that's all we can do." He laid the glass at his feet and levered a round into the Winchester's chamber. "But right now I'm gonna go talk with my intended."

"Uriah, those Arab sailors don't look like they'd exactly welcome your visit," Shawn pointed out.

"That's their problem, not mine."

"Wait, Mr. Tweedy, I'll come with you," Lowth said. "There's strength in numbers."

"You're a mannerly, well-spoken gent, Mr. Lowth, so you're welcome to talk with my future bride," Tweedy offered. Then to Shawn he said, "Just in case things go bad, cover us, young feller."

Four pairs of black, hostile eyes watched Tweedy and Lowth as they walked closer to the women. One of the guards, a big, brawny fellow with a ragged black beard down to his navel, stepped in their way. He managed a slight, artificial smile. "Rum," he said, motioning with his Lebel rifle toward the table. "You go, infidel. Drink."

Tweedy stopped, the Winchester in the crook of his left arm, and moved the forefinger of his right hand back and forth. "No drinkee." He pointed at Julia. "Me talkee."

The Arab hesitated. His lord was still on the schooner with the American and he'd been ordered to pretend a warm welcome to the infidel dogs. After a few moments, he bowed slightly and stepped aside.

"See, Mr. Lowth, all you have to do is talk to them in their own lingo and they'll do anything for you." Tweedy smiled at the stone-faced Arab. "Thankee . . ."

The women crowded around Tweedy and Lowth, all of them asking questions at the same time. Tweedy held up a silencing hand. "Ladies, I'm only here to see Miss Trixie Lee, my intended."

One of the young Mexican girls asked, "Can you help us, señor? Can you take us away from this terrible place?"

Tweedy pretended a confidence he didn't feel. "Never fear, ladies, we'll get you out of here and back to Santa Fe." He grinned. "Never fear. Tweedy is here."

The girl took Tweedy's hand and kissed it, her tears falling on his tough skin. "Thank you, señor. Oh, thank you."

Tweedy, knowing he'd lied to the girl, who was little more than a child, felt like a Benedict Arnold and he was forced to swallow the lump in his throat.

"How are you holding up, Miss Lee?" Lowth asked Julia. "I hope you are not too distressed."

Julia looked at the man, her face empty. She said nothing.

Tweedy, discouraged by his lie to the Mexican

girls, said in an apologetic tone, "We're goin' to save you, Trixie. But it won't be easy or soon. You understand?"

"Save yourself, Uriah," Julia said. "It's too late for me, too late for all of us."

"Never you mind. We'll come up with somethin', Trixie. Damn right we will, on account of how when this is over me an' you is gettin' hitched right away."

Julia managed a smile, but it was distant and fleeting. "Don't get your hopes up, Uriah." She put her hand on his buckskinned arm. "You are all in terrible danger. Tell Shawn O'Brien I said that."

"I reckon he already knows, Trixie," Tweedy said. "Zeb Moss wants to take the slave ship. Men will die, most of them real quick."

"Then leave us. Get on your horses and ride and don't stop until you reach Texas."

Tweedy shook his head. "We're not leaving you, little schoolteacher gal."

"Then you'll all die soon. It's building, Uriah. Either Moss or the sheik will make his move before dark."

Lowth had been listening intently, but made his way to the redhead with the baby in her arms. He smiled. "How is she?"

The woman looked haunted. "The slaver says he'll buy me but not my baby. That man Moss said that was all right and they'd just leave my little Annie on the beach and let the tide take her."

She grabbed the front of Lowth's coat. "Please don't let them take my baby from me."

"I won't let that happen." Even as he said the words, Lowth knew they were as empty as a banker's heart.

"Thank you." Suddenly there was hope in the woman's eyes. "You'll save us, won't you?"

"Yes. Yes I will," Lowth said, hating himself. "You'll see, dear lady, everything will be just fine."

The woman so obviously and so eagerly believed him that Thaddeus Lowth felt himself die a little death.

# Chapter Thirty-eight

The Chinese girls were slowly drifting away. . . .

Shawn O'Brien sat in meager shade, his back against the thin trunk of a spineless young ironwood tree. As drowsy crickets made their small music in the brush near him, he wondered idly why the women were leaving. If they'd paired off with a man and were seeking a place for a rendezvous he'd have understood. But they were slowly walking toward the beach one by one as though afraid their leaving would be noticed.

Shawn's eyes moved to Moss's gunmen. They seemed unconcerned, talking to one another, though every now and then a man would slant a puzzled glance toward the schooner. No doubt Moss and the sheik were still bargaining for the women, Shawn decided. Or, more correctly, Moss was going through the motions, biding his time before he made his move.

Shawn shifted his eyes back to the Chinese girls and saw something else that disturbed him. Apart from the men guarding Moss's captives, the ship's crew had assembled near the schooner and all were armed with rifles and swords.

Suddenly, tension stretched in the air, taut as a fiddle string. The Arabs were not making any hostile moves, but constantly chattered to each other. Then, their black eyes glittering, they fingered their weapons and looked toward Moss's gunmen.

Tweedy, as downcast as a man could be after spinning one lie after another, sat close by, drinking rum.

"Hey, Uriah—" Shawn began.

"I see 'em," Tweedy said. "Trixie said the fun times was fixin' to come down soon and I reckon she was right."

"You reckon the Arabs will open the ball?" Shawn asked.

"Yeah, I do, but not yet. Not without their boss man."

"It would seem like." Shawn looked toward the schooner. There was no one on deck nor any sound but the faint creak of two tall masts in the breeze.

The morning had grown warmer and, except for Silas Creeds, the Moss gunmen had removed their coats, but all wore their guns. They were talking little now that they'd noticed the departure of the Chinese girls and the gathering of armed crewmen near the ship. But without Moss they seemed undecided about what to do. For the moment they were content to remain right where they were. A few of them were drinking rum in earnest.

Like Shawn and Tweedy, the gunmen felt something in the air, as though the atmosphere around them had shifted and become poisonous. Hostility hadn't greeted them gently. It reached out, grabbed them by their throats, and started their alarm bells ringing.

Without even realizing it, the gunmen had spread out a little, each man clearing some fighting room around him.

Shawn rose to his feet. His eyes narrowed and his vision began to tunnel as happens to a man who knows he's about to get into a shooting scrape.

Yet, the Arabs made no moves.

They remained standing where they were, silently looking toward the gunmen around the table as though waiting for something to happen.

Suddenly, the Arabs broke into a cheer.

Tweedy and Lowth stepped closer to Shawn. All eyes were on the beautiful Chinese girl who'd just bowed out of the smaller tent. She held a basket piled high with fruit and dates and she smiled as she walked toward Moss's men.

Shawn was puzzled. Was this a peace offering of some kind?

The girl wore very little and her pert little breasts were mostly exposed, a sight not lost on Moss's men. Grinning, they crowded around the girl, more interested in what she had on show than they were the fruit basket.

"Purty little thing, ain't she, Mr. Lowth?" Tweedy commented.

"Indeed she is, Mr. Tweedy. I believe Celestials as a whole are a pretty race."

Shawn said nothing. His eyes were fixed on the young Arab man who'd also left the smaller tent. He seemed unsteady on his feet and drool from his slack mouth trickled down his black beard. Shawn thought the man was drunk or had been smoking opium, a drug to which his brother Jacob had once been much addicted.

But then Shawn saw something that chilled him to the bone.

The man held a burning brand in his hand. He opened his vest and lit the short fuse of a silver-colored bomb strapped around his waist. Immediately, he shrieked and ran on bare feet toward the Moss gunmen.

Shawn yelled, "Look out!" He drew and fired, but his bullet spurted dust inches behind the assassin's pounding feet.

Alerted to the danger, the gunmen faced the Arab, and bullets slammed into him. The bomber staggered, but kept on running toward them, screaming, "Death to the infidels," his hatred fueled by drugs and sex.

Then he was among Moss's men.

"Down!" Shawn yelled as he dived for the ground and was aware of Tweedy thudding onto the sand beside him.

The bomb blast erupted in a spinning Catherine wheel of scarlet flame and crimson blood. Severed heads, arms, and legs flung into the air and maimed men screamed amid the pornographic violence.

Shrapnel screeched over Shawn and Tweedy and behind them, Lowth yelped and hit the ground hard.

Then it was over.

A dark ribbon of smoke and dust rose in the air spiked with the stink of gunpowder and blood and the day was made terrible by the agonized moans of dying men.

Shawn rose and glanced at Lowth. The man was sitting up, but his forehead was bloody and his eyes seemed distant and unfocused.

"See to him, Uriah," Shawn said.

Then he walked forward . . . into a charnel house.

Seeing the result of the bomb, all Shawn's courage and fortitude went out of him like a gust of breath. He'd been prepared for sprawled bodies and dying men, but not a scene like the aftermath of a demonic feast on the bodies of the damned.

Moss's gunmen had been torn apart by the explosion, as had the Chinese girl, her headless, naked corpse obscene in death. The bomber had been blown to smithereens, as there was nothing left of him that was identifiable as human. A red thing without arms or legs begged Shawn for death, but numbed by horror, he could only stumble away from that terrible place, gorge rising in his throat.

Silas Creeds and the Topock Kid were the only Moss gunmen still alive.

They stood near the beach surrounded by the terrified women who had fled from the blast. Julia comforted a Chinese girl who sobbed quietly on her shoulder.

Creeds and the Kid seemed stunned, unable to believe what had happened. Creeds' hands were in his coat pockets, ready to draw as soon as he could identify the enemy. Beside him, the Kid's battered face was empty, a man trying to grasp a horror beyond anything in his experience.

But there was worse to come.

Moss and Hakim scrambled from the ship and stepped rapidly toward the blast site. Moss had removed his coat and looked tall, handsome, and immaculate in a white, frilled shirt, black pants cut tight in the Mexican style, and English riding boots. He had a blue, ivory-handled Colt stuck in his waistband.

He saw Creeds and without slowing his pace, yelled, "What the hell happened?"

"Bomb," Creeds said, figuring no other explanation was necessary.

Moss swung on the sheik. "Damn you. Did you plan this?"

Those six words closed the final chapter of the book of his life.

He gasped openmouthed as Hakim, moving with flashing speed, rammed three feet of Damascus steel into his belly. Blood stained his mouth as he stared wide-eyed into Hakim's face, unable to comprehend the terrible fact that the Arab had killed him.

"Yes, infidel," Hakim said. "Now I will take your women and make them my own." He withdrew the sword and Moss fell dead at his feet.

Hakim kicked the corpse. "Infidel dog."

Creeds didn't lack sand. His guns cleared his pockets, but he fell to the ground under the weight of the crewmen who'd jumped on top of him. Creeds fought like a cougar, kicking out as he tried to bring his .38s to bear. But a savage club to the head from a Lebel butt knocked him into stillness.

The Kid, surrounded by leveled rifles, made no attempt to draw. He was a paid mercenary and nothing in the code said he had to die to avenge a client. Like Creeds, he was disarmed and pounded to the ground.

Shawn drew his Colt and retreated slowly toward Tweedy, who was wiping blood from Lowth's face.

Without looking at the younger man, Tweedy said, "Don't try to buck a stacked deck, boy. There's too damn many of them."

A dozen corsairs advanced on Shawn and the others, teeth bared, their rifles up and ready.

Suddenly Shawn had had enough . . . enough of blood and guts and violence and the screams of dying men. He tossed his Colt away and said to the oncoming Arabs, "Damn you. Come and get me. I'm through."

# Chapter Thirty-nine

"The ten-o-three to Sonora and points south ain't exactly a cannonball, mister," the ticket agent said. "If I was you I'd talk to the engineer and ask him to let you off at the same place as them other folks."

"The question is, am I chasing after the right folks," Jacob O'Brien said.

The agent scratched his stubbly chin. "I wouldn't know about that."

"Do you recollect those people, the ones that left the train in Sonora?" Jacob said.

"I recollect they had a private Pullman and a passel of women," the agent said. "And that's all I know. There are gents that don't like questions, and I didn't ask none."

Jacob was silent as he absorbed that and the agent said, "Hardcases, that's what they were."

"It sounds like the people I'm hunting," Jacob said. "You hear any names?"

"I don't give out passenger's names to them as has no business knowing them." The agent found himself looking down the barrel of Jacob's Colt. He said quickly, "The man who rented the Pullman was called Mr. Moss, and that's all I know. So you can put the cannon away."

"Zebulon Moss?" Jacob asked, holstering his gun.

"Mr. Moss."

"He's the man for sure. A lot of women, you say?"

"That's what I said."

"Did you see a tall, handsome fellow, kinda favors me in some ways?" Jacob said.

"There ain't no handsome fellas favor you, mister, if you'll forgive me for saying."

"Well, did you see a good-looking fellow, yellow hair, blue eyes, well set-up?"

"A few of the hardcases in the Pullman car looked like that." The agent lowered his head to the ledger in front of him and his eyes were hidden by his black visor. The man's talking was done.

Jacob reached inside his mackinaw and consulted his watch. He snapped it shut and said, "Will the ten-o-three be on time?"

The agent sighed and raised his eyes again. "It's never early, so it's always late. Ten minutes, thirty, who knows?"

"Thanks. You've been a big help." Jacob turned away and headed out the door.

"Maybe we should open a line just for hard-cases," the agent mumbled. "Seems like we're getting enough of them coming through here recent."

Jacob stepped onto the depot platform and sat on a bench, his eyes scanning the bleak landscape around him. He built a cigarette and settled in for a wait, unsure of what lay ahead for him.

Was Shawn with Moss? Or had he already been killed?

Jacob shuddered. That was something he didn't want to contemplate. Dromore without his laughing, handsome brother would be an empty, dreary place. And how could he break it to the colonel? It could kill him.

Aware that the black dog was creeping up on him, Jacob rose and walked to the edge of the platform. He looked at the line, the shiny iron rails vanishing into distance, and saw no sign of the train.

If Shawn was with Moss, perhaps a prisoner, he needed help, and damn soon.


According to the big railroad clock on the depot wall, the ten-o-three southbound was exactly fifteen minutes late. Other passengers had gathered on the platform, Mexican couples with children mostly, and a soldier in a shabby blue and red army uniform who carried a slung Lebel rifle.

After the locomotive chuffed to a halt, Jacob walked along the platform and hailed the engineer, who was leaning out of the cab, studying the line ahead. Jacob questioned him about Moss and asked if he could be dropped off at the same spot.

Yes, the engineer remembered the folks on the Pullman.

Yes, there were a bunch of pretty women on board, Chinese, black, and Anglo.

Yes, he could find the drop-off spot on the line again.

Yes, he could stop the train and give Jacob time to unload his horse.

"But," the man said, "a little something for the inconvenience would not go amiss. If you catch my meaning, mister."

"Would twenty dollars cover it?" Jacob said, steam jetting around his legs.

"Hell, mister, I'll sell you the whole train for twenty dollars," the engineer said. "Climb aboard."

# Chapter Forty

Shawn O'Brien sat in a circle with four other men, Tweedy, Lowth, Creeds, and the Topock Kid. Facing out, their backs to each other, none of them moved. Movement was impossible, bound tightly as they were with ship's ropes.

Lowth's bowler had holes fore and aft, the result of a walnut-size chunk of shrapnel that had burned across the top of his head and drawn blood. "What will they do with us, do you think, Mr. Tweedy?" he said. Before the other man could answer, he added, "I must admit that I fear the worst."

"Well, they took us prisoner instead of killin' us outright, Mr. Lowth," Tweedy said. "I'd say that's a good sign."

Because of the seating arrangement, Silas Creeds was forced to talk over his shoulder. "They'll kill us before they sail. The damned pirates are swarming all over the boat, getting her ready for sea."

Without the threat of his guns, Creeds seemed

diminished, just a tall, skinny man in an oversized coat and battered top hat with fear in his eyes.

"Are you of the same opinion, Mr. O'Brien?" Lowth asked.

"Creeds said it right," Shawn answered.

"Then we're done for." Lowth sighed.

"Damn you, hangman, do you always state the obvious? Of course we're done for." Creeds strained against his bonds. "Damn these ropes. Damn them, damn them, damn them!"

Creeds' outburst earned him a kick from one of their guards. The man pushed the muzzle of his rifle against Creeds' head and said, "Bang!" and the men with him laughed.

Shawn had no illusions about his fate. The Arabs would not let them live.

He looked to where Julia and the rest of the women were crowded together on the beach under heavy guard. The guards and the Arabs on the schooner shouted back and forth to one another and it seemed to Shawn that they were planning to load the women soon.

But a sailing ship needed wind, and the afternoon was dead calm. Unless she could be rowed out in the hope of catching a favorable breeze in the gulf, the schooner was going nowhere that day.

A persistent buzzing he'd been hearing for some time made Shawn turn his head and look at the place where the bomb had exploded. The whole blood-splashed area was thick with flies, black clouds of them gorging on the remains of what had once been men. And a woman, he reminded himself. For her, death had come fast.

"Hey, something's happening." The Kid's swollen eyes strained in the direction of the ship.

The slavers around the ramp bowed low, kowtowing to a creature being led from the ship by the tall man who'd killed Zeb Moss.

"It's a woman," Creeds said.

"No, it ain't," Tweedy disagreed. "It's some kind of animal."

"Wearing clothes, you idiot?" Creeds grumbled.

"Then it's an animal wearing clothes." Tweedy didn't back down.

The creature was sexless, a bent, frail shape wearing a brown, hooded cloak. The feet were large, the long toenails like curled horns and the skinny arm the Arab supported with his was wrinkled and as big around as a willow twig. Its face was hidden by the hood. Even when the creature stopped in front of Shawn and the others they couldn't tell if it was male or female.

"For those of you who don't know, my name is Sheik Abdul-Basir Hakim," the tall Arab said. "I trust you gentlemen are quite comfortable and your needs have been attended to."

"You go to hell." Tweedy spat at the slaver's feet.

Hakim nodded. "A brave infidel, is he not, sorceress?"

So she was female, Shawn thought. And she looked to be about a hundred years old . . . or two hundred.

"Let us see if you are as brave after my soothsayer pronounces your sentence," Hakim said. "I must warn you that she is not a merciful woman."

The woman pushed back her hood and revealed a face deeply furrowed by a long passage of time. Strands of thin white hair fell to her scrawny neck. She had a small hook of a nose and her black eyes were sunken in the sockets.

She stood over Tweedy, sniffed the air, and said something to Hakim in a language Shawn did not understand.

The Arab laughed. "She smells bear, old man. Do you consort with bears?"

Tweedy looked shocked and said nothing.

The crone moved on to Lowth and again she smelled the air around him. She again spoke to the sheik in the language Shawn didn't understand.

The sheik explained. "The smell of death is all about you, infidel. Are you an executioner?"

"I am a hangman," Lowth said. "It is an ancient and honorable profession."

Suddenly the sorceress cackled and she spoke longer.

After she'd finished talking, Hakim smiled. "Ah, that is so exquisite, old woman." He loomed over Lowth. "You will hang your companions from the yards of my ship. In return, you can have your own miserable life."

"And if I don't?" Lowth asked bravely.

The sheik spoke to the witch and she spoke again.

He nodded. "If you don't, the bellies of you and your companions will be cut open until your guts spill, then you will all be buried alive in the same pit."

"Then I'll do as you say." Lowth's face was ashen, like that of a dead man.

Hakim smiled. His hazel eyes looked like mildewed brass. "The executions will be tomorrow at first light before we sail, hangman. One word of advice. Do not tie the knots too tightly. My men will wish to see the infidels dance."

Tweedy, red with anger, nodded at the crone. "Is she your wife, Abdul? She's as damned ugly as you are."

The sheik smiled again. "And you, my bear-loving friend, will dance longest of all."


"Thankee, Mr. Lowth," Tweedy said. "Gettin' hung by a friend is a sight better way to go than a cuttin' an' buryin'."

"He ain't no friend of mine." Creeds turned his head and glared at Lowth. "You do it right, mister. Break my damned neck."

"Or what?" Shawn asked, smiling.

Creeds was silent. There was no answer to that question.

"I am," Lowth said softly, "much distressed. I wish my dear wife was here to give me counsel and succor."

"It's not your fault, Thaddeus,' Shawn pointed out. "The Arab offered you a choice that was no choice at all. You gave him the only answer you could."

"I've never hung friends before."

"There's a first time for everything, Mr. Lowth," Tweedy's face suddenly brightened. "Here, do you think that old hag really smelled bear on me?"

"It would seem so, Mr. Tweedy," Lowth said. "That was a most singular occurrence."

"I bet it's the ol' she bear I slept with during the winter of '82. Her smell must've rubbed off on me." Tweedy bent his head to look at Shawn. "What's your opinion on that, O'Brien?"

"I'd say it seems likely," Shawn agreed. "I reckon you haven't taken a bath since."

"Bathing gives a man the rheumatisms, boy. Hell, everybody knows that."

"Shut the hell up!" Creeds yelled. "All of you! Let a man have some peace."

"Seeing ghosts, Creeds?" Shawn asked.

He expected the gunman to curse him, but Creeds surprised him by saying, "Yeah, every damned one of them I ever kilt. They're out there in the desert, watching me. Saying nothing, just standing there, staring at me."

"Must be quite a crowd," Shawn said.

Creeds tilted back his head and yelled, "I done for all you blackguards once and I'll do you again! Now leave me the hell alone!"

"Easy, Creeds," Shawn advised. "Take your medicine like a man."

Creeds slumped. "Ain't you afraid of dying, O'Brien?"

"Yeah, I am. But there isn't much I can do about it." Shawn nodded to their alert, hostile guards. "Those gents are a pretty determined bunch."

Creeds' gaze moved to the desert where thin shadows stretched among the scrub. "You see them boys out there, O'Brien?"

"No. They're hanging heavy on your conscience, Creeds, not mine."

"Then be damned to you for a preaching fool," Creeds said. "I should've gunned you when I had the chance."

Shawn said nothing and looked over at the

schooner. Sailors swarmed over the ship, readying her for sea, and men were aloft in the yards.

He had until dawn. It was not a long time for a man to live, but time enough to make his peace with God.

# Chapter Forty-one

The huge locomotive glowed red and steamed like a dragon asleep in a cave.

"Mister, are you sure you want off here?" The burly engineer stood beside Jacob in the midnight darkness. "North, east, south, and west, there's nothing but desert and mighty little water, except salt."

"I'll make out." Jacob's eyes searched the gloom bereft of moonlight. "You sure Moss's men took the women west?"

"Damn sure." As though to justify his certainty, he pointed in one direction. "East lie desert flats and then the Sierras." He pointed a finger to the west. "That way is the California Gulf. Maybe they planned to board a ship."

"Could be." Jacob extended his hand. "Well, thank you kindly for your help."

"And thank you for the double eagle." The

engineer had a wide Irish face and a good smile. "You can ride my train anytime."

Jacob swung into the saddle and watched the train leave until the red lights of the caboose vanished into darkness and he was alone. The night closed around him.

He built and lit a cigarette and kneed the dun mustang forward. The little horse was a creature of pure evil that nursed ancient grudges to keep them warm, but he could see in the dark like a cougar and Jacob was content to let him pick the trail.

He had no clear idea how many miles lay between him and the waters of the gulf, but he figured they were plenty. He had the Irish gift, but hadn't sensed that Shawn was ahead of him or behind him or anywhere. The immediate future was a closed book, and that troubled him greatly.

There was no breeze and the desert was hushed as he and the horse ambled on, the only sound the creak of saddle leather and the soft sound of the mustang's hooves on sand. There was no point in trying to hurry the mustang's pace. One misplaced hoof into an animal hole in the sand and he could be without a horse, a death sentence in that wilderness.

Half an hour later, Jacob smelled something odd in the air, like the aftermath of a great battle once the cannons have fallen silent.

Burned gunpowder.

His face was grim. Had a gunfight taken place somewhere ahead of him? Had Shawn been involved? Who were the winners and losers?

Those were questions without answers.

All Jacob could do was keep riding west at a walk and pray that he was in time. In time for what, he did not know.

# Chapter Forty-two

The sloop of war *Kansas* was cleared for action. Her guns, fully armed, were run out, and her marines were already on deck in full battle gear. Commander John Sherburne had ordered the guns loaded with canister—proven mankillers. If possible, he was determined to save the schooner. She was a valuable prize and would add much needed revenue to a navy that a parsimonious Congress kept chronically short of funds.

"We'll find her tonight, Mr. Wilson," Sherburne said. "I can feel it in my water, as they say."

"Indeed, sir," Lieutenant Wilson agreed.

"Your marines ready to go?"

"Yes, sir."

"Champing at the bit, eh?"

"Indeed, sir."

"And you, Mr. Wilson? Are you ready to lead your first landing party?"

Wilson smiled. "Yes, I am, sir."

"Good man. I want a tot of rum for each marine before they disembark. Get them in the fighting spirit, eh?"

"They're in the fighting spirit already."

"Well, the rum will give them an edge."

Seeing the lieutenant's young, round face was troubled, his captain said, "Well, out with it, man."

"Sir, we need to coal at the earliest opportunity," Wilson said hurriedly. "I fear this . . . ah . . . expedition will dangerously deplete our existing supply."

"Slow as she goes, Mr. Wilson. We'll burn but little coal."

"Aye, aye, sir," Wilson said, but he didn't seem convinced.

"See to the gun crews, Mr. Wilson, and tell them to stay alert. We'll get under way at dusk."

The *Kansas* was a glutton for coal all right, and even at a slow speed she'd burn a bunker-load on their trip up the coast. Wilson was right. They had a crisis on their hands and a captain who allowed his ship to run out of fuel could kiss his naval career good-bye.

After the lieutenant left, Sherburne stared at the column of dark gray smoke rising from his ship's funnel and felt a twinge of worry. Was his gut feeling correct? Was the slaver still in the gulf? She had to be. She . . . just . . . had to be.

But hoping didn't make it so, and the captain's worry grew.

The afternoon light faded with agonizing slowness and a couple able seamen came on the bridge to man the searchlights.

"Show me those damned Arabs, lads," Sherburne said. "Keep your eyes peeled."

The older of the two knuckled his forehead in the Royal Navy style and said in a broad Scottish accent, "Aye, aye, Cap'n. If the damned rogues are anywhere to be found, we'll light 'em up for ye, depend on it."

*If they are anywhere to be found.* Yes, there was the rub. Sherburne felt the worry twinge again. He could be taking his ship on a wild goose chase with his career at stake. He found the flask in his pocket and was about to take a swig when he noticed the sailors watching him. He passed the flask to the gray-haired sailor. "A tot of rum with you."

The man knuckled his forehead again and said, "Thank ye, Cap'n." After he'd taken a throat-bobbing swig, the seaman passed the flask to his companion.

To his chagrin, when Sherburne got it back the flask was considerably lighter. He took a drink, and then looked up to a flaming sky, banded with dark blue and jade. A single sentinel star hung to the north, a bright lantern lighting the way for the fleeing day.

It would be full dark soon. Sherburne nodded to himself. It was finally time to get his ship under way.

*Thank God.*

# Chapter Forty-three

Tweedy peered into the fading light. "They're loading the women. Damn them furriners' eyes. They're using whips, loading them little gals like slaves."

"They are slaves, Mr. Tweedy," Lowth pointed out. "Or they will be soon."

Try as he might, Shawn couldn't make out Julia Davenport in the crowd, and a sense of failure lay on him. He'd set out to save the Dromore schoolteacher and had only made matters worse. And Tweedy and Lowth would die because of his incompetence.

"It won't be long now," Lowth said. "With every tick of the clock I'm dying a little death here. I wonder what my poor, dear wife will think when I tell her what I've done?"

"You'll be going home, Mr. Lowth," Tweedy said. "You'll know the answer to that question soon enough."

Lowth took a sharp intake of breath and let out a great, shuddering sigh. "I can't do it. I'll die first."

"You can do it, Thaddeus," Shawn said. "Uriah is right. A hanging beats getting buried alive with your guts hanging out."

"In the course of my career, I've legally hanged fifty-three men and one woman. One would think that four more would make no difference, but it does. I dread the morning light like an unrepentant sinner dreads the opening gates of Hell." Lowth shuddered.

"When the time comes, you'll do what you have to do, Mr. Lowth," Tweedy said. "Here, when this is over will you still follow the hangman's trade or will you go into the women's drawers profession with your wife?"

Lowth shook his head, unwilling—or unable—to speak.

"Well, says I, if'n I was in your place, I reckon I could prosper in the drawers profession. Not that I'm an expert in women's fixins, mind, but I know a fine pair of drawers when I see 'em."

"You shut the hell up, old man," Creeds called. "I can die without your damned caterwauling."

"And what if I don't, Silas?" Tweedy taunted. "Where are your guns?"

"Damn you!" the gunman shrieked as he tried to hit Tweedy with the back of his bald head, but only succeeded in butting thin air.

Tweedy cackled. "Ain't much good without your revolvers, are you, sonny? Is it them dead folks o' your'n that's makin' you so plumb out of sorts?"

Creeds was quiet for a while, then he said, almost wistfully, "I always wanted to read *The Decline and Fall of the Roman Empire* by Edward Gibbon. Now I've run out of time."

Shawn was surprised, and Tweedy expressed how he felt. "What the hell, boy? Are you losing your mind?"

"You think about it," Creeds said. "The fall of an empire between the covers of a book. It ain't natural, I tell you."

"Bishops within, barbarians without," Shawn said. "My brother says that sums up the whole three thousand pages."

"You know nothing, O'Brien," Creeds muttered. "You'll die as ignorant as you lived."

"And you're nuts, Silas," Tweedy said. "Like I told you, them spooks is gettin' to you. That Roman stuff ain't any kind of a book for a man like you to read. Dime novels will improve your mind and they're good readin', every damned one of them."

Creeds was silent for a while, then he said, "They're out there, them spooks, waiting for me to get hung. Damn them. They'll drag me to Hell and me with no breakfast in my belly."

"Don't worry, you can eat breakfast in Hell,

Silas. But don't expect no boiled taters. Everything down there is fried." Tweedy snickered.

The Topock Kid erupted, his voice breaking. "What's the matter with you? How the hell can you sit around and talk about books and taters when we're all gonna be hung come morning?"

"What would you like us to talk about, Kid?" Shawn asked.

"See, we're all goin' to die like you said, Kid," Tweedy said, "but there ain't a damn thing we can do about it. Better to be cheerful afore we breathe our last, I say."

The kid was silent for a while, and then admitted, "I don't know how."

"Don't know what?" Tweedy asked. "If you're on speakin' terms with God, you could pray, I guess."

"Hell, I don't know how to pray."

"Neither does ol' Ephraim, but he dies like a gentleman," Tweedy said. "Maybe you should think on that, young feller."

"I don't want to die," The Kid whined.

"Maybe you won't have to, Kid," Lowth said. "I do believe I'm making headway."

"With what, Mr. Lowth?" Tweedy asked, confused.

"Who knows knots better than a hangman, Mr. Tweedy?"

\* \* \*

The burning sky faded like the colors of a dying fish and darkness fell on the land. The air grew cooler and a slight breeze wandered off the gulf and explored, rustling the dry brush like paper.

Down by the shore the cooking fires of the Arabs shimmered scarlet and every now and then outlined the passing silhouette of a man. The corsairs laughed and spoke to each other in their strange language, sounding as though they were glad to be leaving the heathen shores and returning to their homeland.

Shawn felt a slight tugging on the rope, and Lowth said, "My hands are free."

Suddenly he had the undivided attention of his four companions.

"Can you untie the rest of us?" Shawn whispered.

"Yes, but it will take time. The rope that binds us together is knotted behind Mr. Tweedy's back. Somehow I have to reach it."

"Then do it quick, damn you," Creeds ordered. "Don't waste time talking."

"Patience, Silas," Tweedy hissed. "Mr. Lowth is doing his best."

"Unfortunately only my hands are free." Lowth wiggled his fingers. "The rope around our chests also binds my upper arms."

"Is there anything we can do to help you, Thaddeus?" Shawn asked.

"Turn to me as much as you can, Mr. O'Brien. I'll try to untie your hands and then perhaps you can reach the knot at Mr. Tweedy's back."

"An excellent plan, Mr. Lowth," Tweedy congratulated.

"Thank you, Mr. Tweedy," Lowth said. "And one worthy of you, I should add."

"Cut the talk, you damned idiots, and get it done," Creeds insisted.

"Let him be, Creeds," Shawn said. "He's doing his best."

"Damn you, O'Brien. I want the hell away from here."

"We all want away from here." Shawn struggled to turn his back in Lowth's direction, the rope cutting into his chest and shoulders. "As quickly as you can, Thaddeus. As you can tell, Mr. Creeds is getting quite anxious."

The gunman was furious. "The hell with you, O'Brien."

# Chapter Forty-four

Commander Sherburne stood against the bridge rail as the *Kansas* made her slow way along the Sonora coast. The twin beams of the searchlights probed the darkness like questing fingers, closely examining every patch of brush and the sand between. His eyes burned, glued as they'd been for the past hour to his binoculars. Suddenly a column of white light lifted and briefly angled into the black sky before dipping to land again.

"Damn your eyes, steady there." Sherburne swung his head around and saw that the incident had been caused by the older seaman lighting his pipe. Out of respect for the man's white hair and his previous service in two navies, the captain said only, "Concentrate, lads, concentrate."

The sloop's engines thudded into the night quiet and the normally talkative gun crews spoke only in low whispers. The marines maintained a disciplined silence under the stern glares of Lieutenant Wilson and Sergeant Monroe.

The searchlights illuminated the shore for fifty yards inland, bathing the land in a false dawn. Sherburne twice caught sight of skulking coyotes, their eyes gleaming in the light, but of humans there was no trace, only an endless vista of rocky shore and brush and empty desert beyond.

His nerves worn raw, the captain reached for the flask in his pocket. *Damn!* It was empty. He thought he saw a faint smile touch the lips of the stoical helmsman's face. If the man had smiled, Sherburne couldn't blame him. It wasn't every day a seaman witnessed his captain's incompetent leadership as he searched for a will-o'-the-wisp enemy ship that was probably already around the Horn and flying with the trades toward the African coast.

A chart lay open in front of Sherburne with the rock shoals and sandbars clearly marked. The rocks stayed where they were, but sandbars shifted and were treacherous and could easily ground the sloop. The captain worried more, beginning to question his own instincts and decisions.

Only to hear the reassuring sound of his voice, Sherburne said to the helmsman, "Another hour and we'll swing her around, Dawson."

"Aye, aye, sir." The seaman was stone-faced, his voice neutral, neither approving nor disapproving.

The captain envied him. There was something to be said for simply following orders without question.

Commander Sherburne finally admitted to himself that the hunt was hopeless. There was just too much coastline to search, and the *Kansas* was burning coal at an alarming rate. He called Lieutenant Wilson to the bridge. "You can stand the people down, Mr. Wilson. We're going about."

The young officer searched his mind for something sympathetic to say, but could only manage, "I'm so sorry, sir."

"Sorrow doesn't enter into it, Lieutenant. I gambled and lost and there's an end to it."

Wilson looked to shore where the searchlights still explored the darkness. "Damned desert."

"Damned desert, damned slavers, damned poor leadership," Sherburne said. "Do you have any other damns to add, Mr. Wilson?"

"Damned bad luck, Captain."

Sherburne smiled. "A captain makes his own luck, Mr. Wilson. I've failed, that's all."

"I'll stand down the people," Wilson acknowledged.

"Yes. If you please, and—"

A bullet burned across Lieutenant Wilson's left

shoulder at the same instant the report of a rifle was heard.

"I've got him, Cap'n!" the gray-haired seaman cried. The beam of his searchlight pinned a kneeling rifleman to the darkness like a butterfly to a board.

Sherburne gave the orders to stop engines and yelled, "Mr. Wilson, we have them in hand, by God!"

The searchlights exposed running, shouting men on the shore and the masts of the schooner in a narrow inlet. Rifles fired, flaring in the gloom, and bullets ticked into the *Kansas,* caroming off metalwork, splintering wood. A marine went down, cursing.

"Give 'em a broadside, Mr. Kane!" Sherburne yelled through his voice trumpet. "Step lively now!"

The thirteen-year-old midshipman in command of the starboard guns relayed the captain's order. The sloop heeled to her port side as her ten cannons roared, belching gouts of scarlet flame and smoke.

Onshore, canister shot ripped into the living bodies of men, cutting them like a scythe. The foremast of the schooner shattered and fell to her deck.

The guns were reloaded, run out again, and the dreadful barrage continued. Even above the bellowing roar of the carronades, the screams of wounded and dying men could be heard on board the *Kansas.*

Sherburne danced a little jig of delight and called out to Wilson above the din, "Join your landing party, Lieutenant. Try to spare as many captive women as you can without endangering your men."

"Aye, aye, sir." Wilson saluted quickly and disappeared into the white fog of the cannon smoke.

# Chapter Forty-five

"I believe your hands are loose, Mr. O'Brien," Lowth said.

"Well done." Shawn wiggled his fingers to get the blood flowing again.

"Now, can you reach the knot at Mr. Tweedy's back? Once that is untied we will no longer be bound together."

"I'll sure give it a try."

"Don't *try*, O'Brien," Creeds snapped. "Get it done. And Tweedy, you idiot, help him."

"Doin' my best, Silas," Tweedy said, grunting from the effort. "It ain't easy."

Shawn's hands fumbled with the knots behind Tweedy's back. "Almost there, Uriah. Turn toward me a little more."

"Damn you for a pair of fumbling pansies," Creeds cried. "Hurry! We don't have much time."

Before anyone could say another word, a beam

of light glided across the men, turning night into day. A rifle shot sounded, followed by the excited babble of the Arabs.

"What the hell?" Creeds barked.

A wave from the blast of cannon rocked the ground under the sitting men, followed by a storm of shot that ripped through the camp like hail.

Arabs went down, screaming, and one of the schooner's masts erupted into splinters and fell. Toward the shore men were banging away with rifles. A second volley of shot tore them to pieces and they fell like rag dolls.

Shawn continued to work the knot at Tweedy's back, the tops of his fingers bleeding from the harsh rasp of the hemp rope. He heard a sound like an ax hitting a pumpkin, and then blood and brains splashed across the side of his face. Creeds screamed and the rope tightened as he tried to break free.

The Kid sat still as a fence post . . . without his head.

The bloody stump of his neck jetted blood with every faltering pump of his still-beating heart. Creeds screamed again and struggled to his feet.

Men pounded past them, running headlong for the desert, rifles littering the ground behind them. The beams of light followed the Arabs and the cannons roared again, turning the night into a raking, red-hot hell.

"Got it!" Shawn yelled, and suddenly the tension went out of the rope and it fell to his waist. He rose to his feet, got a hand on Tweedy and Lowth, and hauled them erect. "Let's get the hell out of here!"

"Which way?" Tweedy turned his head in one direction, then the other, looking for a safe way to run.

"Anywhere away from those cannons," Shawn directed. "There's a warship of some kind out there." He turned and headed for darkness away from the searchlights, Tweedy and Lowth at his heels.

Lowth turned around briefly. "Look!" Lowth hollered.

Shawn followed the man's pointing finger and witnessed the last fight of Silas Creeds' life.

For some reason known only to himself, Creeds had headed for the schooner.

Two mounted men came at him, riding the horses of Moss's dead gunfighters. One was the Arab sheik, holding a struggling woman in the saddle in front of him. The woman, who seemed to be unconscious, was bundled up in a blanket and her face was not visible. Hakim's rich robes billowing in the wind, dust spurting from his mount's galloping hooves, he held his deadly curved sword upraised in his right hand. Beside him rode another Arab, armed with a revolver.

Creeds dived for the ground, rolled, and came up with a rifle. Getting down on one knee, he raised the gun to his shoulder. He and the Arab with the revolver fired at the same time. The Arab missed. Creeds didn't. The Arab screeched, threw up his hand, and tumbled off his horse.

With the sheik only yards away, Creeds worked the notoriously balky bolt of the Lebel, but the gun was jammed. He grabbed the barrel and swung it like a club at the Arab's rearing horse. An excellent rider, Hakim swung his mount aside and his sword came down in a glittering arc. Creeds' head jumped from his shoulders and rolled on the ground.

Marines were already landing on the beach, but Hakim trotted back to his fallen companion and called out, "Good luck on your journey, Hassan, my friend." Then he turned his horse and galloped into the desert with the woman.

Unarmed, Shawn could only watch helplessly as the Arab vanished into the darkness.

"Raise them hands, boys, or I'll drop you."

A grim-faced marine advanced on Shawn and the others, his rifle bayoneted.

Tweedy shook his head. "It's all right. We're Americans, just like you."

"I don't give a damn what you are," the marine "Get them mitts up."

"Do as he says," Shawn said, lifting his hands. "After all this, I'd hate to be killed by our own side."

Tweedy clawed for the sky. "Truer words was never spoke, O'Brien."


The left arm of Lieutenant Wilson's coat was stained with blood, all of it his own, but the scarlet spatters across his face were from the Arab he'd killed in single combat with the sword. He was interrogating Shawn, who told his story quickly. "And your Miss Davenport was among the captive women?"

Wilson turned to a marine. "You can put your rifle away. I'll be quite all right."

The marine saluted and left, and Sahwn said, "Are all the women accounted for?"

"Yes," Wilson answered. "But I'm afraid that includes three dead from our shellfire and one missing. That is, according to the other ladies."

Shawn knew the answer to his next question, but asked it anyway. "And the missing woman is Julia?"

"I'm afraid so, Mr. O'Brien." Wilson's round face was apologetic.

Tweedy said, "Damn him, if that Arab has harmed my Trixie, I'll—"

"Trixie?" Wilson repeated, puzzled.

Before Tweedy could answer, Shawn said quickly, "Trixie Lee is, ah, Miss Davenport's stage name."

"I see. Well, all I can do is offer you my deepest sympathy, Mr. O'Brien."

"You're not going to help us look for her?" Shawn said.

"I'm afraid not," Wilson said. "We must coal at the earliest opportunity and transport those poor women to San Francisco. And there's a child involved."

"Is the baby's mother dead?" Lowth put in, alarmed.

"No, she's quite well. I regret to say that the three dead captives were all Chinese women and very young." Wilson met Shawn's eyes. "We can transport you gentlemen to San Francisco, if that is your wish."

"No, Lieutenant, that won't be necessary." Shawn shook his head at the invitation.

"Mr. Tweedy? Mr. Lowth?"

"I reckon I'll find my intended and then ride north with her into bear country," Tweedy said.

"And this quest is not yet over," Lowth said. "I'll stick with Mr. O'Brien."

"As you wish." Wilson hesitated a few seconds and said, "This is hardly the time to ask a favor, but one of the captive women is a very special case."

"How so?" Shawn said.

"She was a bride who was taken by the slavers on her wedding day along with four other women," Wilson said. "The others are happy to go to San Francisco with us, but the bride—"

"Her name?" Shawn interrupted.

"She doesn't speak English very well, but I gather her name is Consuelo. She wants to return to her village." The lieutenant shrugged. "A most singular request since her husband and all the males in the village were killed by the Arabs."

"Where is the place?" Shawn asked.

"On the coast to the south, I believe. She will point you the way."

"Why not just drop her off your ownself, sonny?" Tweedy questioned.

"She's never been on a ship before and she doesn't trust us," Wilson says. "She thinks we may be slavers, and who can blame her?"

"She can come with us," Shawn said. "I don't see how we can refuse."

Wilson sighed in relief. "Thank you, Mr. O'Brien. That's a load off my mind. She's a very pretty girl, and a terrible fate could befall her if she set off alone."

He saluted as a splendid officer in the blue and gold of a navy commander joined the group. Wilson made the introductions and Sherburne listened as his second-in-command told him about the kidnap of Miss Davenport.

"I'm damned sorry, O'Brien," Sherburne said. "That's the most rotten bad luck."

"Yes, I guess it is," Shawn agreed.

The commander turned his attention to Wilson. "You have the butcher's bill, Mr. Wilson?"

"One marine dead and two wounded, Captain. Three of the captive women killed and a few slightly wounded, mostly from flying splinters."

"And the slavers?"

"Eighteen dead." Wilson looked a little uncomfortable. "None wounded."

"The rest fled into the desert, I suppose."

"Indeed, sir."

"Well, a good night's work nonetheless, Mr. Wilson."

"Thank you, sir."

"Now, go see the surgeon and have your wounds attended to."

After the lieutenant left, Sherburne turned to Shawn, "May I offer you and the other gentlemen the hospitality of my ship?"

"Thank you, Captain, but I must refuse. Miss Davenport is an employee at my father's ranch and I promised to bring her back."

"I wish I could assist you, Mr. O'Brien, but I must seek a coaling station."

"I understand, Captain."

Sherburne extended his hand. "Well, good luck to you."

"Thankee, Cap'n," Tweedy said. "Now we're lugging a female along, something tells me we're gonna need all the luck we can get."

# Chapter Forty-six

The dead had been buried, what could be found of the victims of the suicide blast in ammunition boxes. A prize crew under the command of Lieutenant Wilson boarded the slave schooner.

Shawn, Tweedy, Lowth, and Consuelo stood by saddled horses that had escaped the slaughter. In silence, they watched the *Kansas* tow the sailing ship into the channel. In the thin morning light, a mist on the water, the sloop set a course south, dragging the schooner a cable's length behind her.

After a few minutes Shawn and the others were alone on a battlefield, surrounded by fresh rectangles in the sand marking the graves of the uneasy dead.

"Mount up. Let's get it done." Shawn helped the Mexican woman, still dressed in her tattered wedding finery, into the saddle, then mounted himself.

Tweedy swung into the saddle and immediately slid a scavenged Winchester from the boot under his knee. "Stranger comin'."

Shawn's eyes searched the distance to the north. A rider drew closer through the sea mist, holding a rifle upright on his thigh. The man sat his horse like a sack of grain, his range clothes much worn and ragged, and his great beak of a nose overhung a huge dragoon mustache that had not felt the clip of scissors in a three-month. His mount was a scrawny yellow mustang the size of a mountain goat.

Shawn smiled. "It's my brother Jake."

"Hell." Tweedy peered at the man, "Are you sure?"

"Sure I'm sure. Who else on God's green earth looks like that?"

Jacob rode close to the three waiting men and touched the brim of his hat. "Howdy."

Shawn nodded. "Good to see you again, Jake."

"Likewise, I'm sure," Jacob looked at Tweedy. "You must be Uriah Tweedy. I'm pleased to see you've recovered from your wound and are prospering. That's a five-hundred-dollar hoss you got under you."

"He ain't mine, beggin' your pardon, Jake,"

Tweedy said. "Only thing of mine here is the duds I'm wearing an' they ain't worth ten cents."

His eyes wary, Jacob looked at Lowth. "And this gentleman?"

Lowth raised his hat. "Thaddeus Lowth by name, and Thaddeus Lowth by nature, Mr. O'Brien. I am a hangman by profession."

"An honorable calling," Jacob replied. He turned his attention to Shawn again and smiled. "Dare I ask if you've finally taken a bride?"

"No, she's not mine, but she's part of a long story, Jake."

"So I missed all the fun, huh?"

"All but the last act, Jake," Shawn said. "And that's still to come."

"Tell it."

And Shawn did, describing his search for Julia that began in Santa Fe and ended with the cannonade that destroyed the slavers.

"And now you're going after this Arab fella?" Jacob asked.

"He has Julia."

"For a schoolteacher, she's sure caused a lot of grief," Jacob opined.

"She's my intended," Tweedy said. "I'd go to the ends of the earth to find her."

"Spoken like a true romantic," Jacob said. "My hat's off to you, Uriah."

"Thankee, Jake," Tweedy said. "Truer words

was never spoke. Uriah Tweedy is a romantic to the core, fer sure."

"Mind if I tag along?" Jacob asked. "I never took a pot at an Arab sheik before."

"What if I said, no?" Shawn answered with a question of his own.

Jacob shrugged. "I'd tag along anyway."

Shawn smiled. "Let's ride, brother."


They came on their first dead Arab seaman shortly before the sun reached its highest point in the sky.

Bearded and slight, the man had been stripped naked, then hacked to death. His hands and fore-arms were cut to ribbons, bloody testimony to the fact that he'd tried to ward off the savage blows that killed him.

Tweedy stepped out of the leather and kneeled beside the body. After a closer inspection, he rose to his feet. "Them are machete wounds. Seen the like afore on a Mexican feller who got chopped up fer sparkin' another man's woman."

He opened his hand and let some silver coins drop to the sand. "Whoever kilt him was not in-terested in robbery. Them's silver pesos."

"But why was he murdered in such a horrible fashion, Mr. Tweedy?" Lowth couldn't make sense of the murder.

"Your guess is as good as mine, Mr. Lowth," Tweedy said.

Consuelo spat in the direction of the dead man, her pretty face twisted in anger. "Dirty pig."

Tweedy nodded. "He's all of that, honey. And maybe that's the reason for the cuttin'."

Shawn stood in the stirrups and stared across the desert. Far to the east the high Sierras stood out in purple relief against the sky, seemingly as remote as the mountains of the moon. "I reckon we'll find more dead Arabs."

Tweedy said, "Yeah, including that sheik feller."

"Maybe," Shawn said. "That one seems to have more lives than a cat."

Thirty minutes later, they rode up on three dead men. Like the first one, they were mutilated, and one Arab had both his hands chopped off.

But there was another with them. The ancient hag who'd chosen the manner of the white captives' deaths sat hunched over the body of a young man, his bloody head on her lap.

Tweedy couldn't believe what he was seeing. "Hell. It's the damned witch. Looks like she found her long-lost son."

"Or her husband, Mr. Tweedy," Lowth put in.

"I didn't see her after the warship started firing," Shawn said.

"Well she escaped somehow," Jacob said. "Ugly, ain't she?"

Consuelo slid from her horse, crossed herself, and approached the old woman. She said something in Spanish none of the others understood, but she was met with a mute silence. The crone didn't even look at her.

"I guess she doesn't talk your lingo," Tweedy said.

The Mexican woman ripped the top of her dress and removed a thin silver chain and cross from around her neck. She pulled back the crone's hood, revealing an almost bald head with a few wisps of white hair. Grabbing as much hair as she could, she jerked back the old woman's head and pressed the silver cross into her cheek.

The crone screeched and pushed Consuelo's hand away.

"Witch!" Consuelo crossed herself again, hiked up her dress, and remounted her horse. In the saddle boot under her knee was a rifle.

"What do we do with the old dear, Shawn?" Jacob asked.

"Leave her. She'll die out here without water."

Lowth agreed. "I must admit, that I feel a certain animosity toward the lady. She is not a nice person."

"Not a candidate for your wife's bloomers, huh, Mr. Lowth?" Tweedy said, grinning.

"No indeed, Mr. Tweedy. My wife wouldn't sell her undergarments to such a vile person."

Shawn kneed his horse forward. "God, those dead men are starting to stink. Let's get away from here." Behind him, he heard the harsh whisper of a rifle leaving the scabbard and the *chunk-chunk* of the lever.

Even as Shawn turned, Consuelo fired.

Even holding the Winchester straight out in front of her, she scored a hit. The bullet hit the crone's right clavicle and ranged downward into her chest. At close range the big .44-40 had a devastating effect on such a frail body, and later Tweedy would swear the old woman literally exploded.

Before Consuelo could rack the Winchester a second time, Jacob jerked the smoking rifle from her hands. *"Está muerta."*

The old woman lay on her side, her eyes wide open in death.

Consuelo spat in the crone's direction. *"Vieja bruja!"*

Tweedy shook his head. "A lesson to us all, Mr. Lowth. Never ruin a woman's weddin', or even be pals with them as did."

"Indeed, Mr. Tweedy," Lowth said. "Hell hath no fury—"

"If you two old philosophers are quite finished, let's ride." Shawn interrupted. "We've got ground to cover before dark."

They rode away from the place of death and Tweedy again took the point.

Somewhere ahead of them was Sheik Abdul-Basir Hakim, and each and every one of them had a reason to kill him.

# Chapter Forty-seven

The sun was hot and the mighty Sheik Abdul-Basir Hakim, scourge of the high seas and en-slaver of the infidel, was thirsty as a sweating Turkish peasant laboring in the wheat fields of Izmir.

A great lord should never know thirst, and Hakim felt a burning resentment.

He drew rein on his tired horse and stared across shimmering heat to the distant mountains, sharply outlined against the sky like a broken saw blade. He made a face. "Pah!" The mountains were not for him, deserted by God and man. He was a prince of the sea and that was where his destiny lay.

The pursuit must be over, Hakim decided. The infidels would not chase him and the woman far in any case. And if they caught up, what then? The sheik smiled. The unbelievers would not try too hard, for they feared him as women fear the desert lion and dare not venture too close to his claws and fangs. He could turn south and make a loop toward the coast. He had more than enough gold coins in his money belt to see him home.

Pretending a concern she did not feel, Julia interrupted the sheik's thoughts. "Leave me here. I'm only slowing you down."

Hakim smiled. "The thought is tempting and I've already considered it. But I may keep you as a concubine for a while." He nuzzled Julia's neck. "The desert heat brings out the fragrance of a woman's skin as the spring rain does a flower."

Julia's anger flared and she tried to push the man away from her. "Leave me the hell alone!" she yelled, pounding her fists on the Arab's chest.

"A tigress," Hakim grinned. "But I'll soon tame you with the whip."

"You'll never have a moment's rest," Julia promised. "I'll kill you in your sleep."

The sheik thought this vastly amusing and tilted back his head, roaring with laughter as he swung his horse away from the mountains and took the direction he favored. The animal was exhausted, and the sheik drew his sword and slapped its lathered flanks with the flat of the blade. His mount broke into a shambling trot, and Hakim pushed it into a canter.

He'd kill the horse, he knew, but, Allah willing, not until he was within sight of the sea.

An hour later, as the sun hung like a brass ball in the sky to the west, Hakim glanced behind him and the blood in his veins froze. A large dust cloud kicked up by many feet spun into the air just a mile or so behind him. The sheik's eyes narrowed. Was it the infidels? The seamen from the accursed ship that had ruined all his plans?

Damn its soul to hell, his horse was dying under him, wheezing and lathered white. It could not last much longer. How many miles could he beat out of it?

Hakim shook his head. Not many. The sorry beast was on its last legs.

But then a thought came to the sheik that made him smile. The American sailors would not dare chase him across the desert. That much was clear. But his loyal crew would—those who had escaped the infidel cannons.

That was it! His own men were on his trail, raising a cloud of dust as they hurried to be with him.

Hakim grinned. Allah be praised! Now he was no hunted fugitive but a warlord with followers who would die for him.

"Look," he cried to Julia. "Allah be praised! My men are coming for me! We will go greet them so they may once again bask in the presence of their lord." He slapped his horse with his sword and the animal lurched forward.

Shrieking the undulating battle cry of the Bedouin, Hakim beat the horse into a canter and its hooves pounded over hard-packed sand. As he drew closer he expected to hear answering cries from his men. But the dust cloud came on in silence, relentless as a wave at sea.

Suddenly, Hakim was wary. Through gaps in the yellow cloud he caught glimpses of white-clad legs, not the black sailor pants of his crew.

He savagely drew rein and studied the dust more closely and the ugly truth dawned on him. They were rabbits! The filthy Mexican peons he'd hunted for sport.

Once again Hakim's sword slithered from the scabbard. He raised the shining blade above his head and snarled his rage. He would scatter the vile peasant rabble like wheat chaff in a wind.

The mighty lord Hakim threw Julia from the saddle, roared his battle cry, and charged.


The horse was a big American stud named Blue Boy, and he'd been born and raised in the green pastures of Kentucky. Bred for speed and stamina, he'd been a hired gunman's charger since he was four years old and he'd proven himself time and time again in battle or in the chase.

But even Blue Boy's strong heart could not take the punishment Hakim had dealt him.

Fifty yards from the dust cloud . . . he faltered and pecked a couple of times.

Thirty yards . . . his breathing was labored, and his knees started to buckle.

Twenty yards . . . Blue Boy's noble heart burst, and he was already dead when he cartwheeled to the ground and threw Hakim over his head.

Sheik Abdul-Basir Hakim lay stunned for a few moments, his sword a couple of yards away from him. He saw the Mexicans running toward him, blades in their hands, and he dived for his scimitar.

Too late.

Hands reached out for Hakim and tore off his clothes. He sprawled on the sand naked as the day he was born.

Bellowing his anger, he fought the peons and struggled to get to his feet, determined to die like a warrior, not a dog.

But a dozen men, who badly wanted to kill him like a dog, dragged him to a hedgehog cactus and threw him on top of its spines. Men hauled at his wrists and ankles and Hakim was spread-eagled. He roared his outrage at a great and mighty lord being given such treatment.

Then the old women came to him and Hakim began to taste fear.

They were survivors from the village he'd

ravaged and mothers of the men he'd killed on his rabbit hunt. He looked into their faces and saw no mercy, only a silent hate burning in their eyes like black fire.

The lord Hakim did not scream when cactus spines were forced into his skin and set alight, a trick the Mexicans had learned from the Apaches who had taught them much.

He did not scream as the women, solemn as the Sphinx, their faces empty of expression, used their knives to cut slices from his skin.

He did not scream when the wife of the dead village blacksmith showed him the iron hammer that would soon shatter his bones.

But when the honed knives began to carve away his manhood . . .

Well, Sheik Abdul Basir-Hakim screamed then all right.

# Chapter Forty-eight

"They didn't leave much of him for the buzzards, did they?" Uriah Tweedy shuddered as he stopped his horse in front of Hakim's dead body.

"He looks kind of like one of those jigsaw puzzles children play with," Thaddeus Lowth commented, stopping too.

Shawn turned in the saddle. "How long you figure it took him to die, Jake?"

"Too long," Jacob said. "See the cactus spines burned down to his skin? That's an old Apache torture."

Tweedy dismounted and looked at the footprints around the scarlet stain, large as a steer hide, surrounding the Arab's body.

"Judging by the sandal and barefoot tracks, I'd say Mexican peons done fer him." Tweedy nodded to the dead horse. "Deservedly so, if only for riding that hoss to death." He looked around him. "What happened to Trixie? Did the Mexicans take her?"

"I don't know," Shawn said. "But I sure aim to find out."

Tweedy mounted his horse. "Then let's ride. It will be dark soon."

Jacob gathered the reins and said to Consuelo, "The man who murdered your husband is dead."

Consuelo stared at the butchered corpse for a long time, then lowered her head and sobbed quietly.

Jacob, no hand with crying women, turned to his brother. "Shawn, can you help her?"

Shawn moved his horse close to the woman and put an arm around her. She sobbed on his shoulder while he gently stroked her hair and whispered cooing sounds, as he would with a baby. Jacob watched and thought it very well done.

From a distance, came the thin cry of another woman, begging for help.

Jacob's gaze scanned the desert, but it was Tweedy who spotted Julia. "Over there." He pointed to a figure on the ground not too far away. "See her?"

He turned his horse around and galloped in the direction of the fallen woman, Jacob close behind him.

They swung out of the saddles and Tweedy knelt by Julia's side. "Are you all right?"

"I hit the ground hard." Julia stretched out her right leg and hiked up her skirt. "I think my ankle is broken."

Tweedy looked at Jacob. "What do you think, Jake?"

"It looks swollen. We'd better check it over." Jacob kneeled in front of Julia, unlaced the high-heeled boot, and ran his hand over her ankle. "I don't think it's broken. But you've got a bad sprain."

He took her hands and pulled the woman to her feet. He dropped her hands and smiled. Damn, but she was pretty.

Julia tried a few tentative steps. "I'm sorry. I can't walk."

"I'll carry you," Tweedy offered.

"You might hurt your back," Julia protested.

"No I won't. It's the least I kin do fer my intended bride."

"Uriah—"

Ignoring what Julia had been about to say, Tweedy swung her into his arms. "No need to thank me fer becomin' your husband, Trixie. I'm doin' it right willingly."

Julia threw a despairing look at Jacob, who smiled and said nothing.

It seemed that poor old Tweedy was headed for a big disappointment.

\* \* \*

Flies had found the Arab's carcass and Shawn and the others left the place of terrible death and headed back toward the coast.

But after barely a mile, Consuelo suddenly swung her horse around and cantered back into the desert.

"Let her go," Shawn said as Jacob made a move to go after her. "She's heading back to her people where she belongs."

"Seems to me, that little gal just ain't right in the head," Tweedy said. "What's your opinion on that, Mr. Lowth?"

"Sadly, I concur, Mr. Tweedy," Lowth agreed. "The Arab didn't kill her, but he wounded her mind."

"Her people will take care of her," Shawn pointed out as they continued to ride.

"I believe in second chances, Mr. O'Brien," Lowth continued. "Perhaps she'll be given one."

"Truer words was never spoke, Mr. Lowth," Tweedy said. "After what that gal's been through, she deserves a second chance."

"Well, good luck to her." Jacob watched Consuelo disappear in a distant cloud of dust, then swung his horse back in the direction of the coast.

Julia was behind him in the saddle, an extra burden that did not go unnoticed or unpunished by his nasty mustang.

* * *

Thanks to the Irish engineer who stopped his train on the tracks to let Jacob and the others board, two days later they rode the cushions of an Albuquerque-bound cannonball, and Julia broke the bad news to Uriah Tweedy.

She let the old man down as gently as she could. "I'm just not ready for marriage, Uriah. I want to go on teaching at Dromore. I don't think the life you offer is for me."

For his part, Tweedy was stunned. "Ol' Ephraim will be coming out of his winter sleep pretty soon. You an' me should be hitched and huntin' by then."

Julia shook her head. "I'm sorry, Uriah. I like you, but I don't love you as a wife should love her husband."

"Is there another man? Just give me his name and I'll—"

"There's no other man, Uriah. I look ahead to see my future and it's at Dromore."

"Trixie, you're making a bad mistake. Is that not so, Mr. Lowth?"

Lowth laid his cup back on the saucer and glanced around the dining car, as though he feared being overhead. Shawn was pretending to be serious, but Jacob smiled into his coffee cup, his mouth hidden by his mustache.

"Mr. Tweedy," Lowth said, "you're a well set-up

fellow and you prosper in your chosen profession. In other words, you are true blue in every way, shape, and form."

"Truer words was never spoke, Mr. Lowth." Tweedy sat back in his seat and beamed as though Lowth had fairly stated his attributes.

"But," Lowth continued, "Miss Davenport is a fair, delicate creature, not suited for the rigors of mountain camps and bear hunts. Alas, your proposal of marriage must founder on the rock of that truth."

Tweedy looked at Julia. "I understand what you're saying, my love. But I can't give up the only life I know and become the husband of a schoolma'am."

Julia saw her chance and took it. As melodramatic as any actress, she said, "Then we must part, Uriah, and go our own ways."

"I know I've broken your heart, Trixie," Tweedy murmured sadly.

"It will mend in time." Julia continued the melodrama. "At least I hope it will."

Tweedy was lost in silence for a few moments, giving thought to the situation. Perking up, he smiled warmly. "Of course, I could give up on ol' Ephraim and hunt wolves for a livin'. Would that be more to your liking?"

Julia shook her head. "Uriah, you're a bear hunter, strong, reliant, and brave. When I lie in bed at night just before I drop off to sleep, I want to see you in my mind's eye, out there in the wilderness, just you and Ephraim."

"But I don't hunt at night," Tweedy said, confused.

"Well, I'll see you in my mind's eye in the morning light then," Julia responded.

Jacob, grinning, held up his sack of tobacco and papers. "May I beg your indulgence, ma'am?"

"Why, of course." Julia nodded.

Tweedy was dispirited. "Her heart's broken, Jake."

"She'll get over it, Uriah. In time," Jacob promised.

"Time is a great healer, Miss Davenport," Lowth pointed out.

"It is, but not when it's a man like me who captured the lady in question's heart," Tweedy said, a great sadness in his voice.

Shawn coughed uncontrollably and covered his mouth with a fist. Finally, his eyes watering, he gasped, "Anybody else feel like a drink?"

# Chapter Forty-nine

"So Uriah Tweedy is in his mountains, Julia is back in her school, and all's well that ends well." Shawn was in the study of Dromore. His brothers, Lorena, and Luther Ironside sat in various places throughout the room. Colonel O'Brien stood on the pink hearthstone he and Ironside had dug out of the mesa for Saraid when they first arrived on the shaggy range that later became Dromore.

"What happened to Thaddeus Lowth?" Samuel asked.

"He says he's given up the hanging profession and plans to help his wife with her business."

"She makes drawers for genteel young ladies," Jacob informed.

The colonel snorted. "I'd much prefer to be a hangman."

"Oh, I don't know," Luther Ironside said,

"there's a lot to be said for a fine pair of drawers on a woman. Why, I mind one time I was frequenting a cathouse down El Paso way, and—"

"Please, Luther." Lorena cut in. "Keep that particular reminiscence to yourself."

"All I was going to say is that Fat Flora, one o' the whores, wore this pair of—"

"That will do, Luther," Shamus stopped him. "You heard what Lorena said, and my boys are present."

"Hell, Colonel, I've told them the story before," Ironside argued.

"Good, then they don't need to hear it again." Shamus looked at his youngest son. "Do you have any plans, Jacob?"

"Nothing immediate, Colonel. Maybe after the cold months."

"Then perhaps you'll stay at Dromore a while. We could use you on the spring gather."

"I can't stay around for that, Pa," Jacob objected.

"You're a top hand, Jake," Ironside insisted. "Be glad to have you, ain't that so, Sam?"

Samuel nodded. "Jake's always welcome when there's cowboying to be done."

Unhappy about the direction of the conversation, Lorena quickly changed the subject. "Will you play the piano for us after dinner tonight, Jacob?"

"Of course. It will be my pleasure."

Shawn turned to the colonel. "How are the legs holding up, Pa?"

"Pretty good. At least I can walk without pain."

"The colonel has walked so much he's used up enough boot leather to half sole the whole Confederate army," Ironside said.

"Luther is right. I can toddle around quite well." Shamus flexed his knees and smiled. "See, almost as good as new."

The light was fleeing the day and Lorena lit the lamps. Outside, there was no snow, but the night was cold and the wind came from the north.

"We have parlor maids for that, Lorena," Shamus pointed out.

"There are some things I like doing for myself, Colonel, and one of them is lighting the lamps. They're less smoky when I do it myself."

"Where is little Shamus?" the colonel asked. "Will we see him before dinner?"

"He's asleep at the moment, Shamus. I've told Sarah to bring him right down when he wakes." Lorena smiled. "You and Luther wear him out with all your horseplay."

"The boy's got to learn to be tough, Lorena," Luther said.

"And I'm sure that's a lesson you'll teach him very well, Luther," Lorena said dryly.

"Damn right," Ironside replied, pleased.

Shamus stared into the glowing bowl of his pipe, then lifted his head. "It seems that tranquility has once again returned to Dromore. Let's hope it remains this way."

"Amen, Colonel," Samuel agreed.

But then the letter came, and the tranquil days were over before they'd even begun.

It was delivered early the next day by a twelve-year-old boy riding a tired pony who told the butler he couldn't give it to anybody but Luther Ironside.

The boy was silent as the butler led him to the study where the O'Briens and Ironside had gathered once again. He found his voice as he followed the butler into the room. "And Sheriff Clitherow says I'll recognize Mr. Ironside because he's a tall, hard-faced old reprobate with a mean eye."

The boy handed the note to Ironside. "I guess it must be for you."

Shawn laughed. "A letter from one of your close friends, huh, Luther?"

Ironside turned the envelope over in his hands. "You got mud on this, boy,"

"Hell, mister, I rode all the way from Lordsburg. You try riding that trail without gettin' mud on stuff."

"Keep a civil tongue in your head, boy," Ironside commanded. "Or you'll get the strap end of my belt."

"Luther, let the boy be," Shamus said. "He's had a long, hard ride. Why don't you read the letter?"

"I recollect a Clitherow, Colonel," Ironside said. "One time I got unhorsed and he shot a Yankee off'n me who was about to stick a bayonet in my brisket."

"I remember that." Shamus nodded. "His name was Jim Clitherow, a captain of horse artillery as I recollect."

"I wonder if this is from the same man, Colonel."

"There's one way to find out, Luther," Shawn pointed out. "Read the letter."

Jacob leaned forward in his chair. "Out loud, Luther."

Ironside reached inside his vest and produced a pair of wire eyeglasses, perching them on the end of his nose. He coughed, coughed again, then read:

"Dear Luther, I hope you are in good health. I am fine, but for a touch of the rheumatisms in cold weather. Ah well, we're not getting any younger, ha, ha. I was a deputy marshal in Lordsburg until last summer when I took the post of city sheriff in a town called Recoil in the Playas Valley country.

"Well, things were fine for a spell, but recently we've been plagued by night riders who are killing and robbing folks. Last night they shot up my town and killed Fred Rawlings who owns the general store and has a simple son. Now folks are scared, because farms and ranches have been raided and livestock stolen and buildings set on fire."

Ironside looked up from the letter. "He's got his problems, don't he?"

"Please continue, Luther," Shamus encouraged. "You read very well."

"Where was I? Oh yeah, 'livestock stolen and buildings set on fire.'" Ironside continued to read. "The people of Recoil don't lack for sand, but they don't stand a chance against the night riders as they are professional killers. I do what I can, but I'm only one man and the outlaws have no fear of the law.

"But here's the worst part. There are maybe two dozen night riders involved in this terror and the folks around here say they are not human. Luther, this will surprise you, but the outlaws have skulls for faces. Are they alive or dead? I don't know.

"I can't handle this myself and I've sent for a U.S. Marshal but when he'll get here is anybody's guess. Luther, once during the late war in which we were both honored to serve, I was of some help to you and you said that if I ever needed a favor I was to call on you. Well, I'm calling in that favor to save my town and maybe the whole valley.

"Can you come, Luther? I know of no one else who has a gun-fighting reputation like yours and I need you at my side.

"The bearer of this letter will direct you to Recoil should you agree to take up arms again in the cause of justice and liberty."

Ironside folded the letter and said, "Yours respectfully, Jas Clitherow Esq." He looked at Shamus. "I owe him, Colonel."

Shamus made no answer to Ironside, but said to the boy, "What's your name, son?"

"Sam, sir. Sam Brown."

"How old are you, Sam?"

"Twelve, sir, I think."

"Do you have a ma and a pa?"

"No, sir. I'm a foundling. Sheriff Clitherow lets me sleep in the jail cell behind his office. And he's teaching me my ciphers and how to read and write."

"Well, Sam," Shamus said, "you understood the contents of the sheriff's letter?"

"Yes, sir."

"Does he fairly and factually state his case?"

"Sheriff Clitherow told it right. Them night riders are scary, all dressed in black robes, and they're skeletons, not real men. They've killed a lot of folks. I liked old man Rawlings. He gave me cheese and crackers and a soda pop if I'd play with his son."

"I suspect there's more to this than stealing a few dollars out of a granger's money box," Shamus said. "Those boys are human, all right, but what do they really want?"

"There's one way to find out, Colonel. I'm heading for Recoil," Ironside declared.

"Hell of a name for a town," Jacob commented.

"The town was started by a miner who bought a new Sharps Fifty rifle, then fought a battle with Comanches. He said the recoil of the rifle near killed him because he'd been shot in his right shoulder afore." The boy smiled. "Sheriff Clitherow told me that."

"Then it must be true," Ironside said. "You heed Mr. Clitherow an' you'll learn something, boy."

"Lorena, could you take young Sam to the kitchen and see that he's fed? He looks sharp set."

"Of course, Colonel." Lorena ushered the boy out of the room.

"I don't know if I'll be back in time for the spring gather, Colonel," Ironside said.

Shamus nodded. "I plan to give that some thought, Luther. We'll talk again after dinner." He glanced around the room. "All of us."

# Chapter Fifty

"Did you see the night riders, Sam?" Lorena asked.

The boy chewed his ham sandwich, then swallowed. "I sure did, ma'am. The night they killed Mr. Rawlings."

"What happened?"

The boy looked around the kitchen, satisfying himself that the staff was busily preparing dinner. "When the skeleton men rode into town and started shooting, Mr. Rawlings grabbed a shotgun and ran out of his store. He was working late that night because he'd ciphers to do."

"His account ledgers, huh?" Lorena asked to keep the conversation going.

"I guess so, ma'am."

"And where were you, Sam?"

"I was on the boardwalk, walking back to the sheriff's office."

"And what happened to Mr. Rawlings?"

"Well, he upped his shotgun, but before he could draw a bead, one of the night riders shot him." Sam pointed between his eyebrows. "Right there."

"Where was the sheriff?"

"Sheriff Clitherow ran out of his office and shot at the night riders with his Colt gun, but they all rode away, hooting and hollering."

"And they were skeletons, you say?"

"Yes ma'am. One time me and Mr. Rawlings' son came on the body of a dead Indian out by Hatchet Gap, and his face had no skin left on it. That's what the night riders looked like."

"Just bare skulls?"

"Yeah, that's what they were all right, ma'am."

Lorena rose to her feet. "Drink your milk, Sam. And if you're still hungry, ask one of the kitchen staff for another sandwich."

"Well, I'm surely hungry, ma'am."

"Anna, can Sam have some of the roast beef we're having for dinner?"

"Of course, Miss Lorena." The woman's dark face split in a smile. "Been a long time since I fed a hungry boy, now that the O'Brien brothers are all growed up."

\* \* \*

Jacob O'Brien played Brahms on the parlor grand, but his ears remained tuned to the conversation going on around him.

"I don't understand the skeleton thing." Lorena shook her head. "Sam swears the outlaws he saw had faces like skulls."

"Masks probably," Samuel guessed. "I imagine they'd be fairly easy to carve out of wood by someone who knows how."

"Nobody's put a bullet into one of those boys yet," Jacob said from the piano. "That's strange."

Shawn grinned. "Maybe they're bad shots down there on the Playas."

"Maybe," Jacob acknowledged, "but it's still strange."

"Hell, I'll shoot a walking skeleton as fast as I'd shoot any other man," Ironside boasted. "They don't scare me none."

"Now there speaks a true hero of the South."

"Seems to me the bullet would go right through a skeleton," Patrick said, owlish behind his round glasses. "Unless you hit a bone, of course. Plenty of those on a skeleton rider."

"I'm going down there and I'll put it to the test," Ironside insisted. "Damn right I am."

"You're not going alone, Luther," Shamus said quietly.

"I figured Jake might ride with me, Colonel. What do you say, Jake, are you—"

"Jacob is not riding with you, Luther, I need him here at Dromore. Shawn's already been through enough down Sonora way and I want Samuel and Patrick here for the gather."

"Then I'll go it alone, Colonel," Ironside said, his face stiff.

"No, you won't. I'm going with you."

Shamus's statement fell on the others like a blow and for a few moments the parlor was silent as an empty courtroom.

Finally, his words dropping into the quiet like rocks into an iron bucket, Samuel broke the silence. "Pa, your legs won't hold up to a trip like that."

"And it will come to shooting, Pa," Shawn pointed out. "You haven't shot any kind of gun in years."

"Luther, have you anything to add?" Shamus asked dryly.

Ironside grinned. "Be like the old days, Colonel."

Shamus turned to his son at the piano. "Jacob?"

"You're a grown man, Colonel," Jacob said, his fingers moving over the keyboard. "A man's got to do what he thinks is right."

"Hell, Jake, Pa could get killed down there," Samuel argued. He turned to his father. "And the Playas is nothing but miles of empty desert.

How are you going to stay in the saddle, a man of your years?"

Shamus smiled. "A man of my years will manage very well, Samuel."

"Damn right." Ironside nodded his head in agreement.

Ever the intellectual, Patrick pointed out, "There are a few mining towns on the Playas. I don't think it's a complete wasteland."

"That's right, Pat, encourage him," Samuel said.

Shamus, stiff-kneed, poured himself another drink, then sat by the fire. "I believe the town of Recoil, not the Playas, is the key to this mystery."

"Pa, there is no mystery," Samuel argued, "just a bunch of renegades dressed in scary costumes—"

"Robbing and killing people," Shamus said. "The question is why, and therein lies the mystery."

"Probably to get money for whiskey and whores," Samuel said. He was slightly angry and his face was flushed.

"Outlaws rob banks for that, not struggling grangers and small ranchers. Besides—"

"Then let Jacob go with Luther," Samuel railed.

Shamus blinked his displeasure at the interruption. "Besides, Jim Clitherow saved Luther's life. A man who fought beside me, helped me build Dromore, and remains my closet friend."

"Damn right." Luther said.

"And in addition to that, as though any other reason is needed, Clitherow wore the gray, and I won't turn my back on him."

"So you're still determined to go?" Samuel in disbelief.

"I am going, Samuel," Shamus said emphatically.

"Let it go, Sam," Jacob warned. "You know as well as I do that when the colonel makes up his mind about a thing it would take ten yoke of oxen to move him off his position."

"Damn right," Ironside pounded the arm of his chair again.

"Lorena," Samuel begged with desperation in his tone, "Please talk some sense into your father-in-law."

To everyone's surprise, Lorena said, "Samuel, your father must follow the dictate of his heart and conscience." She smiled at Shamus. "Do what you have to do, Colonel, but come back to us. I'll pray for your safe return every single day. And yours, too, Luther."

Ironside smiled. "That was a right nice thing to say, Lorena. Me and the colonel make a helluva team, you know."

* * *

"May the trail be kind to you, Pa," Samuel said, extending his hand.

Shamus leaned from the saddle and accepted the proffered hand. "Take care of Dromore while I'm gone, son."

Jacob removed his hat and slipped his mother's rosary over his head. He passed it to Ironside. "Wear this, Luther, but bring it back to me."

Ironside stared at the beads in his gloved had, his breath smoking in the cold morning air. "Damn, more O'Brien popery."

Jacob smiled. "The Virgin Mary will look after you, Luther, even though you're an unrepentant old sinner and a heathen to boot."

"Luther, that was Saraid's rosary," Shamus pointed out.

"Then I am honored." Ironside slipped the beads into the pocket of his sheepskin. "I don't know about the Virgin, but I know Saraid is looking down on us. Damn right."

"Time to go, Luther," Shamus said. "There's a long-riding trail ahead of us."

The colonel had made it clear that the Dromore staff were to stay inside, fearing a protracted farewell and women's tears. He swung his horse away from the house, raised a hand, then he and Ironside rode into the gray morning under a lowering sky.

Samuel watched until the two men were lost in distance, then turned to Jacob. "They should be sitting by the fire with blankets around their shoulders, not chasing outlaws."

Jacob smiled. "God help the skeleton men."

### J. A. Johnstone on William W. Johnstone
### *"When the Truth Becomes Legend"*

William W. Johnstone was born in southern Missouri, the youngest of four children. He was raised with strong moral and family values by his minister father, and tutored by his school-teacher mother. Despite this, he quit school at age fifteen.

"I have the highest respect for education," he says, "but such is the folly of youth, and wanting to see the world beyond the four walls and the blackboard."

True to this vow, Bill attempted to enlist in the French Foreign Legion ("I saw Gary Cooper in *Beau Geste* when I was a kid and I thought the French Foreign Legion would be fun") but was rejected, thankfully, for being underage. Instead, he joined a traveling carnival and did all kinds of odd jobs. It was listening to the veteran carny folk, some of whom had been on the circuit since the late 1800s, telling amazing tales about their experiences, which planted the storytelling seed in Bill's imagination.

"They were mostly honest people, despite the bad reputation traveling carny shows had back then," Bill remembers. "Of course, there were exceptions. There was one guy named Picky, who got that name because he was a master pickpocket. He could steal a man's socks right off his feet without him knowing. Believe me, Picky got us chased out of more than a few towns."

After a few months of this grueling existence, Bill returned home and finished high school. Next came stints as a deputy sheriff in the Tallulah, Louisiana, Sheriff's Department, followed by a hitch in the U.S. Army. Then he began a career in radio broadcasting at KTLD in Tallulah, which would last sixteen years. It was there that he fine-tuned his storytelling skills. He turned to writing in 1970, but it wouldn't be until 1979 that his first novel, *The Devil's Kiss,* was published. Thus began the full-time writing career of William W. Johnstone. He wrote horror (*The Uninvited*), thrillers (*The Last of the Dog Team*), even a romance novel or two. Then, in February 1983, *Out of the Ashes* was published. Searching for his missing family in the aftermath of a post-apocalyptic America, rebel mercenary and patriot Ben Raines is united with the civilians of the Resistance forces and moves to the forefront of a revolution for the nation's future.

*Out of the Ashes* was a smash. The series would continue for the next twenty years, winning Bill three generations of fans all over the world. The series was often imitated but never duplicated. "We all tried to copy the Ashes series," said one publishing executive, "but Bill's uncanny ability, both then and now, to predict in which direction the political winds were blowing brought a certain immediacy to the table no one else could capture." The Ashes series would end its run with more than thirty-four books and twenty million copies in print, making it one of the most successful men's action series in American book publishing. (The Ashes series also, Bill notes with a touch of pride, got him on the FBI's Watch List for its less than flattering portrayal of spineless politicians and the growing power of big government over our lives, among other things. In that respect, I often find myself saying, "Bill was years ahead of his time.")

Always steps ahead of the political curve, Bill's recent thrillers, written with myself, include *Vengeance Is Mine, Invasion USA, Border War, Jackknife, Remember the Alamo, Home Invasion, Phoenix Rising, The Blood of Patriots, The Bleeding Edge,* and the upcoming *Suicide Mission.*

It is with the western, though, that Bill found his greatest success and propelled him onto both the *USA Today* and the *New York Times* bestseller lists.

Bill's western series include *The Mountain Man, Matt Jensen, the Last Mountain Man, Preacher, The*

*Family Jensen, Luke Jensen, Bounty Hunter, Eagles, MacCallister* (an Eagles spin-off), *Sidewinders, The Brothers O'Brien, Sixkiller, Blood Bond, The Last Gunfighter,* and the upcoming new series *Flintlock* and *The Trail West.* May 2013 saw the hardcover western *Butch Cassidy, The Lost Years.*

"The Western," Bill says, "is one of the few true art forms that is one hundred percent American. I liken the Western as America's version of England's Arthurian legends, like the Knights of the Round Table, or Robin Hood and his Merry Men. Starting with the 1902 publication of *The Virginian* by Owen Wister, and followed by the greats like Zane Grey, Max Brand, Ernest Haycox, and of course Louis L'Amour, the Western has helped to shape the cultural landscape of America.

"I'm no goggle-eyed college academic, so when my fans ask me why the Western is as popular now as it was a century ago, I don't offer a 200-page thesis. Instead, I can only offer this: The Western is honest. In this great country, which is suffering under the yoke of political correctness, the Western harks back to an era when justice was sure and swift. Steal a man's horse, rustle his cattle, rob a bank, a stagecoach, or a train, you were hunted down and fitted with a hangman's noose. One size fit all.

"Sure, we westerners are prone to a little embellishment and exaggeration and, I admit it, occasionally play a little fast and loose with the facts. But we do so for a very good reason—to enhance the enjoyment of readers.

"It was Owen Wister, in *The Virginian* who first coined the phrase '*When you call me that, smile.*' Legend has it that Wister actually heard those words spoken by a deputy sheriff in Medicine Bow, Wyoming, when another poker player called him a son-of-a-bitch.

"Did it really happen, or is it one of those myths that have passed down from one generation to the next? I honestly don't know. But there's a line in one of my favorite Westerns of all time, *The Man Who Shot Liberty Valance,* where the newspaper editor tells the young reporter, 'When the truth becomes legend, print the legend.'

"These are the words I live by."

**Turn the page for an exciting preview!**

*Two outlaw brothers have been leaving a blood trail
on their way to infamy on the western frontier. Until
bounty hunter Luke Jensen catches one of the
black-hearted Kroll brothers away from his gang. But
while Luke is trying to get Mordecai Kroll from jail to
justice, he's ambushed by the Kroll gang and taken
prisoner. And that draws Luke's own brother,
Smoke Jensen, into the fight, guns drawn . . .*

**BROTHERS BY BLOOD. BROTHERS BY BATTLE.**

With Smoke Jensen comes fire—adopted son
Matt and lifelong friend Preacher, who storm
into battle to save Luke Jensen from the Krolls.
With trigger-happy back-stabbers, cutthroat
outriders, and murdering devils joining the
fray, the deadly mayhem paints the harsh
landscape an unforgiving red—a place where
the Jensens' enemies go to die . . .

**THE FAMILY JENSEN:
MASSACRE CANYON**

by William W. Johnstone
*with J. A. Johnstone*

On sale now, wherever Pinnacle Books are sold.

# Chapter One

Luke Jensen pressed his back to the wall of the corridor beside the hotel room door and raised the long-barreled Remington revolver in his right hand until it was beside his head. He waited patiently, a tall, rangy, muscular man with a rough-hewn face and a neatly trimmed mustache that matched the dark, slightly curly hair under the thumbed-back black hat.

Any minute now, the springs on the bed inside that room would start to squeal, and Luke would know that it was time to kick the door open and throw down on Mordecai Kroll. It was a shame to interrupt a man's sporting fun with a particularly good-looking redheaded dove, but Luke would make an exception for Mordecai Kroll.

He would take any advantage he could get over a cold-blooded, rattlesnake-mean killer like Kroll.

There were bad men . . . and then there were men like Rudolph and Mordecai Kroll. If there was a state or territory west of the Mississippi where they weren't wanted by the law, Luke wasn't aware of it. He had seen reward dodgers issued on them from Texas to Montana, from Missouri to California.

Their list of crimes was as long as the list of places offering bounties on them. Murder, rape, robbery, arson, kidnapping, extortion, assault, horse theft, cattle rustling . . . Come up with a violent crime and chances were the Kroll brothers had committed it at one time or another.

At some point they had probably pried the gold fillings out of a dead man's teeth.

As a result, if Luke could bring in Mordecai Kroll, dead or alive, he stood to earn the biggest payday of his career as a bounty hunter. The rewards for Mordecai added up to more than ten thousand dollars. The only way Luke could ever top that would be to corral Mordecai's older brother, Rudolph, who had even bigger bounties on his head.

Of course, if he could get both of them, Luke thought, he would collect enough to give up his dangerous profession. He could afford to buy himself a cattle ranch somewhere, like the Sugarloaf spread owned by his brother Smoke.

But he couldn't buy the goodwill and the friendship that Smoke had earned, nor did Luke know of any store where he could waltz in and buy himself a smart, beautiful wife like Sally Jensen.

No, he was just a bounty hunter, and while he might aspire to more, it was doubtful that he would ever achieve it, especially considering the fact that he wasn't as young as he used to be.

Since that was the case, he would concentrate on doing his job he told himself, instead of standing in the dim, dusty second-floor hallway of a rundown hotel in a little town in Arizona and daydreaming about what might have been. He stood a little straighter as he heard the bedsprings squeak on the other side of the door.

"Get on with it, Mordecai," Luke muttered to himself. "She's a whore. She's not expecting flowers and poetry."

He'd been coming out of an eatery a short time earlier when he spotted Mordecai Kroll emerging from a saloon across the street arm in arm with a rather buxom redhead. The young woman had a shawl around her shoulders against the evening chill, but it didn't do much to conceal the ample bosom that threatened to escape from the low-cut neckline of her dress. She still had her looks, which meant she hadn't been working as a soiled dove for very long.

Mordecai appeared to be half-drunk. He stumbled a little as the two of them moved along the boardwalk, but the redhead didn't let him fall. Both of them seemed to find his rotgut-induced clumsiness hilarious.

Luke had moved quickly into the shadows of

the alley next to the café and studied the two people on the other side of the street, just to make sure he really saw what he thought he was seeing. He'd heard rumors that the Kroll gang had been spotted in this corner of northeastern Arizona, not far from the border with New Mexico Territory, and he had drifted in this direction to have a look around.

It was hard to believe he'd be lucky enough to run smack-dab into Mordecai Kroll like this. Even more astounding was the fact that big brother, Rudolph, and the rest of the gang didn't appear to be anywhere around.

Mordecai must have slipped off without telling the others, Luke thought as he studied the outlaw. He had seen countless posters with a variety of drawings of Mordecai Kroll on them, and the man with the redheaded whore matched up with those likenesses. He had the same angular features, the same bushy eyebrows, the same shock of fair hair, the same lanky build.

That was Mordecai Kroll, all right, Luke had decided. No doubt about it.

He followed them to the Sullivan House, which was a pretty fancy name for a second-rate hotel. Through the front window, which fortunately wasn't as grimy as it might have been, he had seen the clerk behind the desk take a key from the pegboard on the wall and hand it to Mordecai. Luke's keen eyes had no problem reading the number 14 printed on the slip of paper tacked to the wall under the peg where the clerk had gotten the key.

From there it was simple to slip in the rear entrance and go up the back stairs. He found Room 14 about halfway along the corridor with a threadbare carpet runner, faded wallpaper, and a lamp burning dimly on a table at the far end. The hallway was deserted except for Luke.

While he stood there waiting, he heard laughter and voices from inside the room. A man and a woman, and both sounded like they'd been drinking. That confirmed he had the right room. He slipped one of the Remingtons he wore in cross-draw rigs from its holster and waited.

The doorknob of another room clicked as it was turned. The door opened and a man stepped out into the hall. It happened too quickly for Luke to hide, and there was no place to conceal himself in this corridor anyway.

The man stopped short and his eyes got big with fear. He was tall and skinny, with a prominent Adam's apple. He wore a tweed suit and a derby. The clothes had seen better days. Luke pegged the man for a drummer of some sort.

Carefully, Luke lifted his left hand and pressed the index finger to his lips in a signal for silence. The man took in the bounty hunter's rugged face, the dusty black shirt and trousers, the pair of revolvers. He swallowed hard, which caused his

Adam's apple to bob up and down. Then he backed into his room and gingerly closed the door behind him.

Smart man, Luke thought. Whatever was about to happen, that hombre didn't want any part of it.

Luke hoped no bullets punched through the thin walls between rooms. He would do his best not to fire a shot, but that really might be too much to hope for.

The bed noises from inside the room got louder. Luke got ready to make his move. He planned to kick the door open and rush in. If Mordecai was on top, it ought to be a simple matter to wallop him over the head with the Remington and knock him out. If he wasn't on top, that would complicate things. He might be able to reach for a gun before Luke could stop him.

Luke was counting on the booze to slow down Mordecai's reactions long enough for him to get the redhead out of the way. Then he and Mordecai would just have to take their chances against each other.

A thought flashed through his mind as he stepped away from the wall, drew his other Remington, and turned toward the door. With a quarry like Mordecai Kroll, some bounty hunters would start shooting as soon as they kicked in the door. If some of the bullets wound up in the whore, that was just too bad. They could always claim that Mordecai shot her, and chances were that nobody would question the claim.

Luke had never been that sort of man. He hadn't lived a blameless life, not by a long shot, but he liked to think there was a core of decency in him, instilled there by the sheer fact that he was a Jensen, even though for a long time he hadn't used the name and had called himself Luke Smith instead.

He had thought that he had good reasons for doing that. It had taken meeting his long-lost brother Smoke to show him that he was wrong. Now he was proudly once again a Jensen and would remain so.

He lifted his right foot and drove the heel of his boot against the door right beside the knob, as hard as he could. The jamb splintered under the impact and the door sprang open.

Luke leaped through the doorway with both revolvers thrust out in front of him. Either Mordecai or the redhead had lit the lamp on the small dressing table, so a yellow glow filled the room and revealed that the bed was . . .

Empty.

But the redhead stood beside it, still fully dressed, bent over with both hands resting on the mattress. She appeared to be frozen in that position with a look of terror on her face, and in that frozen instant of time, Luke realized why.

She had bounced the bed up and down and

made it sound like both occupants of the room were romping on it, but that wasn't the case. In fact, Mordecai Kroll was all the way on the other side of the room, holding a shotgun that he pointed at Luke.

Flame erupted from both barrels as Mordecai triggered them.

# Chapter Two

Luke's quick reflexes were all that saved him. He dived forward as the terrible boom of the shotgun's discharge filled the room. He hit the floor hard on his belly. The double load of buckshot passed over his head. A couple of pellets stung his legs as the loads spread, but that was all.

He angled the Remingtons upward and fired both revolvers. Mordecai had already darted to the side and barely avoided the .44 slugs, which ripped into the wall.

At least the bullets were traveling at such an angle that they probably went well over the head of anybody in the next room, Luke thought as he cocked the guns to try again.

If Mordecai had fired just one of the shotgun's barrels, he could have finished Luke off with the second one. The weapon was empty, though, so he was forced to swing it as a club. The twin barrels hit Luke's left-hand revolver and knocked it over into the other Remington as the guns discharged again. Still unscathed, Mordecai slashed at Luke's head with the stock.

Luke rolled out of the way of the blow and twisted on the floor so he could hook a booted foot between Mordecai's calves. He jerked hard with it and swept the outlaw's feet out from under him. With a startled yell, Mordecai went over backwards.

Luke started to scramble up, but Mordecai recovered quickly enough to kick him in the chest. That knocked Luke back against the bed. He was off-balance and sprawled against the side of the mattress.

Mordecai had been able to hang on to the shotgun. Even though he was fighting for his life, a cackle of vicious glee exploded from him as he rammed the shotgun's barrels into Luke's belly. Luke doubled over in pain and fell forward on his knees.

Since he was already bent over and low to the floor, he drove forward and butted Mordecai in the belly. The breath whoofed out of Mordecai's lungs as he fell on his butt. Luke surged ahead and planted a knee in the outlaw's groin. Mordecai groaned, and Luke smelled rotgut whiskey and spicy food.

He had the advantage now. He smashed his right-hand gun against Mordecai's jaw. The impact slewed Mordecai's head around. While Mordecai was stunned, Luke cracked the barrel of his left-hand gun across Mordecai's right wrist. That finally made Mordecai drop the empty shotgun.

Luke kneed him again and took some vicious satisfaction of his own from the agonized, high-pitched scream that Mordecai let out. No man could take punishment like that and keep fighting for very long. Mordecai Kroll was no exception. He curled up in a quivering, whimpering ball of pain.

Luke shoved himself up and staggered to his feet. His chest rose and fell hard from the effort and the sheer desperation of the fight. He eared back the hammers of both Remingtons and pointed the guns at Mordecai, even though the outlaw seemed helpless at the moment. Without taking his eyes off his prisoner, he asked the red-head, "Are you all right, gal?"

No answer.

Fearing the worst, Luke backed a couple of steps toward the door and glanced to his right so he could see on the other side of the bed. The young woman lay there, and she wasn't pretty anymore after what the buckshot had done to her face. A pool of blood spread slowly around her head.

Luke cursed bitterly. He didn't blame himself for the redhead's death; Mordecai Kroll was the one who had pulled the triggers on that shotgun. But Luke regretted what had happened, just as he always regretted what happened when somebody innocent got in the way of a cold-blooded killer.

He stepped closer to the mewling outlaw, leaned down, and struck again with the right-hand Remington. The blow knocked Mordecai out cold and shut him up.

The sound of rapid footsteps in the corridor made Luke swing toward the door. His guns came in line with the opening just as a man appeared in the doorway. His eyes widened at the sight of the Remingtons pointed at him, and he took a quick step back.

"Whoa, hold on there, mister!" he said. "Don't shoot!"

Luke spotted the badge pinned to the pudgy hombre's vest and lowered the Remingtons. The lawman had a six-gun on his hip and carried a Winchester, but he made no effort to point the rifle at Luke.

"Take it easy, Marshal," Luke told the newcomer. "The shooting is all over."

To prove it, he holstered the left-hand gun and started reloading the two chambers he had fired from the other Remington. He had to break the revolver open and expose the cylinder to do that.

The lawman stepped into the room and asked, "Anybody hurt in—" Then he stopped short and gulped as he spotted the redhead's legs sticking out on the far side of the bed. He leaned over to look, jerked upright, and a sick, greenish expression came over his face.

"I didn't do that," Luke said. "You can see for yourself that the poor woman was killed with a shotgun. That bastard on the floor is the one who did it."

He snapped the Remington closed again and nodded toward the senseless Mordecai Kroll.

"Who . . . who's that?"

Luke started reloading the other gun. A man in his line of work often needed all the firepower he could get. He said, "That's Mordecai Kroll."

"The outlaw?" The local star packer sounded like he couldn't believe it. "Mordecai Kroll was in my town? Really?"

"You can see him with your own eyes. Surely you have wanted posters on him in your office. You can compare the likenesses on them to Kroll in the flesh if you want, after you've gotten him safely behind bars."

"I'll do that. If that's Mordecai Kroll, I reckon that makes you . . . what? Some sort of bounty hunter?"

"That's right," Luke agreed dryly. "Some sort of bounty hunter. My name is Luke Jensen."

He could tell that the marshal had never heard of him, which was all right. Luke had never sought notoriety. That was one reason he had kept his true identity a secret for many years. He didn't want to bring shame to his family over the failures and tragedies of the past.

He had put all that behind him now. Anyway, there was no way he could ever be as famous as his brother Smoke, who quite possibly was the fastest, deadliest gunfighter the West had ever known. Despite all that, Smoke had built a reputation as a solid citizen, so Luke supposed there was hope that a bloody-handed bounty hunter might become respectable someday . . . but for now he was content to lie low and do his job.

The marshal suddenly looked even more worried. He said, "If that's Mordecai, where are Rudolph and the rest of that wild bunch of theirs?"

"I have no idea," Luke replied honestly. "I just spotted Mordecai on the street a little while ago. He had that young woman with him and appeared to be drunk, so I decided to follow him and see if I might have a chance to take him into custody."

"You don't really talk like most bounty hunters I've run into," the lawman said with a slight frown.

"I read a lot," Luke said simply.

That was true. He always had several books stuck in his saddlebags, and he picked up more whenever and wherever he had a chance. In the lonely existence he had led, sometimes it seemed like books were his only friends. They were certainly the only ones who were always there for him.

The marshal's thoughts must have gone back to what he had been talking about before. He said, "You must not've been able to get the drop on him like you hoped."

"He must have spotted me following him," Luke said, and once again that note of bitterness was in his voice. "He forced the girl to make the bedsprings bounce and squeal like they were busy. Then when I kicked the door in, he was ready and cut loose at me with that greener. I barely got out of the way."

"Yeah, but Sheila didn't," the marshal said with a gloomy expression on his face. He shook his head.

"That was her name? Sheila?"

"Yeah. Not a bad sort, for a whore. She seemed to genuinely like folks. I reckon she probably would've stopped feelin' like that if she'd stayed in the business long enough. Maybe it's a blessin' that she didn't have the chance."

Luke couldn't bring himself to feel that way. Any life cut short before its time was a bad thing. But he wasn't going to argue philosophy with the local badge-toter in an Arizona cowtown.

"We'd better get Kroll locked up while we've got the chance," he said.

"Yeah, we don't want the others to show up

while we're takin' him down the street." The marshal sounded like it would have been all right with him if Luke hadn't captured the infamous outlaw. Now he had to worry about the rest of the Kroll gang riding into town to bust Mordecai out of jail. With a sigh, he added, "I'll have to get the undertaker up here to take care of Sheila, too. Not to mention the damage to the hotel from the blood and the buckshot and the bullets and such."

Luke would have been willing to bet that this wasn't the first time blood had been spilled in the Sullivan House, nor were those bullet holes the first ones that had been put in the walls. He would pay the proprietor for the damages, though. With the rewards he would collect for capturing Mordecai, he could easily afford the expense.

He rolled Mordecai onto his belly and took a strip of rawhide from his pocket. Some bounty hunters carried handcuffs, and Luke had a pair of the metal bracelets in his saddlebags, but the rawhide served well for tying a prisoner's wrists together, too, with the advantage of being compact and lightweight. It wouldn't clink against something at a bad time and give away his presence when stealth was important, either.

Mordecai started to come around as Luke jerked his arms behind his back and lashed his wrists together with the rawhide. He pulled the knot good and tight and wasn't any too gentle about it. Then he took hold of Mordecai's arms and hauled the outlaw to his feet.

Mordecai yelped in pain and cursed.

"Careful," he said.

"Like you were careful when you practically blew poor Sheila's head off?"

"Was that her name? Hell, if she don't have sense to duck, it ain't my fault, is it?"

Luke drew his right-hand Remington, pressed the muzzle to Mordecai's head just behind the right ear, and pulled back the hammer.

"If my thumb happens to slip, it's not my fault, is it?" he grated. "Anyway, all the reward dodgers on you say dead or alive, so it doesn't really matter, does it?"

Mordecai stood stiff as a board now. He must have realized that his callous remark had pushed Luke a little too far.

The local lawman broke the tense spell by clearing his throat and saying, "Uh, Mr. Jensen . . . we said we were gonna lock him up. . . ."

"And so we are," Luke agreed as he got control over his anger. He lowered the Remington's hammer and slid the revolver back into leather. "But if you're smart, Kroll, you'll keep your mouth shut for a while. Just remember . . . dead or alive."

# Chapter Three

Marshal Jerome Dunlap sighed in obvious relief when the cell door clanged shut behind Mordecai Kroll. He had told Luke his name while they were marching the prisoner up the street and into the squat stone building that housed the local marshal's office and jail.

Luke said, "Turn around and back up to the bars, Kroll, and I'll untie your wrists."

Kroll did as Luke told him. When his arms were free again, Mordecai brought them around in front of him and massaged his wrists as he glared at Luke.

"You're gonna be mighty sorry you ever crossed trails with me, Jensen," he said. "That was your name, wasn't it?"

"That's right," Luke said.

With a sneer, Mordecai told Dunlap, "You better make a note of that, Marshal, so you can tell the undertaker what name to put on this dumb bastard's grave marker." Mordecai paused, and then went on. "No, wait, that's right, you'll be dead, too, so you won't be able to tell the undertaker a damned thing."

He laughed raucously. Luke ignored him and turned back to the marshal's office.

Dunlap followed him out of the cell block and dropped the big ring of keys on the desk with a jangling thump.

"I'll have to send to St. Johns for the sheriff," he said. "That's the county seat of Apache County. We can't hope to hold Kroll here in this cracker box of a jail."

Luke thought the marshal was underestimating the building's strength, but Dunlap had no deputies and it was certain that just the two of them wouldn't be able to withstand an attack in force by the entire Kroll gang. The sooner they could get Kroll to the county seat and surround him with armed, experienced deputies, the better.

"Have you got a telegraph office here?" he asked.

Dunlap shook his head.

"No, I'll have to send a rider to St. Johns. Fella who owns the livery stable has a boy who carries messages for me sometimes. Got a fast horse, too."

"How long will that take?"

"Start him first thing in the morning, the sheriff ought to be back here with a jail wagon and some men by nightfall."

Luke nodded and said, "So we've got to wait less than twenty-four hours."

"Twenty-four hours can be a mighty long time when you've got trouble rainin' down on you," Dunlap pointed out.

He was right about that, Luke thought. But all they could do was hope for the best.

"You mind stayin' here while I go roust out the undertaker and tell Benji Porter I need him to ride to the county seat in the mornin'?"

"Go ahead, Marshal," Luke said. "I'll keep an eye on Kroll."

Dunlap nodded. He looked like he would be glad to get out of the office. Luke wondered briefly if the marshal would come back tonight or manage to be occupied elsewhere. He didn't think Dunlap would abandon his duty like that, but you never could be sure about people.

Once Luke was alone in the office, he looked at the few wanted posters that were pinned to the wall. He figured that Dunlap had to have more reward dodgers than that, unless the marshal had been using them for kindling, so he took a look in the scarred old desk. In the second drawer he found a big stack of the posters.

He didn't have to flip through them for very

long before he came across one with a drawing of Rudolph Kroll on it. The man staring out balefully from the penciled likeness was considerably older than Mordecai, but Luke could see a slight resemblance in their craggy faces. Rudolph was dark where his younger brother was fair. His nose was bigger, and underneath it was a thick, dark mustache that drooped over the corners of his mouth. If anything, Rudolph Kroll looked even meaner and more filled with hate than Mordecai, although such a thing didn't seem possible at first glance.

Luke found posters on some of the other members of the Kroll gang in the stack: Fred Martin, Calvin Dodge, Pete Markwell, a handful more. All of them ruthless, hard-bitten, dangerous men, even if their reputations weren't quite as bad as that of the Kroll brothers'. Luke had no doubt that any one of them would have killed him in an instant if given the chance.

He didn't intend to provide them with that opportunity.

"Hey!" Mordecai called from the cell block. "Hey, Marshal, you still out there?"

Luke put the wanted posters back in the desk drawer and closed it. He stood up and went over to the cell block door to ask through the barred window in it, "What do you want, Kroll?"

"That you, Jensen? Where's the marshal?"

"Busy. If you don't want anything, shut up."

"I didn't say that. I could use some coffee. My head really hurts where some big dumb son of a bitch walloped it with a pistol."

He chuckled at his own cleverness, or what he regarded as cleverness, anyway.

Luke had already noticed the coffeepot staying warm on a pot-bellied iron stove in a corner of the office. Several tin cups sat on a small shelf to the side. He supposed it wouldn't do any harm, and since there was a good chance he would have to stay awake all night to guard the prisoner, he decided he ought to have a cup for himself.

"All right, but don't try anything," he told Mordecai. "I'd just as soon put a bullet in you as look at you."

He poured thick, black coffee into one of the cups and took it over to the desk where he picked up the key ring. He had seen which key Dunlap used to lock the cell block, so it was simple to unlock it. He drew one of his guns as he used the other hand to carry the coffee into the cell block.

Mordecai was in the first cell on the left. Luke told him, "Back off all the way over there under the window. Take a step in this direction before I tell you to and I'll blow your kneecap to hell. You'll have a bad limp when you walk to the gallows."

"You're mighty confident," Mordecai said as he backed over to the far wall. "I'm gonna enjoy watchin' you die."

Luke just grunted. He bent, reached through the bars, and placed the cup of coffee on the cell's stone floor. Then he backed up well out of reach and said, "All right, you can go ahead and get it now."

Mordecai did so. He took a sip and made a face, then said, "Has the marshal been boilin' this stuff for a week? It tastes like it."

"I wouldn't know," Luke said. "I can take it back—"

"No, no, that's fine."

Mordecai sat down on the bunk, took another sip, and sighed.

Luke had encountered scores of outlaws during his career as a bounty hunter, and few if any of them had ever given much thought to the havoc they wreaked in innocent lives. Despite knowing that, he asked, "Doesn't it bother you that you killed that girl?"

"It wasn't my intention that she come to any harm. I just planned on killin' you."

"Because you saw me following you?"

"Yeah. See, you thought I was drunk . . . and I was. But I got highly developed instincts, like a wolf, say. I can sense danger. And when I saw that some fella was skulkin' along on the other side of the street, it got me curious. Figured you might be after the bounty on my head. So I decided to set a little trap for you." Mordecai took another drink of the coffee and then added, "I can sober up in a hurry when I need to."

"What if I hadn't been after you?"

The lanky outlaw shrugged.

"If the gal had bounced that bed up and down for a few minutes without nothin' else happenin', I would've said that my suspicions was wrong, and then we would've put the bed to better use. But I wasn't wrong, and you come bustin' in, and . . . well, you know what happened after that."

"Yeah," Luke said. "I do. Finish your coffee."

Mordecai grinned and said, "Now, don't rush a man. I'm a prisoner now. You got to treat me decent." He sipped the coffee again. "You want to kill me, don't you?"

"More than you could ever know."

He didn't say anything else, even though Mordecai took a couple more gibes at him. When the outlaw finished the coffee, Luke had him set the cup through the bars and back off again. Mordecai cooperated. He might be a loco animal in a lot of ways, but he had enough sense to know that if he gave Luke the slightest excuse, the bounty hunter would ventilate him.

Luke picked up the cup and went back into the office. He locked the cell block door and sat down at the desk again with a cup of the strong black brew for himself. A few minutes later, Marshal Dunlap came in.

"Got those chores taken care of," the lawman

reported, almost as if he were the deputy and Luke was the one in charge. "The undertaker's collected Sheila's body, and Benji Porter will be settin' out to fetch the sheriff at first light. All we got to do is sit tight and wait for somebody to show up and take Kroll off our hands."

"And hope it's not his brother and the rest of the gang who show up," Luke said.

"Mister, I'm not hopin'," Dunlap said fervently. "I'm prayin'."

# Chapter Four

Despite the marshal's worries, the night passed quietly with no sign of trouble. He and Luke took turns sleeping and napping on the old sofa on one side of the office, but nothing disturbed them. Early the next morning Dunlap went over to the café and brought back breakfast for both of them and for the prisoner.

"I went down to the stable, too," he said as he and Luke were eating. "Abner Porter told me his boy left for St. Johns before dawn. He's mighty excited to be helpin' out in something like this, Abner said."

Luke frowned over his flapjacks, eggs, and bacon.

"He's not so excited that he'll go spreading it all over town about Kroll being locked up here, is he?"

"Well, you know, I didn't think to say anything

to him about that. I might should'a told him not to say anything except to the sheriff."

Luke bit back the sharp comment that tried to spring to his lips. Marshal Dunlap was just a small-town peace officer who probably never had to deal with anything much worse than a drunken cowboy or miner.

Luke stood up and went into the cell block. Mordecai sat on the bunk eating his breakfast. Luke looked at him through the bars and asked, "What were you doing here in town by yourself? Where's your brother and the rest of the gang?"

"You think I'm gonna tell a no-good bounty hunter where to find Rudolph and the rest of the boys?" Mordecai laughed. "You're plumb dumber than I thought, Jensen."

"Yeah, I suppose you come and go as you please, don't you? You want to come into town for a drink, maybe a poker game, and a little slap-and-tickle with a dove, you don't have to ask your brother's permission."

Mordecai snorted and said, "Damn right I don't. Rudolph knows better than to try to put a halter on me."

"So he doesn't know where you are."

"Hell, no! I don't have to tell him every time I—" Mordecai stopped short and frowned. "Blast it, Jensen, you're tryin' to trick me!"

Luke left the cell block without saying anything else. Even though Mordecai was probably a habitual liar like most outlaws, Luke thought his tweaking of the man's pride had prompted him to tell the truth without thinking. Mordecai had slipped away from the gang on his own. He had probably done similar things before. With any luck, it might be several days before Rudolph Kroll got worried enough to go looking for his little brother.

By that time, Luke would have turned Mordecai over to the sheriff of Apache County and the outlaw wouldn't be his responsibility anymore.

During the day Luke saw a number of townspeople lingering on the opposite boardwalk. They stared across the street at the jail and talked animatedly among themselves. He knew that word had gotten around town about the notorious Mordecai Kroll being locked up in there. It would have been difficult if not impossible to keep that quiet, he supposed, especially considering what had happened to the unfortunate, redheaded Sheila.

Since Mordecai's capture was already a subject of much gossip in town, there was no point in saying anything to Dunlap about keeping such things quiet. Luke just kept his eyes open and waited for the sheriff to arrive.

As Dunlap had predicted, that happened late in the afternoon, after a long, thankfully boring day. The sheriff's arrival brought even more excitement to the town, since he rode in at the head of a posse of a dozen deputies surrounding a sturdy jail wagon pulled by a team of six black horses.

Dunlap unlocked the marshal's office door, and he and Luke stepped out to greet the newcomers. The sheriff, a tall, stern-looking man with iron-gray hair, swung down from his saddle and gave Dunlap a curt nod.

"Marshal," he said. "I hear you've got a prisoner for me."

"You make it sound mighty simple, sheriff," Dunlap replied with a relieved smile. "This ain't just any prisoner. It's Mordecai Kroll."

"So I'm told." The sheriff turned to look at Luke and extended his hand. "Sheriff Wesley Rakestraw."

"Luke Jensen," Luke introduced himself as he shook hands with the lawman.

"I hear you're a bounty hunter."

"That's right," Luke said warily. Most lawmen didn't care much for bounty hunters. He supposed they thought men like Luke were encroaching on their job of bringing lawbreakers to justice.

Rakestraw didn't appear to be that sort, however. His expression was bland and noncommittal. Maybe he was more interested in the fact that a mighty bad hombre was locked up where he couldn't hurt anybody else, rather than in who had brought him in.

"No sign of Rudolph Kroll or the rest of that bunch the Kroll brothers run with?"

Dunlap fielded that question. He said, "Nope, it's been peaceful since last night, sheriff. Kroll's locked up inside, and nobody's tried to get him out."

"Good," Rakestraw said with a nod. "Tomorrow morning we'll take him back to the county seat. It's going to take some time and burning up the telegraph wires to sort out exactly who has first claim on him." The sheriff smiled faintly. "There are plenty of people lining up for a crack at hanging Mordecai Kroll."

Luke said, "It's what, twenty miles to the county seat?"

"Twenty-two," Rakestraw said.

"You brought enough men with you to get the prisoner there safely?"

"I think you'll find that my deputies are the best in the territory, Jensen." A smug look came over Rakestraw's face. "We can handle anything that comes up."

Luke wasn't so sure of that. According to everything he'd heard, the Kroll gang numbered about a dozen men, the same size as the group of deputies Sheriff Rakestraw had brought with him.

But Rudolph Kroll might be able to call on a dozen or more other hardcases to ride with him if he set out to rescue his brother from the law. That might be too much for Rakestraw's posse to handle.

What they really needed, Luke decided, was a whole cavalry patrol. He wasn't sure the army would go along with that, however, even for an outlaw as notorious as Mordecai Kroll. Besides, there was no telegraph office here, so contacting the military authorities wouldn't be easy.

Their best bet would be to hustle Mordecai to St. Johns as quickly as possible, before Rudolph Kroll found out what was going on.

"I think we should move the prisoner tonight," he told the sheriff.

Rakestraw raised an eyebrow and repeated, "We?"

"I'm coming with you," Luke said.

"I don't figure that's necessary. I can put in the reward claims for you, if that's what you're worried about."

"No offense, sheriff, but I'd rather handle that myself."

Rakestraw's weathered face tightened. Despite what Luke had said, he was offended. Luke didn't mean to question the sheriff's honesty, but he was accustomed to handling his own business.

"Suit yourself," Rakestraw said, "but we're not starting back to the county seat until tomorrow morning. You're welcome to ride along with us then if you want to."

Luke nodded. He supposed that would have to do. If nothing else, the jail here would be much better guarded than it had been the night before.

Rakestraw turned to his deputies and ordered, "Dismount and get set up, men. Tom, take the wagon down to the livery stable and see to the team."

The deputies responded crisply. Several of them, each packing two revolvers and carrying a Winchester, went into the jail to watch over the prisoner. The others began positioning themselves around town where they commanded a field of fire all around the jail. If anybody tried to get in there who wasn't supposed to, somebody would be in position to pick him off.

There didn't seem to be anything left for Luke to do here, so he nodded to Dunlap and walked away. He had put up his horse in the livery stable the previous evening, before he stepped in the café to get some supper, and he hadn't had a chance to check on the ugly, hammerheaded dun since then. That was where he headed now.

When he reached the stable he found a middle-aged man and a teenage boy unhitching the team of blacks from the jail wagon. He said to the youngster, "You'd be Benji, wouldn't you? You followed the sheriff and his men back here after fetching them."

"That's right, mister," the boy said. "And you're that bounty hunter. I heard all about you."

"Did you happen to say anything to folks in St. Johns about Mordecai Kroll being in jail here? Other than Sheriff Rakestraw, I mean?"

The liveryman said, "Now hold on a minute. Don't make out like my boy did anything wrong, Mr. Jensen. The marshal didn't tell Benji not to say anything. You can't expect a boy to keep quiet about something this excitin'."

Luke shook his head and smiled.

"I didn't mean to imply that you'd done anything wrong, Benji," he said. "I'm just curious how many people know about Kroll being captured."

"Well, I reckon I did tell a few people about it . . . and you know how things get around. . . ."

Luke nodded and kept the smile on his face, although not without effort.

"That's fine, Benji. I appreciate you being honest with me." He took a silver dollar from his pocket and tossed it to the boy, who caught it deftly. "That's for the fast ride you made today. That was good work."

The youngster beamed and said, "Thanks, Mr. Jensen!"

Benji's father seemed mollified now. He said, "That dun of yours is a good horse, Mr. Jensen. Not much to look at, but I can tell he's got sand. You gonna be leavin' him here another night?"

"Yes, it appears that I will be," Luke said, not bothering to add that he would have preferred to leave for the county seat immediately with the prisoner and the sheriff's posse. From what he had seen, the road between the two towns was good enough to follow in the dark.

The decision was out of his hands, though. He lingered at the stable for a few more minutes and reached into the stall to scratch the dun's head, then left. He hadn't gotten a hotel room before he ate supper the night before, and after that he hadn't had a chance to do so, spending the night in the marshal's office instead. So finding a place to sleep tonight was the next order of business, he supposed.

He was on his way along the boardwalk in search of a better hotel than the Sullivan House when a voice called from behind him, "Mr. Jensen! Mr. Jensen, if I could speak to you for a moment, please!"

Luke stopped and turned. He was curious because the voice that had hailed him belonged to a woman.

But he wasn't expecting her to be a woman beautiful enough to take a man's breath away.

# Chapter 5

She was almost as tall as he was, so she didn't have to tip her head back much for her eyes to meet his. Those eyes were a rich, deep brown, he noted, almost as dark as the thick, dark brown hair pulled into a bun at the back of her neck.

The woman wore a gray hat with a little brown-and-white feather attached to it. Her traveling outfit was the same shade of gray and had a thin layer of dust on it, so Luke knew she had been on the trail. That traveling outfit was snug enough to reveal an intriguingly curved shape.

Her skin had a golden tint to it, and her exotic good looks made her even more striking. Luke wouldn't have been surprised to see a woman like her in the finest restaurant or hotel in San Francisco, but here in this little Arizona Territory settlement, she definitely looked out of place.

At the same time, she had such poise as she smiled faintly at him that he realized she could make any place belong to her, instead of the other way around.

"Do we know each other, ma'am?" he asked, even though he was sure he had never laid eyes on this woman until this minute. He would remember if he had.

"No, we've never met," she said. "And it's miss, not ma'am. Miss Darcy Garnett."

Luke touched a finger to the brim of his hat and said, "Pleased to meet you, Miss Garnett. I'm Luke Jensen. But then, you seem to know that already."

"Of course. You're Luke Jensen, the famous bounty hunter. The man who captured the notorious Mordecai Kroll. Everyone in St. Johns is talking about you today."

Luke managed not to grimace. In his business, having a reputation sometimes came in handy, but most of the time it didn't.

"You came here from St. Johns?" he asked.

"That's right," Darcy Garnett replied.

"Followed the sheriff and his posse all that way?"

"I certainly did."

"Why?"

"To talk to you, of course," she responded without hesitation.

"Then I'm afraid you've wasted your time," he told her. "I'm about the most uninteresting hombre you'll ever run across."

"I don't believe that," she said. "And I'm sure my readers will agree with me."

Again Luke had to control the impulse to make a face. As they talked, he had started to have a sneaking suspicion that Darcy Garnett might be a journalist. He had run into inquisitive newspaper reporters before and sometimes could recognize them before they started asking their questions. Usually he told them he wasn't interested in talking and stalked off, not caring whether or not he was rude.

That would be harder to do with a lady.

"You work for the newspaper in St. Johns, do you?"

For the first time Luke saw a faint crack in the cool, reserved façade Darcy Garnett put up. She said, "Actually, no. The publisher there doesn't believe in female reporters. I told him that back in Pittsburgh, a woman who signs herself Nellie Bly is writing regularly for one of the papers there, but that didn't change his opinion. I'm hoping to sell a piece about the infamous Kroll brothers to *Harper's Weekly,* and your stirring capture of Mordecai Kroll is just what the story needs to cap it off."

"So you want me to tell you all about it."

"If I could get a firsthand account from the man who brought Mordecai Kroll to justice, no editor would turn down the story. Especially if you could tell me about the tragic death of the unfortunate young woman who was killed, too."

Luke felt a flash of anger go through him. He hadn't known Sheila, but she was dead and this woman regarded her death as nothing more than something that would help her sell a story to *Harper's Weekly.*

"I don't think I have anything to say, Miss Garnett," he told her with a shake of his head. The words came out a little harsher than he intended them to, but he didn't really care.

"Please, Mr. Jensen," she persisted. "The people deserve to know—"

"Most people know more than they really want to about the bad things in the world. And those bad things sure include men like Mordecai Kroll."

"Then you won't give me an interview?"

"That's what I just said, isn't it?"

Anger sparked in her eyes. Her mouth tightened into a line and she said coolly, "All right. If that's the way you feel about it, I won't argue with you. Anyway, Sheriff Rakestraw has already promised me his full cooperation."

For some reason, that rubbed Luke the wrong way. He hadn't particularly liked the sheriff. Rakestraw seemed a mite too full of himself, and his confidence when he talked about how he and his men could handle the Kroll gang if need be had bordered on arrogance. Reckless arrogance, in fact.

Even though he didn't really know the sheriff, Luke figured it would be just like Rakestraw to give Darcy an interview that made it sound like he was the one responsible for capturing Mordecai Kroll. Luke didn't much care what people thought about him; if a high public opinion was important to him, he never would have become a bounty hunter.

But he didn't want anybody making any claims that might damage his chances of collecting those bounties. Say Darcy Garnett did sell a story about the affair to *Harper's Weekly* or some other magazine or newspaper, and it made Sheriff Rakestraw out to be the hero. The men in charge of the banks and railroads and stagecoach lines that had put out those rewards for Mordecai might use that as an excuse to drag their feet about paying him.

Luke wasn't going to put up with that, not if all it took to prevent it was talking to an attractive young woman for a while.

"Hold on a minute," he said. "I guess it wouldn't hurt to answer a few questions for you."

She smiled, and this time he thought he saw a flash of triumph in those brown eyes. She had tricked him into going along with what she wanted by bringing up Rakestraw, he realized. Somehow she had guessed that he wouldn't want the sheriff trying to hog all the credit. And he had to admit that she'd been right.

"Excellent," she said. "Were you on your way to the hotel to get a room?"

"I was," Luke said.

"So was I. Why don't we have supper tonight in their dining room? That'll give us a chance to talk."

He nodded and said, "All right." He supposed he ought to clean up a little first, even though he was really too old to worry about trying to impress a woman like Darcy Garnett.

"We'll meet in the lobby at . . . six-thirty?" she asked.

"I'll be there," Luke said.